One
for
Sorrow

Mary Reed & Eric Mayer

Poisoned
Pen
Press

Dedicated to Eric's Grammy, who read *The Wind In The Willows* to him, and to all the Reedies

Our thanks to the following for their assistance:

Sir Rodney Hartwell and Dr. Robert Cleve, The Augustan Society, Professor Robert Gurval, UCLA, Dr. Robert Ousterhout, University of Illinois, and Samuel S. Long II and to Mike Ashley, who introduced John the Eunuch to the world.

One
for
Sorrow

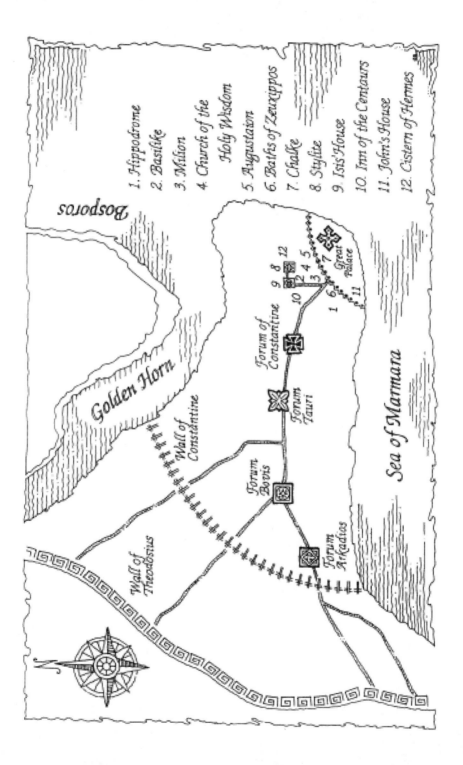

Chapter One

The black bear's huge paw lashed out at its trainer's bottom, almost shredding the man's flesh and the green tights covering it. It could not quite reach the man's furiously wagging buttocks, infuriating the animal and amusing the vociferous crowd lolling under the brazier of the late afternoon sun.

Shifting his lean flanks on the hard marble bench, John felt real sympathy for the wretched bear and its burden of heavy chains. He was likewise pinioned. The weight of the heat beating down on the Emperor's box was nearly as heavy as the richly embroidered court robes John was obliged to wear coming to the spectacle straight from a palace banquet. The occasional tepid sea breeze lazily brushing his face did nothing to alleviate his discomfort. It carried with it the sour reek of the sweating mass of spectators and the earthy smell of animal dung on the Hippodrome's floor, along with a hint of the dead fish bobbing on the swells slapping against the city's seawalls. The stench recalled the rich dishes served at Justinian's imperial table. Their now soured flavors—or perhaps it was that unfortunate choice of fish—made John's stomach roil and gurgle and his head ache. So did the renewed realization growing out of the scene below him that, despite his privileged position, Justinian at a whim could lash out and shred him as surely as the bear could flay its prancing trainer. If it had the reach.

The animal's muscular tormenter was now brandishing a trident as he danced to and fro in front of the bear, a dangerous business had the beast not been securely chained to one of the Egyptian obelisks dividing the chariot track. The man's naked chest glistened with sweat in the hot spring sunlight. He darted in at the captive animal, prodded it with the trident, pirouetted and retreated. Then he danced in again. He was light on his feet for a big man. The massed Romans responded with noisy enthusiasm.

Encouraged, the man broke into a run, circling the obelisk with a comical, high-stepping gait. The bear, though encumbered, pursued him, still hopeful of exacting revenge for its injuries. So intent was it on its pursuit that it did not notice that every turn around the obelisk wound its chain tighter, shortening it inexorably so that suddenly the beast found its body trapped against the hot stone, unable to move.

The bear roared its pain and fury to the unheeding sky as its trainer gave the beast's shaggy back a final vicious dig with his trident.

The crowd responded with coin-throwing enthusiasm as the bear trainer finally departed with his ill-treated charge and slaves, swathed in whirling dust devils, raked the arena's churned floor smooth of the gouges imprinted by the opening chariot races. Soon no trace of chariots or bear remained.

John rubbed his eyes wearily. As Lord Chamberlain, he oversaw the annual May celebrations of the founding of the Roman capital and generally felt he ought to be seen at the public events with which the city had been regaled over the past few days. Today, however ill-advised, he might have settled for a brief, formal bow to the crowd and a quick exit if it had not been for the ill-concealed nervous edge sharpening the voice of his friend Leukos. The Keeper of the Plate was normally a placid, cheerful man. Curious, John had resolved to sit through the afternoon's spectacle and hope to speak privately to Leukos when the rest of the men in the imperial box departed to sample the evening's delights.

His musings were suddenly cut short by the crowd's intake of breath as the teak gate at one end of the Hippodrome slid open. As John stared, an enormous black bull, garlanded in blossoms and ribbons, charged into view. The spectators reacted even more enthusiastically to the animal's raw power than they had to the unfortunate bear. The bull raced around the arena's perimeter, violently tossing its gold-tipped horns.

"Mithra!" John breathed as he beheld the perfect incarnation of the sacred animal of the Lord of Light, John's own god, forgetting for a moment that he was in the imperial box of a Christian Emperor.

A trio of figures followed the bull out of the gate. All three were clothed identically in azure loincloths and beribboned chaplets of flowers. Barefooted, they moved smoothly and swiftly across the chariot track. From a distance, they presented perfect images of bull-leapers from the ancient days of Crete, recreated for the amusement of the city. A moment passed before John realized that one of the androgynous figures was a girl. She was as slim as her two male companions, her long legs as muscular, her breasts small and brown.

The bull wheeled, gilded hooves kicking up clods of earth. As the trio advanced upon it, it pawed the ground impatiently and then charged towards them.

The two young men stepped aside. They were armed with spears, if only for display. Surely, thought John, such weapons would be no defense against the glowering beast now closing in so rapidly upon them.

It was the girl who confronted the bull. John leaned forward, the better to see so slight a woman facing an unchained monster. Such a contest was more interesting than a brute like the trainer mocking a bear safely kept in chains.

The spectators' clamor subsided into a silence like that between breaking waves. In the eerie hush, the snort of the bull carried clearly up into the stands. John could see the creature's massive flanks heaving as its powerful gallop carried it swiftly towards the trio. The girl stepped forward, raising delicate arms as if she might be able to push the animal safely away.

John tried to pick out details of her features, but her face was hidden behind shimmering heat-waves rising from the hot floor of the arena. Was she afraid? Surrounded by thousands, she seemed impossibly alone.

The bull closed in. At the last instant it lowered its massive head, gilded horns flashing murderous intent in the sunlight. For a moment John's eyes blurred. He blinked rapidly, and when he focused on the girl again she had left the earth as easily as a sparrow, grabbing the bull's deadly horns and vaulting over them to land lightly on the onrushing animal's back, facing its tail.

The crowd's thunderous appreciation echoed around the Hippodrome.

The bull wheeled, whipping its head back and forth, but the girl had already swung around to sit astride its broad back, grasping its horns in a hold as secure as that of the ribbons plaited into its tail.

John could not tear his gaze from the girl as the

maddened animal wheeled and galloped back towards the imperial box. The bull's eyes were wild; foam flecked its mouth. As the bull raced by, the girl pulled herself up into a crouch on its back, and then executed a back flip, ending in a handstand on the arena's floor.

But John never saw that somersault, which must have been perfect for otherwise it would have been fatal. Nor did he notice how the spear-carriers expertly herded the animal out of the arena. He was conscious of only one thing: as the bull had carried the girl past the imperial box, in the instant before launching herself from the animal's back she had turned her face upwards and John had looked down into her dark eyes. Eyes in which he had lost himself, years before.

"Did you see her?" the man sitting beside John blurted out. "I have to meet her!"

How many times had John heard the same refrain from his younger friend? But this time Anatolius sounded far away, a voice in a dream.

"John? What's the matter? You look as if you've seen a demon."

The Lord Chamberlain, known more familiarly to residents of the capital as John the Eunuch, was gradually becoming aware that his friend was speaking. Looking into the girl's eyes again, so unexpectedly, had been like falling into a deep well. He surfaced with a shudder, cold, even in the hot sunlight.

"I knew that girl, Anatolius," he whispered, "A long time ago. In another place. We were lovers."

Chapter Two

As the arena emptied again, and his companions fell into conversation, a shaken John retreated into his memories. After a few unsuccessful attempts to draw the Lord Chamberlain in, the others began to bicker amiably about Anatolius' earlier wager concerning whether or not the bear would draw blood.

While the crowd had obviously enjoyed it hugely, the spectacle of the dumb beast's torment had struck those in John's party differently.

"If only our enemies were bears and we could measure the length of their chains," the heavy-set bearded man seated to John's right growled. Felix, the bearded Captain of the Excubitors, had something of the shaggy look of the bear himself.

The elegantly groomed young man to his left offered reassurance. "Don't worry, Felix. You don't have any enemies here. At least not within arm's length." Anatolius had wagered that the bear would not suceed in bloodying its trainer. Now he was counting his winnings while Felix scowled at him with blue eyes as cold as the Bosporos in January.

"Since our enemies don't have chains, our best defense is to learn which way they are going to jump," the man to Felix's right remarked. A pale man. His bald head shone in the harsh sunlight almost as brightly as the precious ceremonial metalwork that lay in his charge, for while John directed the elaborate ceremonies regulating the heartbeat of the court, it was Leukos who bore responsibility for its sumptuous trappings.

Anatolius looked at the usually cheerful Leukos with surprise. "Why Leukos, what enemies do you have?"

"We all have enemies. You might want to consult this soothsayer who has recently arrived in the city. Perhaps he can point out a few of your enemies for you."

"I've heard tales about him," put in Anatolius. "He must be a remarkable man. He disemboweled a chicken for a certain office holder we won't name and was able, from its guts, to assure this august personage that he would not end up like the unfortunate chicken, or at least not for a week or two. I've heard so much about him that I have decided on a visit myself this evening."

"And what will the Emperor say if he finds out that his private secretary is consulting fortune tellers?" growled Felix.

"Actually," Leukos broke in, "I had him cast the augurs for me a day or so ago and he did appear quite knowledgeable. In fact, I'm returning to see him today myself."

Felix shook his head. "Leukos, you of all officials must be aware that the more plausible the rogue, the greater the necessity to guard the silver. It is unwise to trust people in these times."

Anatolius smiled. "Are you thinking of these kidnappings and extortion plots we've been plagued with lately, or the street violence, or… " he paused for effect, "… is it that little tart at Madam's? I understand she took more than some liberties the last time...."

Felix again directed a chilly gaze at the younger man. "You're a gossip, Anatolius. If you don't watch your tongue you'll lose it."

Anatolius pretended to look hurt. "That's unfair, Felix. Gossips are the ones who spread tales about the Patriarch's tribe of illegitimate children—such slander to cast at a churchman—and swear that the Emperor is really a faceless demon in human form. I just pass along the news."

Leukos stood up. "I have to be off now or I'll be late. At least I'll be out of this sun." He fumbled with the leather pouch he carried on his belt, closed it with a sigh, and wiped the sweat from his broad forehead with the back of a pale hand. Then the Keeper of the Plate slipped quietly away.

John, his wandering attention arrested, cursed quietly as he realized his shocked return to the past had made him forget Leukos' odd behavior. Now he'd missed a chance for a quiet word in hopes his old friend would disclose the reason. But even as Leukos vanished into the crowds, their full-throated roar as another chariot race began would have made private conversation impossible. Sighing, John felt Anatolius tap him lightly on the arm.

"You've got one more chance to win a few nomismata on the racing, John. Perhaps. Going to wager on Green again?"

"I'll decline your kind offer this time, Anatolius. Where's Leukos gone?"

"He just went to see a soothsayer, John. You weren't paying much attention to what he was saying, were you?"

John shrugged.

"Still thinking about that girl, eh? I don't blame you." Anatolius grinned. "But, Felix, here's a chance to recoup your losses! If you have a nomisma or two left, are you willing to wager against my having kissed that young bull-leaper before sunset tomorrow?"

Chapter Three

By the time the games ended and Anatolius left his friends to hurry toward his appointment with the soothsayer, the sun was setting behind the seven hills of Constantinople, leaving the city's innumerable columns silhouetted briefly against a fading purple sky that rapidly pulled them into its soft darkness.

"Lovers," he mused. John had said that he and the girl had been lovers.

It was preposterous, of course. Not because of John's condition. He had, after all, once been whole. But the girl was too young. Younger even than Anatolius.

And John was usually the most rational of men. But of course the Lord Chamberlain had been under a great strain preparing for the yearly celebrations. Even the most brilliant of men were human. Then, too, John wasn't getting any younger.

Anatolius emerged from his musings just in time to see a pair of burly litter-bearers hauling their canopied chair down the center of the narrow street. He ducked aside, his back banging against the wooden wall of a tenement. The chair and its passenger were hidden behind sumptuous drapery, tassels dragging in the muck. Who was being borne in such haste and where were they were going? No doubt it was someone he had seen at court, perhaps someone he knew personally.

He stepped quickly back into the middle of the street. Once darkness fell on the city it was common, although illegal, for householders to empty waste out of their windows. Not that the night soil laws were particularly well observed in daylight either.

The games at the Hippodrome had not yet ended and so the streets were still relatively deserted. Less official and certainly less decorous celebrations that would span the night had not yet begun. There was only an occasional group of drunkards to mark the holiday.

Anatolius' thoughts returned to the girl. He recalled her exquisite face, the enormous dark eyes. Truly beautiful eyes, not merely illusions created by the skilled application of kohl.

Anatolius was all too familiar with artifice as practiced by the soft young women of the court. Pallid and slack. This girl, this woman... she was fully alive. Supple and muscular. Tanned. Her tiny breasts smooth and firm as apples. Yes, he had to admit it, he was in love.

And he had to confess, also, that he was glad John was not at his side to inquire about the goddess Lucretia, silken-breasted Lucretia, skin-like-moonlight Lucretia. Anatolius' most recent true love. She who had married a senator last week.

But, no, Anatolius chided himself. He had learned his lesson. He had been younger then, and foolish. Lucretia had been a delusion, but... this girl... whatever her name might be.... He must find out where the bull-leapers were staying. He must meet her. As for his friend John... well, he was clearly not himself today. No doubt he would awake tomorrow, feeling better, and gladly assist Anatolius in his quest.

And the soothsayer might also be of assistance. Yes, the future was even more seductive when you had found love.

Anatolius had been told that the Inn of the Centaurs where he was to meet the soothsayer was near Madam's place. He was familiar with that house of dubious repute since a young man had certain needs even at those rare times when he was not in love— and on those more frequent occasions when his love was unrequited. But when he arrived at Madam's door he could not see the inn.

As he stood, looking around, the door swung open, letting out a puff of warm, perfumed air that touched the side of his neck like the breath of a beautiful woman. For once, he was not tempted. Several men staggered out, obviously intoxicated. For them the celebrations had begun early. A faint tinkling of bells pursued them. The door slammed shut.

Soon, thought Anatolius, the streets would be jammed with celebrants like them. Again the door slammed. More figures spilled into the darkening square.

"The Inn of the Centaurs," Anatolius called out to a corpulent man rushing away in what Anatolius imagined was the right direction. "Where is it?"

"Just around the corner," the man called back over his shoulder, without stopping, as anxious to get away from Madam's as he had probably been to get there.

An alley running behind Madam's house invited Anatolius to take a short cut. But even those who were familiar with the city did well to respect its dark corners. Cutthroats didn't recognize class distinctions. A thief would be as likely to plunge a knife through expensive robes as through a threadbare tunic.

Anatolius, placing safety before speed, followed in the corpulent man's footsteps.

The large, decorative brass plaque sunk into the freshly plastered wall at the inn's entrance was new, although the rest of its appointments were not. This perhaps explained why Anatolius had not noticed the place before. He surely would have remembered the elaborately wrought beast, half man, half horse, engraved on its sign. It immediately brought to his mind a vision of the young bull-leaper, feet planted so surely on the bull's back that she might have been part of the animal.

Passing under the inn's arched entrance Anatolius discovered an enclosed courtyard boasting a gurgling, splashing fountain.

He found the innkeeper's wife, who appeared to be in charge this evening, setting the tables in the dining room. She was as impressive as the inn's brass plaque. Her ample frame was draped in what looked very much like the finest grade silks; she was obviously preparing for some very high born guests. A special celebration, perhaps, organized by one of the city guilds.

"Excuse me. I've come to see the soothsayer."

"The soothsayer? Yes, of course." She sounded annoyed by the query. She glared at Anatolius with what she must have considered a haughty expression. He noticed her heavy rouge, hardly necessary on her plump red peasant cheeks. "He's been very busy today. The old man's paid for a room, not a personal servant to direct his callers. But since you ask, that's him in the corner over there, waiting for his dinner. He'll eat like a horse tonight. I can predict that as well as he can!" The woman gave a disdainful sniff.

The old man the innkeeper's wife had indicated

looked more like a beggar than a seer. Anatolius sat down on the wooden stool next to him. He appeared to be dozing, but opened his eyes, alert, before Anatolius had a chance to speak.

"You must be the young man who wants to know his future?"

Anatolius noted that the soothsayer's voice was low. But, after all, the young man thought, discretion was something all the seer's customers must demand.

"Well, yes. I did make an appointment for...."

The old man interrupted him. "I see you are in love...."

*　　*　　*

As John and Felix made their way through the thronged tenement-lined streets, John found himself wishing that he had declined Felix's invitation to take some wine before "the mob drinks the city dry," as he had put it. There was something in John's look and bearing that normally cleared a path, but tonight the intoxicated and insolent alike blundered into him blindly and Felix had to take the lead, pushing his way through the crowd.

The face of the bull-leaper still floated in the darkness of John's mind. It was the same face to which he had been drawn so many years before. He was certain of it, yet it was impossible. He could almost feel her warm breath against his lips. He had been a different sort of creature then.

Even Anatolius, always the romantic, had insisted it must be a different woman. But John knew better. "Time is gentler with some. And performers wear makeup," he had pointed out.

"She didn't just appear young, John," Anatolius had said. "She was young. Closer to my age than yours."

John couldn't blame his youthful friend for being entranced. Anatolius' infatuation would pass quickly, as it always did.

"Pay attention," Felix scolded. "You look like a poet gazing at the sunset. The girl was a child and no use to you anyway, if you'll excuse my saying it."

Felix was right, of course, and John tried to bring his attention to bear on where he was, rather than where he had been or where he was going. This was always a wise strategy on the city's bustling streets, but somehow his attention kept slipping back to events at the Hippodrome. Fatigue and the afternoon sun had made him less than attentive to what Leukos had been saying before the bear baiting began. What was it? Something about a visitor?

Memory stirred. Yes, that was it. Leukos had remarked, "It isn't just citizens who come to the palace with their hands out. Yesterday there was a barbarian sniffing around my treasure. Said his name was Thomas. He claimed to be an emissary of the King of Bretania. And looking for a goblet...."

The rest of the scene flashed into John's mind.

"You gave him one, of course," he had teased Leukos.

"No, I referred him to you," was the airy reply. "Well, John, he insisted that it was a matter of state. Surely matters of state are your line, not mine. You're in the Emperor's confidence, are you not? So if I were you, I would expect to see my mysterious visitor calling on you tomorrow morning."

Now that his mind was working again, John regretted Leukos' haste in slipping away from the Hippodrome, and his own inattention. He would have liked to know more about Thomas, not to mention learning why the usually circumspect Leukos wanted to visit such a questionable character as the mysterious fortune-teller.

The games having now ended, the festivities had spread out into the city. Fires burned in its narrow streets. Sparks cartwheeled up toward thin swatches of night sky between the buildings. Grotesque shadows groped past blank lower story walls toward open windows higher up. Men sang and cursed. Some paraded in costume, disguised as demons or wild animals. Others lurched along arm in arm, holding each other upright. Groups of Blues, recognizable by their Hunnic hair style, shaved in front and long in back, squared off against one another in mock anger. Fortunately, no gangs of Greens had made an appearance, so no brawls had broken out. As yet.

"This will be a long night for the Watch," muttered Felix. He deftly elbowed aside a staggering duck-headed thing that gave a pitiful cry, collapsed into the gutter, and crawled off. A trio of ruby-lipped women leaning in a nearby doorway laughed shrilly, raucous as ravens afflicted with quinsy. The acrid smell of wood smoke mingled with the odor of unwashed bodies, cheap perfume, and night soil.

The press was thicker still in the small square on which stood Madam's house. This was not the evening to stop and talk with his old friend, thought John.

"Look," directed Felix, "It's the bear trainer."

In the middle of the square the big bare-chested man in green tights stood in front of an iron cage sitting atop a cart. The bear was a dark shadow behind the bars. Occasional illumination from a nearby bonfire glinted off eye, incisor, or claw.

"Who'll be the next?" barked the man, brandishing a stout pole at the milling crowd. "Come on! You call yourselves Romans?"

A young man in a brocaded tunic and cloak stumbled forward, pushed by several laughing comrades. One of them flicked a coin at the bear trainer, who followed its flashing arc to pluck it expertly from the air.

The bear trainer held out the pole to the obviously intoxicated young man, who took it gingerly in one hand. He appeared to feel he needed both hands free to remain standing.

"Give 'er a poke, then," he was instructed.

"You trying to steal Madam's trade?" yelled a wit among the spectators. The young man stood uncertainly, swaying from side to side.

"Go on," repeated the bear trainer. "Give 'er a poke!"

"Go on, Aoinos!" urged his companions. Their friend took an unsteady step forward and gingerly pushed the pole through the bars.

The bear reacted instantly. With a roar, it caught the pole, wrenching it out of the youngster's hands. The suddenly free end whipped upwards, smashing the would-be tormentor's nose. Blood gouted into the air.

The response of the onlookers was as quick, mindless, and vicious as the bear's.

"It's the Blues!" someone bellowed, his words slurred. "It's a trick!"

"Greens!" another inebriate screamed. "Over here! Don't let them get away with it!"

The crowd surged in sullen eddies toward the cart.

"Quick, let's get away from here," Felix urged. The Captain of the Excubitors had come between rioting factions often enough, but always with an armed contingent at his back. But as he and John turned to retreat down a nearby alley the crowd became still, unnaturally silent. As quickly as it had moved forward, the crowd backed away, until the cart was visible.

It was empty. The iron cage had toppled to the

ground and atop it an enormous shadow moved.

A woman screamed.

The bear rumbled deep in its throat and jumped to the ground.

Men backed away from the beast slowly, each afraid to single himself out by attracting its attention.

John froze, gaze darting back and forth. The beast might shamble in any direction.

No longer the tormented, the bear lurched forward. A man in the short, simple tunic of a laborer found himself in the monster's path. His head turned first one way and then the other, but he could not make himself move. His eyes gleamed huge in the bonfire light. A gurgle of fear escaped his throat and he crumpled to the ground. The bear, heedless, stepped over him, accidentally crushing his forearm.

The beast's head swung from side to side, and then stopped, its bright, hard eyes focusing intently. It turned, advancing purposefully toward Madam's doorway.

That was where the bear trainer cowered.

The man whirled around nimbly, doubtless seeking to escape through the door into Madam's house, but the bear was already moving. This time no chain brought it to the ground, short of its goal. As the trainer's hand scrabbled at the door, the bear's massive jaws were already tearing out the side of his throat. Blood spilled down the trainer's chest.

While the bear occupied itself, drawn swords and daggers glinted and a few onlookers, cautiously, moved toward the oblivious animal.

"Hurry up," Felix urged. "The alley behind Madam's. We can get away down there before there's more trouble."

The two men half ran past the angle of the wall and found themselves in darkness. The cobbles were slippery underfoot. John steadied himself by running a hand along the rough side of the house. He heard a rat skitter out of his way. The alley stunk of human waste and worse.

His boot was caught by something soft but bulky and he toppled forward, his knee banging down painfully on the stones.

Darkness shimmered before his eyes like a veil of black silk as he scrambled to hands and knees. At least, he thought, the cobbles here were dry. He was blinking, trying to see what had tripped him, when a shuttered window above was thrown open. A woman's voice demanded to know who was waking good citizens.

In the sudden flood of lamplight John looked down at a pale face. The eyes were wide open, the features slack, blue lips drawn back.

"Leukos?"

His friend, lying on his back in the filthy alley, did not answer. Leukos was dead.

Chapter Four

It was late when John returned home, and as he approached his iron-studded door he heard from within a cracked sobbing. His old servant Peter had waited up. The mournful noise was Peter's rendition of a Christian hymn, and one written by Justinian at that. John had heard Peter sing the same hymn while scrubbing the lavatory.

The sound stopped at John's first knock. The door creaked open, and Peter's leathery face peered out from the dim orange lamplight illuminating the hallway.

"Trouble, sir? I can see from your face it is trouble."

"Yes," John said sadly, watching Peter secure the door bolts. "Leukos has been killed."

The old man made the Christian sign. "The Keeper of the Plate. You spoke well of him. I'm sorry." His expression darkened. "I wouldn't walk the streets at night. The devil's abroad. It's not like ages past."

John reflected that it was the old servant's Christians who had invented the devil, but said nothing. Peter served him well despite his being a free man. John would not have employed a slave.

"The Prefect of the Night Watch is a prickly character. He's retained the dagger that was in Leukos' ribs, but when I used a little… shall we say persuasion… he finally agreed to have Leukos' pouch sent to me after the authorities have examined it."

"His family would want that," nodded Peter, assuming this was John's purpose.

"Yes," agreed John. No doubt Leukos had family somewhere. Like so many in the capital, the man who had risen high must have arrived alone from a distant corner of the empire to seek his fortune, or flee his fate, or do both. Like John, he rarely spoke about his past. Perhaps that was one reason John had been at ease with him.

Out of concern for his old servant's feelings, John said nothing about the entwined serpents on the hilt of the dagger which had killed Leukos. Peter was superstitious and would doubtless interpret the design as an evil omen, especially since it was obviously of foreign origin.

John retired to his study and Peter brought him the harsh Egyptian wine he favored.

"I am sorry to hear about your friend," the servant said as he turned to go. "I will pray for his soul."

※　　※　　※

The Lord Chamberlain sat at his desk and poured wine into a clay cup decorated only by a ruby-stained crack in its lip. He was troubled by the murder of Leukos and, as powerfully, by the bull-leaper he had glimpsed at the Hippodrome. Surely it was wrong that the image of those dark, bright eyes should keep pushing from John's mind the fixed stare of his dead friend. Mithra, he wondered, is it enough for a man to control his actions, or are you pleased only with those who can control their thoughts as well?

John forced his attention toward Leukos and the circumstances of his death. Surely that was where his duty lay. He had spoken to the man nearly every day. They often worked together. On a few occasions Leukos had visited him to share a meal and some wine. He had been aware of John's pagan beliefs, not an unusual thing at court if the truth were told, but equally not a thing one would confide to an enemy. Yet John knew very little of the personal circumstances of the man he had called a friend.

One thing he certainly knew was that no man deserved to die in such a fashion. Still, death in the street, at the hands of a mob or some anonymous cutthroat, was hardly more unnatural than death by a pox. An accident. Terrible, but hardly unexpected. But was it an accident?

Then there was this foreigner whose visit Leukos had mentioned. He had said the stranger was to call on John in the morning. And now Leukos was dead. A coincidence? John downed another gulp of wine.

The man had told Leukos he was an emissary from Bretania. Wandering storytellers had filled the countryside with tales of a great Christian king who had united the Britons. They spoke, when they were safely outside the walls of Constantinople, of a court rivaling Justinian's in splendor and of a round table, apparently of some ceremonial significance.

John took another sip of wine and smiled bleakly. He was fortunate he would never have to arrange banquet seating at such an infernal table. Men who toiled in the strict hierarchy of Justinian's court killed to sit one place nearer the Emperor than a rival.

But could it possibly be true that a great king had sprung from the stinking sloughs John recalled from his days on that barbaric island?

The trembling light from the lamp on John's desk animated the elaborate wall mosaics the house's former owner had left to the austere Lord Chamberlain. At the base of the wall a goatherd tended his flock, hunters loosed dogs, a farmer chided a reluctant donkey, and three ducks took flight while children played with a miniature cart.

Above these pastoral scenes, however, lusty old Roman gods and goddesses rioted in a manner which the most jaded courtesan might find a good argument for Christianity. Moreover, the artist had pressed the mosaic's colored glass tesserae into the drying plaster at such angles that subtle changes in color, when the tilted glass caught lamplight, revealed scurrilous details thankfully invisible by the light of day.

As always, however, John's attention was drawn to one figure. Among the bucolic mortals shown gathered below the heavenly company, a young girl aged perhaps nine or ten stood apart from two boys playing knuckle bones. Her eyes were very large, almond-shaped, reminding John of the ancient funerary portraits he had seen during his time in Egypt.

There was a touch of naturalism about the girl the other figures lacked. She alone seemed to have been drawn from life. She might have been the artist's daughter, John thought. Though the girl gave no overt sign of noticing the heavens, her mouth was drawn up in a grimace of pain, suggesting knowledge and suffering beyond her years.

For no reason he could name, John thought of her as "Zoe." She was, he knew, a stoic. Much like himself. At times, he could feel her presence in the room.

John lifted the cup again. The rough wine burned the back of his throat. He had been known to ask Zoe questions which he always answered himself, but on this night he did not ask what she would make of a friend stabbed in an alley, or a vision of a lost love, or what sort of royal emissary might travel from barbaric

Bretania to the Golden Horn.

Zoe stared out from the mosaic at him. The flickering light catching the tesserae forming the corners of her lips hinted at movement, but she did not speak.

✻   ✻   ✻

Elsewhere in the city, another girl, lips trembling, warily pushed open the heavy, rotting shutter of a second floor tenement room. The air of Constantinople was fetid, smoky, sour with the stench from the alley beneath the window, but still more breathable than the air inside the tenement that was laden with the smell of humanity and cooking odors. The girl's husband rolled over in his sleep, muttering, disturbed by the noise of the shutter. He flung one heavy arm out, barely missing the pot of night soil the girl had set next to the window. He was big and could almost reach across their space, one of several created by subdividing an already small room with thin, rough boards.

During the day he worked as a laborer at the new church Justinian was building. Or had until his fall.

"The dome alone will rival the heavens," he had told her. "Imagine such a wonder!"

"But why do we need a dome like heaven when heaven's already over our heads?"

"Heaven may be up there, but you can't appreciate it in the tenements." He must have been sorry to see her frown, because he continued, "You don't regret leaving the country with me, do you?"

"You're my husband." It was a simple statement, carrying everything within it. "We're not country folk now. This is Constantinople, the greatest city in the world. Our home."

She had made herself smile.

Then one afternoon he had fallen from high up

in that great dome. That he had survived had been a miracle. But perhaps a short lived one. His fever had returned.

Now she bent to pick up the heavy pot, averting her face. She was exhausted. But then, what a night it had been. The second time she had opened the shutters, after her first fright, it had been even worse. What had she seen but a corpse apparently looking straight up at her. And to think she'd had the pot in her hand. It seemed indecent. She had almost dishonored the dead.

She forced herself to peer down into the alley. This third time, at last, it seemed deserted. She emptied the pot, leaning over the sill. Its contents splashed on the cobbles below.

She sank wearily down next to her husband and hoped for dreams of the country.

❊   ❊   ❊

Though the night was far advanced, the liquid sounds of syrinx and flute still filled the perfumed air of the vast imperial dining room as a scantily clad girl danced down the middle of a long table that was draped in purple and gold. Not that she really knew how to dance. But she moved her narrow hips, imitating older performers, directing her bare feet as nimbly as possible over and around plates of pomegranates, figs, and boiled duck. The young men on the couches flanking the table laughed as she went by, trying to look up her short green tunic. They seemed pleased.

She was only a girl, young enough so she could remember when men had not noticed her. This new power she had been granted fascinated her. She could sense the probing thoughts of the men and their attention exhilarated and repulsed her at the same time.

One of the men had grabbed her around the waist and thrust her onto the table. She could smell sour wine on his breath. As he embraced her, his stubble brushed the side of the breast that her tunic, tied only at one shoulder, had left exposed in what the great lady who had prepared the girls had explained was the ancient manner.

"What's your name, little one?" the man had demanded.

"They call me Nymph," she had replied, mindful of the great lady's admonition to give only that name and not to reveal her real name, which was Berta. She was puzzled when the man burst into laughter.

"Dance for me," he'd commanded, and so Berta had danced.

Perhaps she would please one of these men so that he would bring her to live at the palace. It could happen. Look at the Empress herself. That's what all the girls at Madam's said. Consider Empress Theodora. You never knew.

She had been hand-fed a few morsels from the table, a slice of an unfamiliar fruit more succulent than anything she had tasted before. All was luxury here. Even her indecently brief tunic was of silk, smooth against her skin. Her underclothing, too, the same.

As she danced amid the plates, bare feet still retaining their instinctive childish agility, she felt the smooth material caressing her between her thighs. She shaved there. Madam demanded it of all her girls. She was from Egypt and that was the Egyptian custom for those in the profession.

The flutes played even faster, cymbals under-scoring their sinuous rhythm. The girl danced in time, skipping between chalices, ducking under a huge golden bowl of fruit suspended by chains from the ceiling. She felt sweat running down her ribs. A flush rose on her cheeks. Surely this was heaven. But then, wasn't the Emperor a god?

Her attention was caught momentarily by an unwelcome figure. A garishly dressed page leered at her from a corner. Odious little boy. He'd pawed her earlier.

Distracted, she failed to clear the roast boar.

Her foot caught on its platter. She toppled off the edge of the table into an obviously male lap. Recovering her senses, she rolled over to look up into the face of whoever had broken her fall. Perhaps he would take her to his house tonight.

Berta assumed her most dazzling, ingratiating smile. And gasped. The face looming above her was creased with years but its opening lips revealed surprisingly white teeth.

"I am a soothsayer, but I need no chicken entrails to tell me what a lovely creature you are," declared the ancient man. "Would you like to earn a trinket?"

Chapter Five

"Lord Chamberlain." The stocky man spoke curtly as he pushed by Peter into John's study, filled now with the watery sunlight of early morning. "Felicitations," he added clumsily, in heavily accented but understandable Greek.

John half bowed in acknowledgment, gesturing his visitor to a wooden stool by his desk. He had slept little, but, as an ex-soldier, it was something to which he was accustomed. Peter had introduced the burly redheaded visitor as "Thomas, an emissary from Bretania".

Thomas sat down stiffly. "I am Thomas, a knight from the court of King Arthur."

Although his visitor spoke in the Greek commonly used in the capital, John noticed with curiosity that he used the Latin "eques" for "knight," a class which dated back to the early days of Rome. "You say you are a knight?"

"Indeed. The High King has trained a cavalry after the Roman fashion and so has given us that title, although, I understand, it is a long time since Roman knights rode in battle."

"I have heard of King Arthur," replied John. His

visitor shifted on the stool. "I see you're uncomfortable, Thomas. Afflictions of the joints come with the climate of your land, as I recall."

Peter poured ruby Egyptian wine into two silver goblets and withdrew. A breeze brought the pungent smell of the Sea of Marmara through the open window.

"I suffer myself," John continued, "and sometimes, on damp mornings like these, it feels as if Cerberus is gnawing my leg."

"This leg of mine... it's an old wound. But you know Bretania? It surprises me to find someone familiar with my country in this place." Thomas' glance flicked uneasily over the rollicking gods depicted in the mosaics on John's walls. He looked aghast.

John's first impression was that Thomas would not last long in Justinian's court. Too open and perhaps too honest, despite looking the complete barbarian with scuffed leather boots and rough wool tunic, leggings, and cloak stained by travel and weather. His woven belt was, however, swordless. John, a cautious man, would not knowingly permit a weapon in his house, although he did not doubt that most visitors carried at least a small dagger concealed about their persons. He did himself.

"The mosaics were commissioned by the former owner of this house," explained John. "A tax collector. So efficient was he that the Emperor finally had to hand his head to the populace, although he never returned their gold. My own tastes, as you can tell from my furnishings, are considerably less extravagant." The Lord Chamberlain gestured toward the few pieces of unadorned wooden furniture scattered about the opulently walled room. "But, as to your country, I was there in my youth."

John thought it tactful not to mention that he

had served as a mercenary. For all he knew he might have made his visitor's acquaintance in battle. An odd thought, but the world was full of odder things.

"A wild land," he continued, "Beautiful but wild. And I have the scars to prove it." The men exchanged soldierly smiles, brothers in arms. "And so, it has been a while since you left your homeland?"

"Well over a year now. I'm a soldier, not a courtier, but even so, it's been a long journey and a difficult one."

"And even a soldier longs for home eventually. You will, of course, dine with me later? My servant Peter is a passable cook."

"I regret I have pressing business today. But I'd be pleased to accept one of those figs." He nodded toward the bowl of dried fruit on the low table by the door.

"Of course." said John. "I am told you visited Leukos, Keeper of the Plate?"

"Yes." Thomas, who had risen awkwardly to help himself to a fig and returned to his seat, grimaced slightly. "Leukos directed me to you, Lord Chamberlain." He was blunt. "I've not been able to gain an audience with Patriarch Epiphanios. But I understand that you are very knowledgeable in matters of state and in matters of religion as well."

"I am flattered. Many have the same knowledge. Of course," John pointed out, "this is a Christian court. Still, there are many religions, and I know a little about some. It has been an interest of mine. You should know, however, that Leukos was slain last night."

Thomas regarded John steadily, but said nothing.

"You don't seem surprised," said the Lord Chamberlain.

"Nothing surprises me in this city."

John found that most unlikely, but he made no comment.

"I must offer you my sympathy," said his visitor. "If you would prefer I could return?"

"No."

"Well, then. To be direct, it is your sacred relics that interest me."

"I can tell you something of them, certainly." John did not add that he was more interested in what his visitor could tell him of his recent travels. Aside from his own curiosity, John could hardly afford to allow others in the palace to gain information he did not possess. And, it occurred to him, Thomas was also one of the last people to have spoken to Leukos.

Thomas lounged sideways, looking out the window toward a cobbled parade ground in front of a barracks. His troublesome leg was extended. The breeze ruffled his red hair, worn longer than would have been considered fashionable, even among those who were followers of the Blues. He suddenly nodded at a large, dark bird sitting hag-like on the roof of the barracks. "Tell me, do you have ravens here too?"

"Ravens?"

Thomas turned his sea-deep gaze to John, continuing in the same even tone. "Whatever bird that is, if I were superstitious, I would be looking to hear ill tidings."

"Alas, a common enough event in men's lives these days. But why so, particularly?" John asked as he refilled their goblets.

"In my country," his visitor went on, with a crooked smile, "it is said that to see a raven, a single raven, mark you, is to foretell sorrow. But for the fortunate one who sees two, this means joy. And so on, and so on." Thomas took a deep draft of the wine. "Six, now, that means gold."

"Let's hope certain court officials don't get wind of that. The imperial treasury would be inundated in requisitions for funds to capture sextets of ravens and pinion them to the roof in hopes their predictions of wealth come true." John's tone was dry. He was not sure, now, what to make of the foreigner.

"I don't think that would work. For one thing, whatever the priests say, the gods aren't so easily swayed by the machinations of men."

John eyed Thomas. A strange comment, he thought, coming from a member of a renowned Christian court.

"For another," his guest continued, "if Fortune is so fickle as to favor those with good eyesight, it would seem likely that the ravens would have to be free to come and go or men would stare at the roof all day."

"You sound like a devotee of the Athenian philosophical school." John wondered where this strange discussion was taking them. "It would appear then, if this is correct, that a blind man is doubly ill-treated by Fortune, for he can see neither his present nor his future."

Thomas considered this philosophical problem. "Well", he opined at last, "men must be aware, if not beware, of ravens. For Fortune may prove a more implacable foe to the soldier than Persians."

There was silence in the sybaritically decorated but spartanly furnished room. Was the stranger's juxtaposition of ravens, soldiers and Persians accidental? All were ranks of Mithraism. John recalled his visitor's interest in figs. The fig tree had fed and clothed Lord Mithra, as followers who climbed the ladder of secret knowledge knew. Was the outwardly simple barbarian speaking in codes?

Outside the lone black bird rose silently into a cloudless sky, soaring away until it was a speck over the twinkling swells of the sea.

Thomas abruptly broke the silence. "I am here on

delicate business. It is common knowledge that Constantinople has many glories. The churches, for example. Precious stone mosaics, solid gold lamps and marbles of green and blue." He shook his head at such extravagance.

"That is correct."

"Yet there are here in the city greater treasures still. Moses' staff, even a fragment or two of the True Cross, so I hear."

"Yes, a fragment, at least."

Thomas winced slightly as he leaned forward. "But what I am in search of is the Grail."

"Ah, yes, according to legend, the cup from the last meal before the Crucifixion. Though some say it is a platter, such as those from which we eat, or—what else?—a precious gem is yet another possibility. I must confess I have not heard that the Grail is here, if indeed it exists at all. But if it were it would surely be in the Patriarch's charge."

"Well, Lord Chamberlain, not all treasures are where we would look to find them. And many which are in their rightful place are not necessarily, shall we say, authentic?"

John glanced outside as a loud shuffle of feet below marked the progress of a detachment of excubitors toward their next watch. He caught a glimpse of Felix as the burly captain emerged from the barracks. Evidently he saw John as he raised a hand in acknowledgment before barking out orders to his men. Perhaps, thought John, he should humor his visitor in hopes of finding out more useful information later. "What makes you believe that such a relic, surely the most holy of all, is here in the city? And where do you think it is?"

"I heard about it from an old man. I met him... well, let us say, fairly recently." Thomas was apparently a cautious man. "He told me an interesting tale, and swore further that it could be found within the Great Palace."

John's eyes narrowed. "The palace grounds may be extensive, but still, I find it hard to believe they conceal such a gem so completely it is unknown to me."

"A soldier's oath, my lord. The High King has sent out his knights to seek the Grail, and to bring it home. Like mistletoe in the old religion, it will heal all."

"Is that what they say? But even if it were here, surely you realize that Justinian would never part with such a treasure?"

"Of course. My plan is to find out where it is. Then I shall return home and the High King can negotiate. I fear there isn't enough gold in all of Christendom to buy it, and judging as a soldier, your city's location, not to mention its walls, would render any siege futile."

"It sounds as if you have studied our defenses."

"Yes, well, it is prudent to keep one's eyes open here, isn't it? At any rate, what I say is, let those in high places make the decisions. But," he leaned forward confidentially, "make no mistake, Lord Chamberlain, more than you might suppose hinges upon this."

John looked down at his goblet, turning it slowly in thin fingers. There was no more dangerous zealot than a mistaken zealot. All the same, if there was some truth in the tale.... "Tell me," he asked, "do you not see how old these goblets are? I got them years ago in one of those lanes off the Augustaion. The man who sold them to me, a Syrian, swore they were a hundred years old. There are older in the imperial collection. The one you seek is even older. Could such a fragile thing have survived?"

"Who can say? In any event, that is why I am

here seeking your help. Perhaps you could give me a personal introduction to the Patriarch? I will be at the Inn of the Centaurs for a few days yet. May I expect to hear from you?"

John looked at his guest silently. The Inn of the Centaurs was where Leukos had gone to meet the soothsayer.

Thomas added, "I ask it of you as a Raven."

The Lord Chamberlain's eyes narrowed. "You are an adept then? A follower of Mithra?"

His visitor smiled wordlessly.

How, John wondered, had Thomas come to guess the Lord Chamberlain's secret beliefs? Or, perhaps more to the point, who had told him?

"But why should a follower of Mithra risk his life for a Christian relic, or serve a Christian king?" John asked.

He knew what the rejoinder would be immediately the words had left his lips. Thomas did not disappoint him.

"I could ask the same of you," smiled the foreign knight.

Shortly thereafter, Thomas left with an introduction to the Patriarch. John sat brooding for a while, staring at the fantastically detailed mosaic and the little girl Zoe. She had listened to their conversation so solemnly and silently.

"What do you think then?" John asked her. "Is this Thomas trustworthy? Is it only a coincidence that Leukos died the same day he met the man? Yes, yes, you are right, Zoe. It is my task to find that out."

Chapter Six

A hot blade of sunlight bit into the back of John's neck as he entered the courtyard of the Inn of the Centaurs. It was the obvious place for him to begin his investigation, since it was where Thomas claimed to be staying and where Leukos, according to Anatolius, had an appointment on the evening of his death. Had death caused Leukos to miss that appointment as well? Although the image of the bull-leaper constantly intruded into John's thoughts, he was determined to devote the day to following the last footsteps of his murdered friend. His own feelings, he told himself, had to be put aside.

An enormous woman in the inn's kitchen, evidently the innkeeper's wife, grunted unpleasantly when he asked for the soothsayer and directed him back to the courtyard.

"Look for an old beggar, fast asleep. That'll be him. More popular than the Emperor, he is!" she had sniffed.

If Thomas had returned directly to the inn after his visit to John's residence that morning, he was nowhere to be seen. John bowed his head in respect as he passed the fig tree that shaded a marble fountain. Beside the fountain an old man in ragged robes sat dozing on a bench.

As John drew closer with the silent tread that came naturally to him, the old man opened his eyes—large eyes, bright and shrewd, under bushy brows. The eyes of a man who had seen a lot and lamented over much of what he had observed. John realized the other had not been asleep, but rather resting watchfully. Despite the heat, yellowed robes which had been bone-white many dusty years before were drawn closely around the old man's bird-like body.

"I greet you, sir." The soothsayer's voice was surprisingly resonant for one so slight. He gestured to the bench next to him as if he were giving an audience. "How may a humble traveler help a man of your eminence?"

John was careful to display no surprise at the seer's prescience. Although the Lord Chamberlain was not wearing his most opulent garments, it would not be difficult for an observant person to deduce his status from the fine embroidery on his robes.

John sat down next to the old man. The marble bench was warm. He noticed a small striped cat perched on the edge of the fountain basin, engrossed in trying to catch ripples with its paw. It was leaning alarmingly close to the water, or at least what would have been considered alarmingly close were it a human bending, Narcissus-like, to look in the fountain. For an instant John could not help but picture himself leaning precariously over the water. A shudder ran through him.

The old man smiled. "I should not worry about the cat. Unlike humans, they have many lives."

"Cats don't like water, though," replied John. "And some say even humans have lives after this one."

"Perhaps, perhaps." A smile flashed whitely in the soothsayer's earth-brown face, a wrinkled map of the countless roads that had brought him from his distant homeland to Constantinople. "But tell me, what is your business here? I doubt that a man of your rank has taken time away from his duties to have his fortune told!"

"A man makes his own fortunes, or so I believe. But you are correct. I have come to see you, informally, on a matter of business."

There was a burst of shouting from the kitchen. A portly man emerged, half-supporting another who was red-faced and cursing.

"With the celebrations, some of Master Kaloethes' customers have been making rather too familiar an acquaintance with the wine jug," observed the soothsayer.

This particular troublesome customer was, by appearance, a charioteer, still dressed for the races in his short sleeveless tunic although his crossed leather belts and puttees were now askew. He was hardly in any condition to race, for his legs seemed inclined to give way at any moment. With a grunted apology to the two men sitting on the bench, the innkeeper steered the inebriate to the fountain and taking a firm grip on one of the unfortunate man's leather belts, dunked his head several times in the water. The cat ran off, its tail arched in apparent terror.

Tepid water splashed the back of John's hand. To him it felt cold, as frigid as the roiling waters of a swollen northern beck. He quickly wiped his hand on his tunic.

A moment later the innkeeper shoved the cursing charioteer out into the street.

The old man had observed John's startled reaction to the water but remained silent.

Having accomplished his task, the hulking innkeeper trod heavily back to where John and the soothsayer were seated.

"Now there is a man who will wake with the Furies in his head," Kaloethes remarked, regarding John with eyes as small and bright as a rat's. John noted his appraising look. "I'd guess from your fine dress you've come from the palace. What can we do for you here at the Inn of the Centaurs?"

"I've come to speak to the soothsayer," John said mildly.

Kaloethes looked disappointed. "Well, we pride ourselves here on keeping a high class establishment. Perhaps you may want to sample one of our fine wines later, excellency? If so, we would be honored to serve you."

John watched him move slowly back toward the inn. As soon as the innkeeper had vanished inside, raised voices began to emerge.

"As I was saying," John continued, "I am here on a matter of business. I have some questions."

"I shall anticipate one," the old man smiled, "My name is Ahasuerus. My family was originally of Antioch, but I left several years ago."

"I seem to recall that there was an earthquake there. Were you driven from your home then, never to return?"

"No, my lord, although I appreciate your concern. I am, in fact, the last of my line. Since I left, I have traveled on many roads, casting augers, offering advice. Yet for all my wanderings, this is the first time I have seen Constantinople. It is certainly a city of splendor."

John inquired what had brought him to the city.

The old man shrugged. "I felt... how shall I put it... this was where I should be. And so I journeyed here."

John eyed the cat, which had returned and was dabbing a paw at water spilt around the fountain basin, examining it with interest. "I am told you are a soothsayer," he stated. "Do you find trade brisk?"

"I do. I was kept up late last night, telling fortunes. All men seek their fortunes at the dead of night, especially at an inn or wherever wine flows freely. I find people of all walks of life are interested in knowing what lies ahead, those who sell themselves on the streets as well as the highest born ladies." Ahasuerus smiled. "Not all come to see me to acquire fore-knowledge of their fate. A large proportion of the ladies ask their questions for purposes of entertainment. Or so they say. Lately I have been invited to many gatherings to amuse the ladies."

"Yes, I have heard excellent reports of your readings from more than one source." John silently petitioned Mithra to forgive the lie. "But from your mention of the ladies, I take it you do not use the ancient Roman method, reading entrails? Too much blood?"

"Oh, yes, certainly. For a man, no, but for the ladies, I usually read currents in a bowl of water or wine, or sometimes I cast pebbles, that kind of thing. I'll tell you this in confidence," he glanced around the deserted courtyard, seeking overly-interested ears. "Just recently I was at a formal gathering at the home of a very highly placed lady. Now, I can't say which lady this was, you understand, as I imagine her husband would be very distressed to hear of it. But apparently she wanted to impress her guests, for I was given a handful of gems to use instead of my pebbles."

"Certainly that must have been impressive." John wondered briefly if the old man had managed to make off with a gem or two. He was of the opinion that a man's actions foretold more about his future than did a length of intestines pulled from a chicken. "And how does this method work?"

"Ah, my son, it would take years to impart such knowledge. Did the Delphic Oracle attain enlightenment in a moment? Of course not! But for myself, I learned it from my father, and he from his. We have been wanderers, travelers for generations. But," he leaned forward, "I can tell you, sir, that to read the signs is a gift." He raised a hand briefly in thanksgiving to the cloudless sky. "And yet, even after many years, what more often surprises me is the person asking the question, rather than the question itself."

John raised his eyebrows.

Ahasuerus glanced around again before continuing in an even more confidential tone. "Recently I told fortunes at a celebration held by another lady of high-rank, satisfactorily so far as I know for I have not had a demand for my fee to be returned, or at least not yet. But surprisingly, she not only insisted on a traditional reading, but provided a chicken for the purpose." He shrugged. "I doubt that she told her husband either."

John thought that while the woman's spouse might not have known about it, the slaves and servants who had cleaned up after the reading certainly did. "Have you had any clients from court?"

"It is possible. Not all my clients say who they are, but one can deduce from small things at least something about their station in life. I look at their bearing, accent, jewelry. Do they arrive alone or with attendants? Based upon such observations, I would say that I have had several visitors these past few days who could well be connected to the court."

"Tell me then, among those visitors, do you recall a large man, pale, completely bald?"

Ahasuerus reflected for a few seconds. "I did cast pebbles for a man such as you describe very recently. He had concerns about his health. I was able to reassure him that he would be in good health all his life. Also, if I remember rightly, that he might come into sudden wealth."

John noted the past tense. Perhaps it was nothing more than clumsy grammar on the part of one whose native tongue was not Greek.

"He isn't complaining about his reading, is he?" the old man continued. "Perhaps he wants his money back?"

"No, no. Your prophecy has turned out to be true enough, so far as I know." True enough that Leukos was in perfectly good health until he was murdered. As to wealth, given the brevity of his life following the reading of his fortune, any wealth he might have gained would have had to appear very suddenly indeed. John's thin lips curved in an ironic smile. "Tell me, do you fare well enough at your trade?" His quizzical gaze swept over Ahasuerus' well-worn robes and dusty sandals.

"Oh, I manage well enough. Despite how I look, they pay me, you know, not the other way around." The soothsayer gave a slight chuckle. Then his expression became serious. "But I can tell there is something else engaging your mind. Someone, or something else, which you seek."

A shrill voice pierced the hot air in the courtyard. John looked around and saw the innkeeper's wife in its doorway gesturing impatiently.

Ahasuerus climbed to his feet with surprising agility. "I am being informed that the meal is prepared. I have found it best to be quick to table when she calls or there is nothing left to eat."

"Then I must let you go." John watched the old man hurry away across the dusty courtyard. It struck him as humorous, the old oracle being as eager for his meal as a child.

It was growing ever hotter in the courtyard. The heat reflected from its walls made the air move in shimmering waves. It would be almost easy to immerse himself in the water at the baths on a day like this. Fortunately the city's many cisterns kept them well supplied during even the worst droughts.

John followed the old man to the kitchen where he found the innkeeper. He spoke to Kaloethes only to make a brief farewell.

Leaving, John's thoughts turned back to the bull-leaper. He did seek someone, and not just Leukos' murderer. How did the soothsayer know? Almost immediately John chided himself for being drawn into the old man's game. Wasn't everyone always seeking someone or something?

He went out into the clamor of the street, turning his steps toward his next task. He knew now that Leukos had kept his appointment with the soothsayer. He had a vague feeling that he had learned something even more important during his visit, but was not able to say exactly what it was.

※　　※　　※

Looking out of the kitchen window, Kaloethes watched the Lord Chamberlain leave and felt relief and regret wash over him, mixed like wine and water. The thought reminded him that he would have been more than glad, the Lord only knew, to sell even one bottle of the very expensive wine his wife insisted they stock expressly for such visitors. Unfortunately, such wealthy and discerning people never ventured into the Inn of the Centaurs. Yet one satisfied customer from the palace might well lead to others, as she was always telling him.

Then again the next visitors from the palace hierarchy might just as easily be tax collectors, building inspectors, or perhaps even worse. So he was relieved that the tall, austere man's questions had been perfunctory. As if he would have noticed some bald man amid all the noise and chaotic revelry that had filled the inn the night before.

Thankful that his sharp tongued wife had temporarily vanished on some errand or other, Kaloethes lowered his exhausted bulk onto the wooden bench next to the soothsayer, who was worrying a chicken bone across his plate like a starved cat.

Watching the old man, it occurred to Kaloethes that the inn had in fact had visitors from the palace recently, but unfortunately only to have fortunes told rather than to drink expensive wine.

But perhaps such visits could be used to his advantage.

"Tell me," he asked Ahaseurus, "why don't your clients linger a little longer at our establishment? What's so shameful about having your fortune told? They creep in and slink out, hoping nobody sees them, no doubt. Pretty soon, I'll need a back door like the one at Madam's."

The soothsayer dropped the cleanly stripped bone onto his plate. "I am afraid the authorities of the official religion frown on such gifts as mine. Perhaps they feel it is better to be cautious. And who knows but that they may be correct?"

Kaloethes made a rude noise. "It's a bit unnatural to know your future, if you ask me. A lot more unnatural than most of what goes on at Madam's."

The soothsayer wiped his plate with the last bit of his bread. "Yet it is not unnatural to have a future."

The innkeeper was not convinced about that, considering his own financial situation, and said so. "So what's my future? A place at the palace at last, do you supppose?"

"It is what your wife desires, is it not?"

"Takes no fortune teller to see that. But will it ever happen? Is there ever going to be an end to this incessant labor?"

"I can't give you a proper reading here." The soothsayer had finished his bread and was staring, somewhat mournfully, down at his plate.

"Look at you! You clean your plate like an obedient child. I remember my mother insisted that I clean my plate. And what did it make me? Not big and healthy, just fat. The butt of jokes." The innkeeper sounded genuinely hurt. "Still, though, seeing as there's just us here and nobody to overhear, what about this future of mine?"

"Sometimes knowing your past is to know your future."

"Don't give me that nonsense, old man! I'm not from the palace and I don't have time to fret over fancy words that don't mean anything."

The soothsayer glanced up at him, sighed, and then said he would need his fortune-telling tools in order to cast augurs. "The pebbles are quicker to cast, but a chicken reading is more certain, more detailed," he ended.

"Well, you've got part of a chicken there, at least." Kaloethes nudged the fleshless chicken bone with a pudgy finger.

The soothsayer's glare startled him. "I will tell you this. It takes back-breaking labor to build a church, but at the end it is filled with song."

Kaloethes stared at the old man's leathery face, trying to fathom what was meant. "I can see where someone with spare coins might pay you well, you old fraud." he finally admitted with admiration. "How much do they pay?"

"Enough to pay for my meals and board here."

"But surely, a little more than that would be helpful? Is there anyone who couldn't do with a little more?"

"I believe so, but I know you would not agree."

Kaloethes, suddenly struck by a profitable scheme, ignored the remark. "How about this? When your fancy palace clients come here, you might suggest that their future holds a fine wine from downstairs. Or—better yet—that some great good fortune might just await them at the Inn of the Centaurs, but at some unspecified time in the future. To get them to come back, you see? They might even bring a friend or two along with them, with any luck. Naturally I'd slip you a few coins out of what they spend."

"I would betray my gift if I agreed to do that." The soothsayer got to his feet. "Now, if you'll excuse me, I must resume my meditations."

The innkeeper persisted. "How about this? You could serve your clients some of our fine wines. It would make them more comfortable, not to say credulous. I'll give you a break on the price. What do you say?"

The soothsayer bent down to his plate and passed his hand over the chicken bone, then shook his head and said solemnly "I regret that I must inform you that such a plan is not in my future, Master Kaloethes."

With that the old man returned to the courtyard and, thought the innkeeper enviously, the shade of the fig tree.

The only shade Kaloethes was likely to see in the near future was that of his wife when she loomed over him with some new complaint. Where had the slim young thing he'd courted disappeared to, the girl who had seen in the poor, overweight boy abilities others had overlooked? When had her encouragement turned to nagging, her dreams to obessesions?

He picked up the soothsayer's plate, tossing the chicken-bone out the window to where the small striped cat waited. It would be disappointed the bone was bare. He looked down at the plate. Silver. Imagine that. The woman's pretensions were intolerable.

But so was her nagging tongue, and he had to find a way to appease it. He sighed and forced his thoughts back toward more practical matters. Mules, it seemed, weren't meant to be philosophers. He was already late paying several taxes and he was afraid the revellers who had filled the inn during the May celebrations had caused enough damage to their rooms as to reduce his expected profit considerably. What exactly was he going to do? What was that the soothsayer had said about it all ending in song. Not likely. He decided he had to go out for awhile.

He thought again about the elegantly robed man from the palace who had questioned him so briefly. The man had not identified himself, but it was obvious he was a highly placed official, powerful and extremely rich. They always seemed so clever and and self-assured, those men. If only you were half so clever as I, they seemed to say without actually saying it, you would not be toiling away your pitiful existence under the twin lashes of your creditors' demands and your wife's contempt.

Kaloethes wondered wistfully what it was his visitor knew that he did not. Surely that was the key to wealth? But then he comforted himself with the sour thought that the man probably knew nothing, had doubtless been born to his position. But he could not quite convince himself that was the case. He would have been amazed to know that, at that moment, John was just as puzzled, in his own way, as was he.

Chapter Seven

Thomas, standing near the bustling dock, was just as puzzled. To passersby he must have resembled nothing so much as a bewildered, ginger-whiskered child. The bright sunlight washing over him was clearer and warmer than the dank fogs of his native land, but it was the only thing in this place that was clear.

In his travels over the past twelve-month he had heard stories of the great civilization of Rome. Yet now, after only a few days of its hospitality, he longed for the wilderness that was Bretania. It seemed to Thomas that in civilized Constantinople anything not prohibited was regulated. It must be a constant headache, albeit creating a livelihood, for the army of administrators, scribes and secretaries whose days were devoted to interpreting and applying regulations governing everything from the price of bread to the width of the streets. Thomas had encountered more of these official ants that morning than in all his life hitherto.

And how did a foreign visitor treat an officiously obstructive, pasty-faced secretary who seemed to talk down and through his nose at the same time? If some ruffian had challenged him on the public road, Thomas' blade would have cleared the way quickly enough. But he couldn't very well skewer some poor cod of a secretary.

"Thomas!"

A familiar voice interrupted his thoughts. It was the Lord Chamberlain who was approaching, holding a half-eaten chunk of grilled fish evidently freshly purchased from one of several itinerant vendors whose braziers were strung out along the dock.

"This is the last place I would have expected to find you dining, Lord Chamberlain," Thomas said in surprise.

John wiped a spot of grease from the corner of his thin lips. "Ah, but it's good soldier's fare."

Thomas was struck anew by the strength of the man's voice. He had, after all, heard that the Lord Chamberlain was not really a proper man. Yet he did not speak like a woman.

"I didn't expect to see you again so soon, Thomas."

"Nor I you," Thomas replied, haltingly. Somehow he could not get his thoughts to march properly in Greek.

"I trust your endeavors are going well?"

"I've had no good fortune at all. You have too many rules here. Everything and everywhere is forbidden. It's too much for a simple man like me."

"True enough," agreed John. "But you must learn to negotiate the maze. Take this delicious fish, for instance. It's only available because the Emperor decided fish merchants were entitled to maintain their monopoly. By that, he meant not to have their prices undercut by fishermen. Even though it's the fishermen who actually brave Poseidon's wrath to land his bounty, mark you."

Thomas gave John a puzzled look. Was the Lord

Chamberlain making fun of him? He cocked an eyebrow, trying to appear skeptical, just in case. "How can that be?"

"In order to protect the merchants, the Emperor has forbidden fishermen to sell fresh fish. But you see these vendors? At other times they're fishermen. The sale of cooked fish is not prohibited. Why don't you try some?"

Thomas chuckled. He tossed a copper coin to a nearby vendor who started to pocket it. At a stern look from John, however, the man clipped a piece from the edge of the coin, returning it to Thomas along with a wooden skewer of partially blackened fish.

Thomas eyed the misshapen coin. The Emperor's nose had been amputated. It was not very dignified for a ruler to have his image so rudely handled, and Thomas marveled that he would allow it rather than forbidding the practice. As a visitor, however, he decided it would be impolite to state his opinion and popped the coin into the pouch at his belt. He turned his attention to the fish. "Why is this sold so cheaply?"

"You look as dubious as your namesake," the Lord Chamberlain replied. "But try it anyway." He took another bite himself. "Have you been to see the Patriarch?"

"He refused to see me, even though I presented his secretary with the introduction you so kindly provided this morning."

"My apologies."

"I suppose there was nothing untoward in it, was there?"

"You didn't read it? You are indeed an honest man, Thomas."

Thomas regarded the ground. "Lord Chamberlain, if there is one thing I guard above all else, it is my dignity. Still, I suppose I should be honest with another... believer. I am unable to read or write. They are not skills I have much use for."

John seemed unsurprised. "Then I shall speak with the Patriarch personally and see what can be arranged. Perhaps there has been a misunderstanding." John dropped the remains of his fish into the gutter. "Meanwhile, if you are not going anywhere in particular, I think you might be interested in visiting a friend of mine, a lady. I think I can promise you she will be more hospitable. I'm on my way there now. I have a few questions to ask. Would you care to meet her?"

"Well, why not? The inn was in a ferment last night. The noise went on almost to dawn. I can't say I'm in a hurry to return."

"Was there a reason for the excitement?"

"It's the charioteers," Thomas replied. "Apparently a lot of money has been changing hands this past week and no small fortune is riding, if I may use the phrase, my lord, on the racing tonight."

"I was at the inn this morning. Evidently one of the charioteers had been celebrating too much. He got well-dowsed in the fountain, and thrown unceremoniously into the street, to boot."

"And, of course, some of the Hippodrome performers are staying there as well," added Thomas. "They tend to be very loud, but then they are all very young."

"Ah, my friend, we were all young once," John pointed out with a smile.

"Sometimes it seems a long time ago," his companion lamented.

"Indeed it does. But let us depart before the crowds become impossible, not to say impassable."

What remained of Thomas' skewered fish joined John's in the gutter. "I do hear that some of the

Hippodrome entertainers performed especially for the Empress," he mentioned.

John's mouth set in a hard line. "Indeed?"

"Oh, yes. It seems she has taken a special interest."

"Are the bull-leaping troupe staying at the inn?"

"Only the two men. However, there's also a young lady with trained chickens." Thomas looked thoughtful. "They say... well, they say she has trained them to peck grain from her naked body. I can hardly believe such a thing."

"You have not lived in Constantinople long enough, Thomas. We can go this way, if you'd like to come along?"

Suiting action to word, John plunged into a network of short, narrow alleyways, finally emerging into a small but busy square. Chanting from a church on their right accompanied the two men's footsteps up to the front door of a honey-colored building at the far side of the square.

❄   ❄   ❄

John noticed the house had been redecorated since his last visit, transformed from the court of the King of Persia into a Temple of Venus, or at least an Egyptian-born madam's idea of how such a temple might appear.

Thus the two men were greeted by the sound of pipe and lyre in the cool, shadowy, marble-floored entrance hall. Their delicate melodies, mingled with the muted tinkling of ankle bells, emerged from behind a curtained archway. The capitals of the Corinthian columns flanking the archway were inlaid with gold leaf—the work, no doubt, of a grateful local artisan. While Madam's house was one of the better-known and more richly appointed in Constantinople, it was patronage from such craftsmen—more wealthy on average than those who resided in, say, the bronze-makers' quarter along the eastern Mese—as well as visits from numerous courtiers that allowed her to indulge her taste for the theatrical.

Though he set his mouth into a stern line, Thomas couldn't stop his eyes from widening.

"Your country's courtesans do not live so elegantly?" inquired John.

Thomas grunted. "How would a knight know such things?" he parried.

John knew the different style of decoration would mean a change in the girls' names and mode of dress as well as the role taken by the doorkeeper.

"Darius," John greeted the bullish, long-haired, and highly perfumed Persian who blocked their path. "What am I to call you today?"

Darius' bearded face curved into a jovial smile. "I'm Eros for the moment."

John gave a short laugh. Darius, winged costume notwithstanding, hardly looked the part of that chubby and youthful godling.

Reverting to his official role, Darius continued: "I must remind you gentlemen that weapons cannot be carried into the Temple of Venus. Or at least not the sort you might raise in anger."

John surrendered his dagger. Darius added it to the international selection piled in an alcove: a stiletto with an Egyptian motif on its blade, two swords in worked scabbards of Persian origin, and what looked like a palace-issue excubitor's sword.

"Well, now, Lord Chamberlain, you are truly disarmed." Darius turned dark eyes toward Thomas.

"You can trust these people, Thomas," encouraged John.

With obvious reluctance, Thomas handed over his weapon.

"You Britons always hesitate", commented Darius. "But you wield the iron handily once you set your minds to it, I'm told."

"Darius is an expert on international travelers," John informed his companion. "I'm here to see Madam, Darius."

"She is unoccupied at the moment. You know the way." He nodded toward a rosewood door carved with doves and myrtle, sacred symbols of the Goddess.

"And you might arrange to introduce my friend Thomas to Roman culture?"

The big Persian smiled slightly, striking a brass gong beside him. A girl, blonde hair piled high in the Greek fashion, emerged from behind the gauzy curtains. She wore a short green chiton and was adorned in barbaric fashion with brass and green-stone necklets and bracelets. Her cheeks and lips were ruby-painted and she carried a timbrel.

"Berta, we have a distinguished visitor from the court of Bretania," Darius informed her expansively as he relieved a newcomer, a corpulent middle-aged man, of his dagger.

"Hey, Berta, forgotten me already?" called the man as he passed, ducking between the curtains as the music grew louder.

Berta favored her admirer with the same studied lack of attention Empress Theodora might have given a whining cur seen from her carriage as it went along the Mese. The girl was, John guessed, all of fifteen. When she took Thomas' hand the knight reddened, looking like a little boy hiding behind an auburn mustache. She led him upstairs.

John looked thoughtful for a second. "The big fellow, wasn't that the innkeeper from the Inn of the Centaurs? I'm surprised he dares to stray so close to home." He vividly recalled the leather-lunged woman ordering old Ahasuerus to dinner.

"His wife doesn't care about such things," noted Darius knowingly. "He's prosperous. He keeps her happy with what she does care about. May I suggest it might be best to visit Madam before she's occupied?"

As John lifted his hand to knock on the carved door there emerged from within a thunderous bellow, the scream of the Great Bull when Mithra plunged his dagger into its neck. Or of Zeus in extremis.

John prepared for a polite withdrawal but to his surprise, the door flew open and the madam greeted him enthusiastically.

"Come in, come in, John." She pulled him toward a plumply cushioned couch drawn up to a low table burdened with a jug of wine and filigree silver plates of fruit, nuts and sweetmeats. She was an ample woman whose face still showed traces of the beauty she had once been. "I was just playing with my new toy."

"Yes, so I heard. I'm happy to see you again, Isis." Only Madam's friends were allowed to address her by her real name rather than by her title. Few people even knew her name.

Isis gestured toward an odd contraption set between two carved screens at the back of the room. A dozen or so gleaming bronze pipes of varied lengths rose from a polished wooden box on legs. There was a keyboard on the front of the box.

It was, John realized, a miniature of the organs he sometimes employed ceremonially at processions and in the Hippodrome. They were, of course, not permitted in churches.

"It's called a hydra," Isis was explaining. "It'll give me something to do, now I'm retired, or at least semi-retired. Do you know any music instructors at court?"

John, used to her fads, murmured noncommittally. He leaned back on the couch and looked around the cluttered room. This was her sanctuary, the place from which she ran her business. Here she interviewed her girls and kept her accounts; even wealthy madams sometimes had to pay protectors, if not the tax collector. And here also she occasionally entertained favored male friends. She regarded John in this light, for he paid her well, not for physical favors but rather for information.

"Not but what I would be glad to give freely to one who knows my own country," Isis had once sighed. She was fond of John. Like all exiles, she loved to talk about her home land to someone who knew it.

She was an Alexandrian with eyes as dark as her raven-colored hair. Belying her profession, she eschewed cosmetics. She invariably wore a lapis lazuli fertility amulet suspended from her thick gold necklace, which amused John. Fertility would be the last thing to cultivate in her line of business.

"Wine?"

John declined. He had drunk a goblet or two that morning during Thomas' visit, and was already chastising himself for his weakness. Isis shrugged and took a long draft of her wine. John could not recall having seen her drink so deeply.

"You seem busy today, Isis."

"Festivals always put people in the mood. And we've probably had a few guests who heard about that unfortunate man found in the alley last night. That sort of thing puts some in the mood too." She sighed at the foibles of man, but her eyes were shrewd as she peered at John in the afternoon sunlight filtering in through the closed lattice shutters.

"The dead man was from the palace." John answered her unspoken question.

"We see plenty from the palace, guards, scribes,

that sort of person. Not usually from the upper echelons, however, except for you. John. You're here because of the death." It was a statement.

John nodded. "Leukos was a friend."

"Ah." Isis occupied herself with a silver fruit knife, cutting a dried apple into neat segments. "I suspect you are going to ask if he was here the night he died? I've already asked my girls. None remembered him. 'Course," she popped a segment of apple into her mouth and chewed slowly for a few seconds. "'Course, even so, he might have been here. You learn not to see faces. He wasn't a Christian, was he?"

"He was, as a matter of fact."

"Osiris preserve him! If he'd known how close he was to death I'm sure he wouldn't have wanted to be spending his last hours indulging in sins of the flesh! Or perhaps he would. One man's sin, you know...."

Isis daintily popped another segment of apple into her mouth. Red, green, and blue fire blazed from elaborately worked rings as her chubby hand rose through a shaft of dusty light falling across the room. Few but John, used to dealing with minute but all-important ceremonial details, would have noticed the thin gold marriage band worn in Egyptian fashion on the middle finger of the left hand.

Isis had never revealed whether or not she was or had been married, and if so, to whom, for although she spoke freely, especially to John, she actually revealed very little unless for a price.

"We seem to hear a lot about sin," John commented. "It must be something in the air."

"Sin's always in the air, at least up as far as heaven. Who was that who arrived with you, John?"

"That was Thomas. A knight, he says. He's passing through on a chase for a wild mare's nest. He calls it a quest."

Isis regarded him with silent curiosity, her mouth full. Now that she was earning a living by her business sense rather than her physical charms, she could finally afford to indulge her culinary appetites. She raised her goblet to her mouth again.

"He's looking for a relic, a Christian relic." John continued. "He told me at great length on the way here that he is supposed to be, among other things, chaste and sinless while on this quest. However, I believe he may have fallen by the wayside by now. He seemed quite taken with young Berta. Or taken by her, at any rate."

Isis chuckled, then noted, "Well, there are plenty of holy relics in Constantinople. Did you hear we've acquired another staff of Moses and two more apostles' limbs? What's that, thirty limbs in all?"

John and Isis shared pagan laughter at the follies of the faithful.

"But our little Berta seems to be the woman of the hour," continued Isis. "Did you know she was at the palace last night? She's been showing off this pendant she got there. It's got what they call a bloodstone, although actually it's green. She dotes on green, you know. Anyway, she was telling the girls it was worth more than all the relics in the city put together. Didn't stop her rolling onto her back for a few coins... "

"Just a moment, Isis," John halted the flow of words. "What was that about the palace? Business, was it?"

"Why else? It was part of the festivities. Not an official part, you know, but a private affair Theodora was holding. Just a few select guests. Raising money for that pet project of hers, elevating streetwalkers to polite society. Ironic, isn't it? There aren't enough emperors around to elevate them all, like she was." Isis sniggered quietly, recalling common rumors about the Empress' less than respectable past. "I hear quite a lot of high-born ladies were there, too, showing off their jewelry, so Berta told me. Of course, they're paid better than us."

"I did hear about a celebration. There were complaints about the extra work. Not just ordinary fish or fowl were considered good enough, it seems." John raised his usually quiet, modulated voice to a shrill falsetto, mimicking the indignant tones of the imperial cook. "What was it that the cook said? 'It had to be venison and larks and all manner of sweetmeats, not to mention pepper and spices in unlimited amounts!' Something to that effect. I gather it was a classic case of owls to Athens! And then, adding the final insult, apparently most of the guests ignored the food when the entertainments began, what with fire-eaters, dancing dwarves, and who knows what else."

"Well, Berta said the ladies were eating as much as beggars on bread days."

"What was Berta there for? Does she dance?"

"Yes, but not in any way that would have entertained high-born ladies, or at least not in public. It was at the Empress' behest. Later on, Berta and a few of my other girls carried jugs of wine around. Supposed to be nymphs, you see. That was just Theodora's unpleasant sense of humor, though, since for most of the ladies my girls served, they'd already served the husbands—and not just with wine."

"Did you hear anything else about this celebration?"

"There was a fortune-teller there, some ghastly old man. A foreigner. Justinian will be furious if someone is foolish enough to mention it to him. Not quite the thing, is it, for barbarians to go about telling imperial fortunes? Mind you, it was quite all right in the old days when prophets did so for patriarchs." Isis drained her goblet. John wondered how much she had drunk. Normally she was abstemious. She said she needed her wits about her at all times, and who would argue with that given her line of work?

"Ah me, religions." She giggled at some secret joke. "Heart of Horus, what tangled webs they weave!"

John agreed. Thank Mithra for a simple soldier's religion, he thought, with none of these strange literary wanderings and contradictions and fleshly rites and strange penances. It was enough to drive men insane, and, by all accounts, it sometimes did.

"Did Berta hear anything that the fortune-teller said?"

"Let's see. Something about how the Empress would shortly hold a great treasure in her hands. Well, even Berta could've predicted that! But then the powerful always hear the fortune they hope to hear, don't they?"

"Yes, even barbarians want to keep their beards, as they say, not to mention their heads."

Isis raised her goblet to her lips again, found it empty, and set it down clumsily, banging it against a silver platter. Pistachios rolled across the table.

"Getting back to the point of my visit," John changed the subject abruptly, "we can be fairly sure that Leukos wasn't here last night?"

"No. On my honor. In fact, the Watch searched all the buildings along the alley, including this one. I understand he would have bled a lot. Oh, I'm sorry...."

"No matter. I have seen death before."

"Anyway, they found nothing. So, you see, you've had a bit of a wasted journey. But I always enjoy talking to you. Drop by when you don't have to be here on business and we'll talk about old times in Alexandria."

Isis automatically included John in those bygone

days, although they had not actually met in that
teeming city.

"And now and then it's good to hear a round
Egyptian curse or two," she added. "It must be my
advancing age!"

"Of course not!" John reassured her, meaning it.
"Sometimes even the sunniest disposition can be
afflicted with melancholia, especially in festive times
and far from home. And speaking of festivities, I must
drag Thomas away from his."

He clicked a coin onto the table top. Friendship
was friendship. Business was business.

❊   ❊   ❊

Outside, shadows from the balconies that jutted out
from nearly every house had plunged the narrow street
into premature twilight. The sky, glimpsed through
gaps between the houses, was still half bright.

John made his way through the press of laborers
in rough woven tunics, brightly dressed Greens, ragged
beggars, bent old men in patched robes. He was forced
to dodge a litter borne by four slaves. The aristocrat
concealed behind the litter's curtains might have been
surprised to know that the thin Greek who stepped so
nimbly into the gutter might, with a word to the
Emperor, have had him exiled for the carelessness of
his bearers. Justinian had granted John greater favors.
The Lord Chamberlain, conscious of the abuses of
power, never asked for indulgences so cruel.

Thomas limped along behind him, complaining
about Berta. "Good heavens, John, she was a proper
wag-tongue. Talk, talk, talk! She went on and on about
this talisman she had, and finally persuaded me to try
it on my leg. Didn't seem to do it much good, though.
Where do they get these ideas?"

"You don't think there's anything in it, then, do

you?" John smiled over his shoulder.

"What? Oh!" Thomas frowned. Illiterate he might be, but his intelligence was quick enough. "You mean the 'all heal' aspect of the... er... my... uh... object?" He was also exercising caution, John noted with approval. "That's different," Thomas protested, sounding shocked. "It would be for the good of all. To save the kingdom. It would never be used to cure one man. That's blasphemous!"

John shrugged. Sometimes Thomas sounded the devout Christian, despite his private denials. He did not inquire what else, if anything, had transpired with the girl, and Thomas did not say. They strode along in silence.

It was as they neared the Mese that the street noises around them seemed to John to slowly recede into an echoing cavern far away.

Thomas' seemingly genuine indignation had put an interesting thought into his mind. Up until now he had regarded the foreigner as deluded, although harmless enough. But what if the Grail were really what Thomas claimed, as unlikely as that might be? And what if it actually was to be found in Constantinople, as Thomas appeared to believe?

Could such a wonder exist? At times it had seemed to John that his splendid civilization was but a toy boat floating precariously on the bottomless sea of a reality beyond man's understanding. And concerning religion, did he take the tales of his own Lord Mithra at face value? If a fig tree had truly fed and clothed Mithra, might this holy relic Thomas sought have power to heal even the most grievous of wounds?

Chapter Eight

At the Baths of Zeuxippos, Anatolius was one of the few who did not make a point of averting his gaze from John's injury, either in revulsion or pity, but when he made his customary visit to the baths the next morning, as usual, he lingered in the disrobing room until John had immersed himself. What Anatolius was being careful to overlook was John's difficulty in climbing into the pool.

During his time in Bretania, John had nearly drowned in a rain-swollen beck; a comrade had been less fortunate. John had spoken of it to Anatolius only once. Now, years later, despite a conscious exertion of his will, bodies of water still terrified him, and Anatolius knew how large an effort it took for his friend to step into the pool. It was a battle John fought and won every day, although he still refused, Anatolius had noticed, to use the cold pool.

Anatolius sat down companionably. He was anxious to relate the news preoccupying his mind, but forced himself to deal with official business first.

"The Emperor sends his condolences, John. He knows that you and Leukos were friends. Perhaps he will authorize a small tribute to Leukos. A commemorative diptych, something like that."

"Yes," John said simply.

"You look as if you need a few days away from imperial matters," Anatolius told him, realizing how strange his comment would sound to most. The average citizen of the empire, if he were fortunate enough to see the Emperor even once during his life, would catch only a glimpse, from a distance. A glimpse both brief and dazzling, like a falling star, never to be forgotten.

That was one of the Lord Chamberlain's responsibilities, to insure that when Justinian appeared in public he never appeared less than the divinely appointed being he was believed to be.

"And so what did you do yesterday, John, instead of resting?"

Anatolius listened as patiently as he could while John recounted his interviews with the knight, the soothsayer, and Madam Isis.

Anatolius had not known Leukos well. To the younger man, Leukos had seemed an unimaginative sort, much older than John, although the two had actually been the same age. It was not clear to Anatolius what the two men had in common beyond palace duties and personal reticence. And so far he knew they had rarely met outside their official duties, such as their recent attendance at the Hippodrome. To the gregarious Anatolius that seemed odd.

Thinking about it, Anatolius wondered why John, who had suffered so terribly at Fate's whim himself, could not accept that another might be struck down, for just as little reason. But he did not dare to voice that thought.

"Is there any reason to think Leukos' death was anything more than fate?" he asked John.

"No, no reason. Or no reason that I can put my finger on. He seemed to have something on his mind when we were at the Hippodrome."

Anatolius said nothing. John had already questioned him at length about Leukos' puzzling demeanor on the afternoon of his death but had had no insights to offer.

John slid down until water lapped his chin. Only Anatolius would have noticed the slight narrowing of the lips as John set his jaw.

John was, Anatolius thought, quite an exceptionally handsome man. A lady of the palace might envy his high, sculpted cheekbones and slender frame, yet he had a sinewy toughness attesting he had once borne arms. Anatolius was happy not to have John as a rival in love.

The young man's thoughts leapt naturally to the girl from the Hippodrome. Lithe and lovely, how easily she'd tamed the wild beast. He would celebrate her victory in poetry just as Pindar had celebrated the Olympians of another age. He would strew her path with the garlands of his words and she would hear the sweet lyre of his love.

"There was something," John was saying. "Something about his death, I'm not sure what, that suggests murder. The pouch he was carrying—the Prefect of the Night Watch, who is investigating the matter, is having it delivered to me. I want to see what was in it. It might, just possibly, suggest a course of investigation. Anatolius, are you listening?"

"I'm sorry, John. I was thinking of the bull-leaper, thinking I would be Pindar to her Aristomenes."

"Aristomenes? The wrestler? The bull-leaper did not strike me as such. And as for Pindar," John added wearily, "was it not he who reminded us that man is merely the creature of a day, the dream of a shadow?"

Another bather, climbing clumsily into the pool, sent a wave rippling across the surface and John abruptly pulled himself up until his face was safely above its surface.

"Perhaps someone saw it happen?" suggested Anatolius, his mood considerably subdued by John's remark.

John shook his head, tiredly. "Unless one of the Prefect's men happens by at the right time, or a mob catches the fellow immediately and tears him to pieces, street crimes are never solved."

"True enough. And it could just as easily have been one of us killed in that alley." A thought came to Anatolius. "Unless it were a deliberate murder. If it were, what about this Thomas? Is it possible he could have had a hand in Leukos' death?"

John paused as if considering the suggestion. Anatolius wondered if he had managed to point out a possibility John had overlooked. In recounting his interviews John had had much to say about backgrounds and philosophies but little about whereabouts and motives. His friend sometimes pondered too deeply, he thought, and thereby missed the obvious. Anatolius never missed the obvious.

"He seems too open and naive. Too honest, if I dare say that." John finally said.

"But?" Anatolius recognized uncertainty in his friend's voice.

"He purports to be a Mithran."

"It is a soldier's religion, after all. Still, a strange one for a man seeking a Christian relic. Perhaps he is simply acting the fool. "

"Indeed. Although I think the man is genuine, I did not invite him to our forthcoming ceremony."

Aantolius had nearly forgotten about the ceremony, distracted as he had been by other events. He glanced around nervously. Even he realized it was not politic to mention such events in public. He need not have worried. The pool was still nearly deserted, as John had surely noted before speaking.

"And how about the madam? Can you trust her? Leukos was found practically inside her place, after all."

"Oddly, I think I can trust her, on this at least."

"But if her livelihood were threatened?"

"The soothsayer strikes me as more suspicious. Only the gods know our futures."

"Did he have any inkling of how short Leukos' future would be? What did he say when you told him Leukos had died so soon after his visit?"

"I didn't mention it."

Anatolius looked surprised. "Did you ask the old man where he was when Leukos was killed?"

John shook his head. "That would be the Prefect's way. You wouldn't expect a murderer to tell you the truth and I don't have a small army to go about the city knocking on doors and verifying stories."

"But you could have observed his reaction when you broke the news."

"If murderers were so poor at disguising their feelings there'd be fewer victims. At any rate, of those I've spoken to, I am most troubled by the soothsayer. Only the gods know our futures.""

"That may be," said Anatolius, "but on the other hand they may communicate with us in whatever way they choose. Even through garrulous old wanderers."

Eager to finally be able to tell John his news, his face brightened as he continued. "I kept my appointment with old Ahasuerus and I found him as amazing as Leukos said."

"And when he told your future, what did he say?"

"He immediately augured I was in love."

"A safe wager!"

"Perhaps, but he was quite accurate. He poured some colored pebbles out of a leather pouch and when he read them, he proclaimed I would be lucky in love."

John laughed. "And how do you know this prediction will turn out to be true?"

"Well, when we were talking afterwards he told me where the female bull-leaper is quartered. On an Egyptian ship at the docks."

❀   ❀   ❀

Like the city, the port of Constantinople was nothing if not cosmopolitan. Drawn up in rows along the docks were the maritime prides of many a nation. Dark-sailed dorkons sweetly redolent of old cargoes of spices from the east rose and fell on the same swells as many-oared triremes. Oppressive heat poured over the harbor's raucous ant heap, where teams of sweat-streaked slaves unloaded imperial prizes: exotic foodstuffs, silk, cases of purple dye from Tyre.

John stood uneasily at the edge of the dock, dark eyes narrowed against the harsh light, toes curled in an unconscious attempt to cling more securely to his boots. Looking down into the cluttered flotsam moving to and fro at his feet, the litter of the city slapping sullenly against the dock's wooden supports, he felt a familiar tightening of his stomach. The water looked cool. Here, in the brazen hours of the day, it would almost refresh one to dive into it. Almost....

Anatolius, shading his eyes with his hand, was staring at the horizon where dark clouds lay in a sullen stripe across the sea.

Noting an imperial dromon gliding by, oars moving with well-oiled grace, he remarked, "There will be a bad storm soon. It would take a braver man than I to go to sea in it."

"Imperial matters wait for no man, although occasionally they must wait upon the tide." John's mouth was as dry as his tone.

He should never have come here. He had seen the girl from a distance, for an instant. There must have been something about her that his memory grasped so that in the dim solitude of his study it had seemed possible that he had found his old love again. But now, in brassy sunlight, it was easy enough to see it had been nothing more than self delusion. Now he had come to the docks, only to be disappointed.

They found the vessel the soothsayer had named, the *Anubis*, an Egyptian ship identifiable by the protective Eye of Horus painted on its side. Anatolius had told John that, according to the old man, while the other performers had been quartered ashore, the young bull-leaper had been allowed—or compelled— to lodge on the *Anubis*, safely away from the city's numerous dangers and innumerable temptations.

The vessel in question lay between a weather-beaten fishing boat and a chelandion, both of which were swarming with activity. The *Anubis* was as silent as the dead its eponymous jackal-headed god conducted to the underworld. A man dozed at the foot of its mast.

The gangplank was not in place. Waves sloshed loudly at the bottom of the gap between dock and ship.

"Hey! Watchman! Visitors to the *Anubis*!" yelled Anatolius. But the man continued dozing. Exasperated, Anatolius suggested John try.

"I don't have the voice for it." Leaning down, John picked a shard of pottery from the litter strewn about the dock and lobbed it at the boat. Its clatter did not awaken the sleeper, but brought forth from the ship's bowels an angry boy. The Lord Chamberlain had seldom been announced in so undignified a manner.

He soon found himself standing in front a low-lintelled door. If there were any sounds to be heard from inside, they were masked by the regular fretting of waves against the ship. He raised his hand to knock, noting with wry detachment that his fist was shaking.

"Go on," urged Anatolius with the impatience of youth.

"Mithra, it's worse than waiting for the cornu to sound the attack," John muttered. He rapped briskly. Light footsteps sounded within. The door opened.

"Cornelia!"

The woman was near his age, a hint of gray in her dark hair. Close up she looked less slender than she had seemed at the Hippodrome, although she was apparently still slim enough to vault and leap over razor-sharp horns. He had not finished formulating his impressions when she stepped forward, pulled him into the cabin, and dealt a stinging slap to his face.

"And they say Cretans are liars!" she hissed. "By the Goddess, you took long enough! And what do you want now, anyway?"

"But, Cornelia, I came to see a young woman, a girl...."

"No doubt!"

There was a sleepy stirring from a corner of the cabin.

Cornelia lowered her voice. "How did you know where we were? No, don't tell me, there are spies all over the place, like as not. And what do you think you're doing, coming here? And, now I think of it, what are you doing for a living these days? And where have you been all these years?" Although she had continued talking she was shaking, and all the blood seemed to have drained from her face leaving her features as white as the moon in the night sky except for an angry spot of red on each cheekbone.

"Still the same Cornelia, all questions and never a pause for breath so I can answer!" John wiped tears from his eyes with a quick swipe of his knuckles.

"The John I knew wouldn't have cried," Cornelia said. Her voice cracked.

"The Cornelia I knew was gentler."

She laughed. "Sit down, John. Take the owner's seat, he's ashore now. In what house I couldn't say." She looked John over appraisingly. "From your clothing, I suspect you're accustomed to finer quarters than these."

John reached for her hand, hesitantly. He half-expected his fingers to pass through hers, as through a mirage, and it was a shock when they were stopped short by the warm solidarity of her flesh.

The cabin floor rolled slightly with the sea's increasing swell. John felt disembodied, a man holding hands with a vision from his past. Yet she was flesh and blood, with an angry face and shoulders set in rigid outrage.

"But I am not the John that you knew, Cornelia. Let me try to answer your questions."

Cornelia said nothing. There was pain beneath the anger in her eyes.

"Do you remember I promised you something special for your birthday? I wanted to buy you silk, to go with your silky hair. But its sale was restricted, and I couldn't afford to buy it. Then I heard that it was possible to get it easily, up on the border. That is where I went. Unfortunately," John's tone wavered slightly, "I accidentally ventured into Persia and was captured. They have savage ways there. A few years later, I was sold back across the border to traders who had gone there to purchase slaves for the palace. Gelded slaves."

"So that was why you never came back." The

woman's voice was softer. "And so you are now...."

"Yes, I am. And I'm still employed at the palace, although at a somewhat more dignified level." John's tone was even. He had long since come to terms with his affliction. Even so, he suddenly felt sick in the pit of his stomach. Perhaps it was just the motion of the sea, rocking the ship.

"If you only knew how I prayed to the Goddess for word from you! But it never came."

"You stayed with the troupe, though, didn't you? They saw that you were clothed and fed?"

"Yes, of course. There are not many of the old company left now, though. Just a few. You will remember Dionysios? We lost him in Thessalonika, to the bull."

"I see." John paused for a second. "You know, Cornelia, when I saw you bull-leaping, I thought how kind the years had been to you. You looked just as young as you did when we first met."

Cornelia laughed quietly. "Your tongue is still as smooth as ever, I see. But in fact—"

The heap of coverlets in the cabin corner stirred again. "Mother? Who is it?"

"Don't worry, Europa, it's an old friend who's come to see me. Go back to sleep."

Shock washed over John in a cold tide. "You have a daughter?" As soon as the words were out of his mouth he regretted them. There was no reason why Cornelia should not have taken a lover in the years since he had been forced to abandon her.

"She is the one you saw bull-leaping, John. As you will see, she looks a lot like me, my daughter." Cornelia paused for a second, then spoke resolutely. "Though there are those who say she looks more like her father. I have often wished that the resemblance was more pronounced, John, for then she would... look like you."

The ship lurched as an unusually large swell pushed it toward the dock. Anguish, rather than disbelief, washed over John. He closed his eyes, feeling lightheaded, as if he were about to topple into a chasm suddenly opening at his feet. It was not the vertigo which had so recently seized him at the dock, but rather an instinctive reaction to the sudden yawning of unfathomable depths as terrifying as those revealed when the split earth disgorged Hades, intent on abducting Persephone.

Struggling with his emotions, John realized he was not what he thought he was. Half of his being, his identity as a man, had been wrenched away from him and twisted around and then thrust back into his dazed grasp, all in the space of the second it took for Cornelia to say two words. "Like you." Europa was his daughter.

Yet the thought which made him so lightheaded had also loosed a gray miasma of apprehension. How would his child—he tasted the word—his child react to meeting the father she had never known? And, fleet of foot, an equally unwelcome thought ran close behind: could she, and could her mother, be used against him by his enemies?

A second or two of silence and then John, with years of practice in presenting the serene public face necessitated by life in Justinian's court, finally gained a death-grip on his emotions.

Cornelia, looking up at him, read his face with a lover's familiarity. "Have you learned to control your emotions since we were together, John? Or have the passing years mellowed the fire in you?"

John did not reply. He had just remembered his companion, still standing by the door and listening with great interest.

"Cornelia," John said quickly, gesturing for the

man to come forward, "I must introduce you to my friend Anatolius."

Cornelia looked alarmed. "I didn't notice someone was with you."

"Don't worry," Anatolius assured her, "Going unnoticed is a talent one develops being secretary to the Emperor."

Chapter Nine

John awakened with a start, to darkness and the sound of raised voices.

He had been dreaming. Not of Cornelia, strangely, nor of his daughter, but of his childhood. He had been running across a summer field. Not pursued and with no destination. Simply running, seeming to skim over the top of the wiry grass. The stones and tussocks, the sun-hardened depressions where cattle hooves had sunk into mud, none of these tripped him. He glided over all of them. Although he was running and not flying, he felt at the crest of every hill that he might take to the sky and soar. He was tireless. His legs did not weaken. His breath did not grow labored. He could run, effortlessly, forever.

Now he was awake, his heart leaping, his breath catching in his throat. The careers of palace officials ended as often with unexpected midnight visits as with presentations of commemorative diptychs before the assembled senate.

John rolled off his bed, grasping the dagger he kept close to hand in an instinctive reaction acquired in hundreds of encampments. He moved toward the door, not pausing, or daring, to light a lamp.

Voices echoed from the marble-walled reception hall downstairs. He dressed hastily.

As he moved quietly down the wooden stairs, John noted Peter, looking perturbed, standing by the door holding a small lamp. Beyond Peter stood a slight figure fantastically dressed in beaded tights and colorful plumes. John caught the heavy smell of perfume. Recognizing Hektor, a court page and one of Justinian's decorative boys, John thrust his dagger back into his tunic belt.

Hektor caught sight of John at the same moment. He feinted to his right, and then darted around Peter's left. The old servant's slow swipe at the agile boy found only the bobbing end of a feather.

"You, John," shrilled Hektor. "Your master wants you, this moment!"

"You don't give orders to the Lord Chamberlain," protested Peter, outraged.

"I speak for Justinian, old fool."

"Never mind, Peter," John reassured the old man quickly. "Bring my cloak." He turned his attention to Hektor, who was posturing insolently at the foot of the stairs, hands on hips. The boy's ruby lips shone in the flickering light from Peter's lamp. "What does the Emperor want of me in the middle of the night?"

"You'll find out when we get there. Hurry up!"

John pulled on the cloak Peter offered him. The old man scowled at Hektor.

The boy's rudeness meant nothing to John. It was the Emperor who concerned him. Few in Constantinople were closer to Justinian than the Lord Chamberlain, but the Emperor was no man's confidant. Sometimes it seemed that he presented more faces to the world than Janus. John had watched the Emperor joke affably about favored charioteers with courtiers whose glib tongues and evasive eyes would be sitting at the bottom of a torturer's bucket before the next sunrise.

Outside, the cobbles underfoot glistened dimly in the light of the moon, a thin clipping from the edge of a silver coin. Hektor raced ahead, oblivious to the dangers of the night. John followed.

As they began to near the Octagon, John could see light in its windows. Lights always burned in the Emperor's residence. Justinian did not sleep like other men. Perhaps he didn't sleep at all. Perhaps he wasn't a man. It was whispered abroad that at night he wandered the hallways, a faceless demon.

John did not believe such tales. Knowing Justinian as he did, he understood that the Emperor had an abnormal capacity for imperial business. And, it seemed to John, part of Justinian's success lay in the fact that his sleeplessness having given him more time to learn, he had already lived, and had time to master the lessons of, a natural lifespan. It was a thing John might have envied had he allowed himself such weakness.

The page, he realized, had led him on a round-about route along flagged paths and through darkened halls and ornamental gardens. It was not efficient, but John thought it wisest to simply follow. Many of the guards they passed had acknowledged John; it was to him their immediate superiors reported. Some, however, were strangers, no doubt under the direct command of the Master of the Offices.

Soon enough John was ushered into a small plaster-walled room at the heart of the Octagon. Here in his private quarters Justinian had discarded his amethyst-studded collar and brocaded cloak and was dressed in a simple tunic and hose. He had, however, retained his imperial pearl-studded red boots.

"John," he said, turning away from a desk piled with codices and scrolls. "How good of you to arrive so quickly." He assumed, for a moment, the smile John had seen him give to allies and condemned men alike.

John inclined his head. "My good fortune, Caesar." He doubted the Emperor had any idea of the late hour. "I see you are busy."

"A new theological treatise. At the Hippodrome celebrations—was it only a day or two ago?—it occurred to me how I might help reconcile some of these quarreling sects who are so troublesome. Have you given much thought to the nature of Christ? How is it possible to intertwine the divine with the human? A tangled knot, indeed."

"They say Alexander took the expedient of cutting the Gordian knot."

"Yes, a simple enough solution for a mere conqueror, but I am an Emperor after all. I will have Anatolius make a copy of my conclusions for you. I know you study such things."

"You flatter me."

Physically Justinian would have been lost in the crush of the rabble which was never allowed to approach closely enough to see his face. He was of average height, his face pudgy and splotched red as if he drank to excess, although in fact he abstained from wine entirely. He was of such unprepossessing appearance that more than one ambitious man had forgotten that the life of every person in the empire hung on the fragile thread of Justinian's whim.

"I am sorry about your friend Leukos," Justinian continued. "Replacing him will be a vexing problem for me. He was a most trustworthy man. Meanwhile, I intend to give you free rein, John, to honor him to the height of your ability, which will be very high honor indeed. But first, there is the question of the manner of his death."

The Emperor paused. "Ah, I see you anticipated that what is only the prologue would be the matter itself." He shook his head and continued. "No, Lord Chamberlain, the concerns which have brought you here tonight are not only the honors to be bestowed upon Leukos, but also the circumstances of his death."

"I understand that an investigation has already begun," John said softly.

"An official investigation, certainly."

"It would appear to be nothing more than a common street murder."

"You know as well as I do that appearances lie." Justinian directed a wintry smile at John. "You have handled sensitive matters privately for me in the past. I remember when I called on you after the riots, when the mob had burned down half of Constantinople. The blessed fragment of the True Cross is once again in the possession of Patriarch Epiphanios, and no one in the city save the three of us knows that it was ever lost, or that you, Lord Chamberlain, were responsible for its recovery."

"Whatever investigation is required, I assure you I shall be discreet."

"I wish you to ascertain who was involved in this so-called street murder, and the real reason for it."

John nodded. "I will report to you, and no one...."

"I'm sure you need your rest now," Justinian cut in.

Dismissed, John turned to leave, but arrested his step when the Emperor added, "About that ill-concealed weapon beneath your cloak, John."

John felt the blood drain from his vitals. Half asleep, he had forgotten the dagger thrust into his belt. He forced his suddenly clumsy tongue to move. "Caesar, in my haste to see you, I must have forgotten...."

Justinian's expression was as smoothly blank as the walls of the room. "If I did not know you so well...." He paused and his full lips tightened slightly, although his eyes betrayed no emotion. "But then, how well can one man know another?"

"I will be more careful."

"We must all be careful, Lord Chamberlain. Especially an Emperor."

    ※   ※   ※

John's heart was still pounding when he reached the blessed darkness outside. How could he have been so careless? The Emperor could have had him executed on the spot. Of course, he reminded himself, the Emperor could have him executed on the spot for no reason at all. It was little comfort.

Agitated as he was, he had walked some distance back toward his house before he realized he was being followed. At first it was merely the sensation of another presence intruding into his consciousness. Then, senses alerted, he began to distinguish quiet movements mirroring his own.

John continued walking at the same pace, betraying nothing. Ahead, the path lay dark and deserted. Although the palace grounds were heavily patrolled, he saw no guards, and only a fool would discount the possibility of some cutthroat or other having managed to slip into its maze of buildings, pathways, and gardens.

He forced himself to continue at an even pace. Listening hard, he thought he could discern only one set of steps. Against one man he would at least have a chance. Once he had been a trained fighter. But his quiet shadower was perhaps a military man, probably one much younger than he and with more recent training. Justinian might have decided to have him killed after all, but on the grounds rather than in his private quarters. On the other hand, John doubted that he would leave such a task to a single guard. The Emperor was nothing if not cautious.

A low archway punctuated the stucco wall his path paralleled. John ducked through it into a small garden. He considered lying in wait to one side of the archway, but decided any trained military man would be alert to such an obvious ploy. He heard the gurgling splash of a fountain. Faint moonlight, falling toward the rooftops of the tenements visible beyond the wall encircling the palace grounds, silvered dwellings, water, and the marble fountain alike. Beyond the garden he had entered, he could distinguish a line of trees, a black mass of branches.

He moved toward them. The footsteps turned after him into the garden, as he had expected. The trees appeared to be figs. John waited until he had almost reached them, then broke into a run. He stopped suddenly, turning back toward his pursuer. He could now see a bulky outline, moving forward quickly. He took a step to the right, then, pretending to be confused, to his left.

With a burst of speed he knew his legs would regret later, he raced around to the other side of the line of trees, then doubled back. But they were too widely spaced to conceal him. He would be visible to the man chasing him, and, what was more, by detouring around the trees he had lost valuable time, time he might have used to escape.

John's pursuer, seeing his chance, took the direct route, straight through the row of trees.

There was a resounding splash and the clatter of a metal blade on marble.

"God's blood!"

John recognized the voice of Thomas.

The burly redhead had emerged from the sunken pool by the time John reached it. Thomas was still spluttering, cursing, and shaking water out of his ginger mustache.

"Thomas, I see you have discovered one of the Emperor's little jokes. It was especially designed to catch trespassers. Though usually they creep in here to steal, not to pursue Lord Chamberlains."

"I wasn't pursuing you. I was out walking and saw you. I didn't want to be shouting about in the middle of the night, and you walk faster than a Pict in full retreat."

Several guards, attracted by the noise, arrived at a run. John dismissed them without explanation. No doubt they would soon be weaving lurid tales in their barracks about his strange assignations with foreigners in garden pools in the middle of the night.

"Why were you walking about the palace grounds at this time?" John asked, wondering exactly how Thomas had managed to get inside the palace grounds at such an hour. "I thought you were staying at the inn?"

"Who can sleep in this city, what with rattling carts, and all those barking dogs and people shouting and such?"

"You have refined sensibilities for a soldier. And why was your sword drawn? In greeting?"

Thomas looked at the sword in his hand, as if just realizing it was there. He snorted and resheathed it. "It came out when I fell into the water," he claimed, somewhat unconvincingly. "But you are right, it wasn't the noise of this damnable city that kept me awake. In truth, John, it was that girl. Berta. The one I, uh, saw. At the house you took me to. My mind's been troubled since then."

"The soldier's simple life has been changed, then?"

Thomas said nothing, but looked abashed. He ran his fingers through his dripping hair, squeezing out rivulets of water.

"Come back to my house and get dry," John offered. "You can return to your inn in the morning. You're likely to get arrested, wandering about the palace grounds at this hour of the night."

❊   ❊   ❊

The flame of the candle in the niche beside the door had hissed and sputtered into a pool of wax before Peter heard John's familiar rap.

"Thanks to the Lord," he murmured, hurrying to admit his master. It had been too long a night for the old man. The ghastly page's arrival to summon John to the Emperor had been frightening enough given Justinian's absolute power over Constantinople's population. More alarming, Justinian was a Christian, whereas John, as Peter knew, was a pagan. Although paganism was widespread and largely tolerated, one could never be sure which sect might become proscribed next. Peter often worried about his master. Worried about his body and his immortal soul. Though, the old man sometimes told himself, his master's god was so like his own true Lord in so many ways that John was perhaps guilty only of getting the name wrong. Still and all, he had been afraid when John was suddenly summoned to the Emperor during the night.

Once John and that disgusting boy had gone out into the darkness, as he sometimes did when he was alone in the house Peter had stolen up to the master's lavatory. Through the slit of a window there, it was possible to see the lighthouse. It was the only vantage point in the house from which it could be glimpsed.

Leaning against one wall, Peter had looked at its

light, a golden carpet across the surface of the sea. At times, it reminded him of his Lord, who was mankind's beacon. At other times it brought to his mind more earthly visions of those distant places that lay beyond the sea, places which he had never seen, and so barbaric by all he heard he devoutly wished he never would.

He had been occupied in this manner when the Prefect's messenger arrived and pounded at the front door. It had given him a terrible fright. He had known at once, from the manner of the knocking, that it was not his master.

Now, he opened the door to see not only John but also a sodden and disheveled companion beside him. On reflection, however, he felt such an unconventional sight was hardly to be wondered at, for he had not liked Thomas when he had first come calling. A shiftless character if you'd asked Peter, which, unfortunately, John had not. Tonight's apparition merely pointed out how right he, Peter, had been.

"I prayed for your safe return the whole time you were gone," Pete informed his master, while directing a glare, which John affected not to notice, toward Thomas, whose wet clothing was making puddles on the floor.

It was only after he'd been dismissed and was climbing the narrow stairs to his tiny room that Peter remembered he'd forgotten to tell John about the messenger's visit.

❊   ❊   ❊

John ushered Thomas into his study, where Peter had kept a small fire going in the brazier. Thomas had been fitted out with, or rather had squeezed into, one of John's tunics, and now the two men sat drinking wine, sitting under the riot of the fantastic mosaics. John poured again, with a liberal hand.

"Ah. This warms where it's needed most," remarked Thomas with appreciation. "We do not have such fine wine in my own country, I must admit. But you are still shivering. And not even wet."

"I was awakened in a rather unpleasant manner, my friend. And later followed with evil intent, or so I thought. And, of course, there is Leukos' death."

John again refilled their goblets. Changing the subject, Thomas ventured that women were troubling.

"It has been a long time since I was troubled by them, Thomas."

"You are troubled now, though?"

John nodded.

"It is not a soldierly thing to be so troubled." Thomas commented. "Yet it is a manly thing, and to be a soldier one must be a man."

"Perhaps this particular jug of wine may contain the answer to that riddle. Men have looked into many others for the answer, and yet not found it."

"The greatest men are troubled in this manner," mused Thomas. "There is, for example, your great general Belisarius. They say his wife Antonina rules him by magic."

"The magic she uses she keeps beneath her chiton."

"Even so. But you... dare I say it, John, as a friend? You have the advantage on ordinary men."

John agreed that he was not easily swayed by feminine magic.

"Nor persuaded to swerve from the path of righteousness," Thomas replied. "Who was it said there are those who make themselves eunuchs to better serve Heaven?"

"One doesn't serve by refraining from that which he cannot attempt. And my condition is not of choice, I can assure you." John found himself refilling his goblet. "At any rate, a man's lust is not a useful guide to his intent, since it always points in the same direction."

Thomas indicated that he needed to use John's lavatory.

"Just off the kitchen."

Thomas stood stiffly and made his way clumsily out of the room.

John realized that he had become as intoxicated as Thomas. He couldn't remember when that had last happened. Certainly not since he had begun his ascent at court. The little girl in the mosaic, Zoe, looked out at him, reproach in the glass facets of her eyes.

After some thumping and the clatter of a displaced utensil or two, Thomas returned. John took his turn, banging his shin hard against the low brazier beside the entrance to the cramped cubicle that served not only for a lavatory, but also as a place to dispose of kitchen scraps and other waste. It was convenient enough, but when the sewers which eventually led into the Sea of Marmara became blocked, not even a roasting leg of mutton could mask their stench. Upon his unsteady return, he noticed Thomas was staring at him, looking, as he sometimes did, like a small boy with a ginger mustache.

"What troubles you now, aside from Berta?"

"I wouldn't presume...."

"No, no. We are friends, are we not?"

Thomas dribbled wine. "Well. I couldn't help wondering. What... what is it like?"

"What is what like?"

"I mean, functioning. You're not as other men." The wine had robbed Thomas of all tact.

"You mean because I am a eunuch?"

Thomas' face dipped down to his goblet. His words were becoming increasingly slurred. "Yes, I know, but...

how much are you not like other men?"

"You are asking whether my genitals were entirely removed?" Thomas looked at his feet. "The answer is yes."

"But how do you... ?

"One learns a different sort of control. That was one of the most difficult things, Thomas. And perhaps my most important skill. Usually you can tell eunuchs by their smell."

"I meant no insult, John."

"No, it is true. The use of heavy perfume can mask only so much. I was fortunate in being able to learn to master myself afterwards."

"I'm sorry. I shouldn't have reminded you, with your just having seen your... uh... your friend again...."

"I had forgotten her for a few moments, actually."

"My apologies."

"But you will want to know how it happened?"

"No, really, I...."

"But your curiosity has jogged my memory," John insisted. "Let me see, now. My lover and I were with a troupe of bull-leapers. We'd come from Alexandria, I recall, and were very much in love. Odd to think of it now, is it not? I wanted the best for her. It was her birthday. I was young. I was impatient. I made inquiries, and heard of a man who sold silk. Illegally, of course. But I wanted my Cornelia to have silk. I bragged to my friends in the troupe that if all those high-born ladies could have it, then so would my Cornelia." He paused, remembering. "As I said, I learned you could purchase silk, with no awkward questions asked, up near the border.

"I had been drinking that night too, and the idea suddenly seized me that I must obtain silk before the sun rose again. So I went. The roads up there are little more than ruts. Amid the defiles and brush, in the darkness, I took a wrong road.

"The man I sought was encamped at a crossroads at the base of a prominent hill, or so I had been told. All the hills looked prominent and none of the roads I took crossed others. Still, I convinced myself I was moving in the right direction. I went on and on. I have learned since that it is better to turn back sooner rather than later.

"I was caught. I wish I could say I killed at least one. In my time, I have killed men. But I was taken by surprise, knocked to the ground, a boy being manhandled by his older brothers."

Thomas grunted uneasily. "There's no need to...."

"I insist, my friend. You wanted to know. I will spare you my captivity. I was not enslaved alone. After some time we became a burden. We were to be killed. It was Fortune that brought traders, because to them we were of some value, properly prepared. Eunuchs, you see, are considered by many to be more dependable than other men, unburdened as they are by family loyalties or normal appetites.

"We were stripped, bound. Flies were already feasting on congealed blood and what was in the bucket. They used a dagger."

Thomas face was chalky. "Please, John, I've heard enough."

"But you wanted to know, Thomas. They grab your flesh casually and brutally, like grasping the neck of a goose to expose it to the knife. When you are young you feel invulnerable. You think you are not like the others. Oh no, not you. Others may die, but not you. So, this being so, surely you could not be deprived of what makes you a man so easily?

"It was a searing heat, I recall. Not clean. And at the end he ripped what was left free by brute force. I suppose I was insane with pain for a time. They inserted a plug and waited for me to heal. The agony is indescribable. At some point the plug is removed. If the healing is such that you are able to void, you must continue to live, as best you can. If not, then you die, mercifully, but in the most terrible torment."

Thomas raising his goblet to his lips, choking on the wine. "But how can one live through such an ordeal?"

"We live or we die. It is not our choice."

Thomas struggled to his feet, lurching hastily from the room, thudding against the hallway walls. Faintly, John heard his friend sending his wine to the Sea of Marmara.

"And now," the Lord Chamberlain concluded, addressing Zoe, who had listened to his tale with perfect equanimity, "I can give Cornelia as much silk as she could ever desire."

Chapter Ten

John winced at the sunlight that shouted through the small rectangular panes of his kitchen window. His head pounded and he could feel a vein in his temple squirming under his skin as if it wanted to get out. On the other hand, he could not stomach Peter's proffered mixture of owls' eggs and wine, the traditional cure for over indulgence of the grape. Evidently he would just have to suffer.

Anatolius, newly arrived, inquired about his friend's health.

"Too much wine," John groaned, proceeding to describe his evening. Peter had seen Thomas out before John awoke. Rather unceremoniously, he gathered. The old servant did not seem to like the redheaded foreigner.

Now John could hear Peter cleaning out the lavatory. A particularly unpleasant job this morning, he supposed, which doubtless would further diminish the old man's already low opinion of Thomas.

Anatolius wrinkled his nose as he sat down at the kitchen table. "Smells like an alley," he remarked, then added a quick apology. "I forgot, Leukos was found in an alley."

"Don't apologize, Anatolius. No one could have had looser lips than I had last night."

"I'm surprised to hear it, John," the other replied, adding with a smile, "Perhaps you should carry an amethyst, for it's commonly said they are a marvelous antidote to intoxication."

Leukos' leather pouch lay on the scarred wooden tabletop. John explained that the Prefect had, as promised, had it delivered the previous night, but that Peter had forgotten to mention its arrival until that morning.

"Perhaps you should wait until later to see what's in it?" suggested Anatolius. His expectant expression belied his words.

"No. It has to be done and I should have done it last night, instead of drinking and reminiscing with Thomas. But I must request that you tell no one I have it, Anatolius." As he spoke, John poured the contents of the pouch into the painfully bright rectangles of sunlight lying across the table.

Something rolled across the table top, fell over the edge, and ticked down on the tiled floor. Anatolius retrieved it. It was a small, polished green stone. John frowned, puzzled.

"I have one like that," Anatolius offered. "The soothsayer gave it to me after he told my future. It was one of the pebbles he used. He said I should keep it for good fortune."

John could hardly believe his own good fortune. "So we've learned something already! Leukos must have kept his appointment with the soothsayer. The old man claimed he had, but objects are not so prone to lie as people."

The other contents of the pouch were more commonplace. There were four coins, three of silver and one gold, the gold coin having been clipped, which John theorized might indicate that Leukos had made a purchase on the last afternoon or evening of his life. But on the other hand, it might also indicate that he, or the coin's previous owner, had purchased something earlier.

"Nothing to be learned from the coins, then?" queried Anatolius.

"Actually they tell us quite a bit. For one thing, it wasn't robbery."

"You mean because they weren't taken? Perhaps the thieves stole something Leukos had just purchased. Perhaps they were scared away as they were in the process of robbing him. That could have happened easily if they were interrupted by a passerby, or someone opening a window and seeing them. Someone might even have come out of Isis' house and disturbed them."

John sighed. His head throbbed even more. "Yes, something like that could easily have happened. I don't think it's what occurred, though. I didn't believe Leukos' death was connected with robbery, and to me these coins confirm that thought."

The other contents of Leukos' pouch were less instructive. What could be made of a square of linen embroidered with the palace mark, and a silver necklace?

"What do you suppose Leukos used this for?" Anatolius said, picking up the cloth. "Surely he wasn't raiding the imperial storerooms?"

"Hardly." John's tone quelled the young man, who had the grace to look ashamed at making such a remark so soon after the man's death.

"Well, he was such a perfectionist perhaps he used it to wipe stray spots off the silver?" Anatolius mumbled lamely.

John said nothing, but picked up the necklace. It was heavy. At the end of its thick silver chain hung two intertwined fish. Both men knew that the fish was a Christian symbol, and that Leukos had been a Christian.

"A trinket for a lady friend?" suggested Anatolius. "Surely the pendant is for a woman?"

"Not necessarily. And do you ever recall seeing him with a lady friend?"

Anatolius shook his head. "No, now that you mention it."

"Don't forget Leukos and I were always interested in finding accomplished craftsmen to carry out palace commissions," said John. "We often collected samples of their creations. I'd have assumed it was something like that, but consider the workmanship. Crude, don't you think? I would have said it isn't anything that would normally have attracted Leukos' attention."

"You think too hard, John. Even with wine-hags in your head, you're concocting explanations just so you can demolish them. And most of them are ideas that would never occur to anyone else."

John agreed it was possible.

Peter continued to crash around in the tiny cubicle off the kitchen. He was now singing to himself, a low atonal dirge that he probably supposed was inaudible.

"I'm sure there is a simple solution," Anatolius offered.

"Probably, probably."

John carefully replaced the objects in the pouch. Had it really been just a robbery which had ended in murder? People died on the streets every day. People who had taken a wrong turn at the wrong hour. One moment on their way home to their families, looking forward to all the joys and trials of the years ahead. The next, dead. And for no reason. It was nothing to do with them or the lives they had led, except that a cutthroat thought they might be carrying something valuable. But strangers died for no reason. Not friends, and certainly not John's friend Leukos.

"I don't know," John worried away at it. "Something's wrong. It doesn't make sense."

"Does it have to?"

"Yes," John snapped, regretting his tone even as he spoke. "Yes, it does."

❅   ❅   ❅

Leukos' funeral was a simple affair. The Keeper of the Plate had no known family, a thing not unusual in Constantinople where the ambitious, not to mention the desperate, arrived alone from all corners of the empire, intent on making new lives for themselves. Thus it had fallen to his servants to prepare his body for burial. Now Leukos lay on the couch in his reception hall for the short time it took for his few acquaintances to pay their last respects. Light from the candles illuminating the shuttered room danced across the dead man's rigid features.

John was grateful that none of the mourners engaged in commonplace histrionics. There was no hair-pulling or breast-beating. Christians, John understood, did not favor such crass emotional displays. He credited them for that. Waiting in the hall, he found the incense infusing the air with the promise of Paradise made his eyes and the back of his throat burn.

But the puzzle of his friend's death would not leave John's thoughts. The Prefect seemingly had dismissed the murder as a common street killing, unlikely to be solved. But even though he knew it was irrational, John could not bring himself to accept that. So, even while feeling it was disrespectful, John sought out the young woman who had been in charge of Leukos' handful of servants.

Euphemia, barefoot and dressed in a short tunic, looked up at John with fear in her large brown eyes when he requested her to accompany him to a sitting room.

"I washed him with water mixed with spices," she told John anxiously. "And then we anointed him with perfumes. Poor master, he never wore perfume when he was alive."

The Lord Chamberlain, realizing that even in one of his less opulent robes he was an impressive and awe-inspiring sight to the young servant, reassured her kindly enough. "I'm sure you've done everything correctly. I just wished to ask you some questions."

He motioned her to a stool. He noticed that the water clock sitting in the wall niche had run dry. Euphemia must have followed his glance.

"Sir, I forgot to fill it," she apologized. "We didn't need them in the country. We had the sun there. Not so many walls pressing in on us."

"You are from Caria?" John had recognized her accent. The girl nodded. There was an unhealthy pallor to her face. "And what will you do now that your master is dead? Return?"

"Oh yes, sir, as soon as I can without disrespect to the master. Constantinople isn't for me. So big and dirty, if you'll excuse my saying so, sir."

"I am from the country myself."

"But you have achieved great office, just like the master."

"I had no choice."

From the reception hall came the sound of hushed voices, and a faint odor of perfume. Euphemia looked down at her clasped hands.

"Tell me, now. Did you see anything unusual recently? Did your master say anything to you?"

She shook her head. "It isn't for a master to confide in his servants, is it?"

"No, but they occasionally do."

"Oh, no, sir, not my master."

"Do you think he had something to confide?"

She looked at him questioningly. Again, there was anxiety in her eyes.

"I just wondered why you mentioned confiding," John explained.

"No, there was nothing. We were not... friends."

"I didn't mean that," John said, kindly enough. "Did he seem agitated at all, recently? Was there anything odd about his actions?"

She shook her head no.

"Did Leukos have visitors?"

"No, sir. Never. Sometimes he went out in the evening." Agitated, the girl rose and went to the window, open to a garden where a few spring flowers were beginning to bloom. She turned her face toward their scent and breathed deeply.

"Do you know where he went?"

"I'm a servant. He didn't tell me."

"Might he have been going to the baths?"

"Well, I could tell when he'd visited the baths." John looked at the girl quizzically. "He always used the gymnasium too. You know he was so pale," she explained, "and when he got back he was still flushed, right up to the top of his head."

John considered this insight into his friend's life. Leukos had never mentioned any evening activities to him. Of course, there was no reason why he should. But one would have expected, at least on occasion, to be regaled with a description of a visit to the theater or of a particularly lively dinner party. There again, Leukos had been unmarried and his destinations may have been the sort a scrupulous man does not reveal.

There was nothing wrong with that, certainly.

"And you are sure he had no visitors?"

"No. Except...." Euphemia turned from the window. "Well, it wasn't like real visitors, but a few times, instead of the master going out, a man would come to the door."

"Did you see this man?"

"I don't mean any particular man. Different men. They seemed soldierly, somehow. But not dressed that way, exactly. It was something about the way they moved. You have something of that yourself, sir, if I may say so."

"And they did not stay?"

"No. They just brought him things. A bag, or a scroll, or whatever it might be."

"Did he go out on those nights?"

"Sometimes." The girl folded her face into a frown. Her hands, held at her sides, balled into fists. "It's all so complicated in this dirty city," she finally blurted out. "All comings and goings in the night and nobody saying what they mean and dark alleyways and who knows what hiding in them. It isn't what I thought. I thought it would be so grand and all. And mice. There are so many nasty mice." She shuddered.

"But surely, there are mice in the country?" John's voice was gentle.

"Oh, but sir, they're country mice."

❊   ❊   ❊

Leukos' coffin was borne up the Mese on a donkey cart. The small procession accompanying him on his last journey followed on foot, winding through the crowded streets until finally turning past the Wall of Constantine into an area in the shadow of an aqueduct. Here the landscape was dotted with unkempt patches of cultivation, several small cemeteries, and some of the cisterns that kept the city supplied with water. In the more populated quarters of Constantinople, such cisterns were buried beneath other structures. Here only the dead were underground.

It was hot. The cemetery in which Leukos was interred smelled of spring vegetation and of freshly turned earth. Birds sang unheedingly as Anatolius gracefully delivered the oration. John disliked public speaking, and avoided it wherever possible.

As John listened to his friend's artful phrases he remembered the numerous times he had accompanied Leukos around the city. They had never traveled out here, to its outskirts. Now here they were, together. Before, their journeys had always been to workshops, keeping abreast of the efforts of Constantinople's artisans so that they would know where to turn should Justinian suddenly demand regalia for some new office-holder or Theodora evince a desire for a new diadem.

The guilds were numerous, their workshops scattered here and there. Silk alone consumed the efforts of six separate guilds, and John could not even recall how many were involved in the manufacture of an earring since its setting, wires, and enamels all required different expertise. Leukos, an expert on such matters, had always been a fine companion, enduring tedium with good humor.

Now Leukos was done forever with tedium.

And all his knowledge of the minutest details of every sort of imperial goods had vanished. A man, John reflected, is more perishable than a silver chalice or a pair of golden earrings.

John looked at Euphemia across the dirt mounded above Leukos. She stood, head bowed, holding her processional lamp. In the sunlight she looked less pale, less fearful.

"Did I render him due honor, do you think?"

Anatolius wondered, as they left. "He was, after all, a Christian. I'm not sure I understand their beliefs."

"I don't think they do either. Or at least they seem unable to agree on what it is they believe if you must listen to what Justinian has to say about it, as I do. He believes he can reconcile them all, you know. But what does it matter now to Leukos whether Nestorios was correct and their poor Christ was both human and divine? Or for that matter, whether their Christ's divine nature had superseded his humanity as Severus of Antioch maintained?" John retreated into his grief, shrouding it in scholarship.

"And men have died for such beliefs."

"Yes."

They lingered for a short while, enjoying the sun and the bird song amid the plaster covered vaults of the graveyard.

Anatolios bent to pick a small yellow flower.

"Europa would enjoy a bunch of these." He stopped short, frowning. "I'm sorry. I shouldn't be thinking of such things, here."

"Don't apologize. Europa and her mother have been on my mind also."

"We take all our joys within sight of death, don't we?"

"A poetical way to put it but true enough."

Anatolius let petals fall. "I wonder what flower that is?"

"Leukos could have told you."

"Leukos? I thought the Keeper of the Plate was an expert on man-made treasures?"

"He was that, but he used to name for me all the exotic blooms Justinian has imported for his gardens. We often discussed delicate business in the gardens, safely away from prying ears."

Anatolius wondered where Leukos could have

come by such knowledge. John shook his head.

"He never said."

"Reticent, for a friend."

"No more than myself."

"I wouldn't call you reticent. You've told me all about your past."

"You think so?"

They had come to one of the towering arches of the aqueduct. The shade beneath was almost chilly. "I know my friendship with Leukos puzzles you, Anatolius. Remember, when I arrived in this city I was a slave, as well as a eunuch. When I became a free man and took up a lowly position at the palace, Leukos was the first to treat me with respect."

"I can see how you would be grateful."

John let his gaze wander out of the shadow under the arch and into the suddenly dazzling sunlight beyond. There was a period of his life into which his memory rarely ventured, years when he was no longer what he had been but had yet become what he would be. He had managed to forget most of that time.

"Do you know, Leukos was student of the Christian philospher, Augustine?"

"An ascetic sort, wasn't he? The keeper of the Emperor's treasures would seem an unlikely disciple."

"I take it, Augustine was no more ascetic than a strictly observant Mithran. Leukos used to compare the philosophies."

"Perhaps he hoped to convert you."

"Indeed, he often told me how Augustine had come to his faith later in life."

"But knowing a man's philosophy, is that the same as knowing the man?"

"It depends upon the man, does it not?"

Something black moved in the weeds amidst the plaster-coated vault roofs. A single raven, thought

John. One for sorrow, as Thomas would say.

Then the black shape leapt up on to a fresh mound and John saw that it was a large mangy cat with a sore on its belly. It made him think of Euphemia's horror of city mice. Which was worse, the vermin or the hunter?

Chapter Eleven

"Five!"

"Six!"

Felix swore across the table at the young charioteer who had opened his fist to display four fingers. Added to the two gnarled fingers raised by Felix, that made six. The other man's quick hand closed over the last few coins on the table.

"You're too quick for an old soldier, Gregorius. I don't know if it's your eye or your tongue," Felix grumbled.

"It's strategy," revealed the other, dropping the coins into his leather pouch.

"They say an older head can beat a young hand. Another try?" suggested Felix.

Gregorius shook his head. "Don't mind losing, Felix. I'll win your money back for you at my next race. That is, if you place your wager on me. But I must be off. I still have that appointment to keep."

"Very well." Felix affixed his official seal to the parchment the young man had come to his office to request. "If anyone stops you, show them this. It's a pass."

"I can read, you know."

"You'd be surprised how many can't."

A third voice broke into the conversation. "Ironic isn't it? Some possess the keys to the palace, but not to knowledge. Which do you think would be preferable?"

As the charioteer exited the whitewashed box of a room, he nodded respectfully to the man who had appeared in its doorway. To the youth just departing, the newcomer looked lean and ascetic, unprepossessing in appearance and yet, as the charioteer sensed, a man of great influence. The younger man trailing in after him, on the other hand, struck him as nothing more than a court dandy.

"John!" greeted Felix. "And Anatolius. Come in. Since you ask, I'd say anyone who has keys either to knowledge or to the palace can't complain, since few have access to either. Anyway, a sword always knows more than a pen when you come down to it."

"Very sensible viewpoint, that," Anatolius put in blandly.

Felix pushed his seat back and walked around the table to stand in front of the room's one window, which gave a narrow view of a courtyard and dry fountain. A silver cross hung on the wall behind the table. It was an official decoration; otherwise the plaster walls were bare.

"What can I do for you, John? Is it official or... " his gaze moved in the direction of Anatolius "if it is about the matter of the ceremony... ?"

John raised a tanned hand to halt Felix. "No, I expect we'll see you there later. Nothing has changed. Anatolius and I have official business to attend to, but since you're on our way I stopped by to ask about someone you may have seen the day before Leukos' death."

"Who is that, then?"

"Do you recall Leukos was telling us at the Hippodrome that a traveler called Thomas had come around asking after goblets?"

"Yes, and, in fact, I did see the man that morning. It was just as Leukos said. He came looking for a pass. You need one to enter Leukos' domain, of course."

"You granted him access?"

"Well, yes. I sent him with an escort. What does that have to do with Leukos' death?"

"Nothing, probably."

"I see. Well, I'll ask my men if anyone observed anything odd at the time. But I'm sure your murderer is roaming the streets. More the Eparch's job to find him than ours, I'd have said."

"And what did you make of Thomas?"

"Seemed genuine enough. He had a soldier's bearing. Honest and straightforward."

"The sort you'd trust to play at micatio in the dark?" suggested Anatolius slyly.

Felix scowled, unhappy to be reminded of his very recent losses at that game.

"With my luck, I might as well play it in the dark," he muttered. "Here, John. Give it a try." He offered a closed fist. "Ready? On three."

John shook his own fist twice, then held up three slender fingers.

His softly spoken "Four" was almost drowned by Felix's booming "Six!" But Felix had raised only his first finger, which made him lose yet again.

"Once is mostly luck," John soothed the soldier's ruffled pride. "The strategy only comes in if you play long enough. Show me your right hand, Felix."

Mystified, Felix displayed his gnarled hand. The fingers were strong and stubby. A livid scar ran along the knuckles and the third finger was hump-backed as the result of an old injury.

"I'll wager you have a little less movement in that third finger, my friend?" John remarked.

"Nothing to complain about."

"But if you can't straighten it quite as readily as the others, you see, you might just be inclined, without thinking, to show one or two fingers more often than three or four."

Felix considered the suggestion. "I never thought of that."

"I wouldn't be at all surprised to learn some of your opponents had come to the same conclusion. It tips the odds in their favor, does it not?"

"Now don't race off to test this theory," cautioned Anatolius. "At least not until you've been paid! Besides, you know you should be saving up to see that little blonde at Isis' place again, shouldn't you?"

"Berta?"

"The same. One can't help hearing tales, you know."

"You mean *you* can't help hearing tales," sneered Felix. "And, as a matter of fact, I haven't caught a glimpse of her since that party at the palace the night of the celebrations."

"You were invited to the Empress' gathering?" John was surprised Felix hadn't mentioned it to him before.

"Of course not! I meant I was there in my official capacity. And I thank Mithra that it was only in my official capacity, because I can tell you that I didn't like what I saw. Especially the way they had Berta done up, and wriggling about on the table. Everyone was pawing her. She ended up in the lap of some filthy old man who plied her with... well, I don't know what it was, but she was enjoying it. I had to remain at my post, of course, and lucky for him, the dirty old bastard!"

"We all have to do what's expected of us, despite our personal feelings," sympathized John. "You must have seen the sun up?"

"It was a long night. At least Berta stayed where I could keep an eye on her, unlike some of the other girls."

"Let me know if you hear anything, will you? I rely on your discretion."

"Of course." Felix flexed his big hand. He noticed, again, the deformed finger John had brought to his attention. "You might be right," he said, changing the subject. "Perhaps that's why I always lose the game."

John sighed, wishing he could see the cause of Leukos' death as easily.

After they had departed Felix turned to look out at the dry fountain. A single raven was perched on its cracked basin and had begun to work at whatever had attracted its attention.

He thought about Berta. A kind-hearted soul. He could offer her a good life. What woman would not jump at the chance to leave an establishment like Madam's for the opulence of the palace? Not that Felix lived opulently himself. He intended to speak to her. But first there was the ceremony. Maybe it would make a man out of that soft, gossip Anatolius, though he doubted it.

Felix examined his hand again. Yes, perhaps it was that crippled finger that betrayed him. He would keep it in mind next time. It wasn't the money, he reminded himself, that attracted him to wagering. It was that he missed the heady potion of terror and euphoria that every soldier downed on the eve of battle. Wagering gave him at least a shadow of that old excitement. Oh, there was danger enough in Constantinople, but it was of the furtive and debilitating sort. There was no glory in the way Leukos had died.

When Felix looked from his suddenly trembling hand back into the courtyard, the raven had gone.

✳   ✳   ✳

Berta was delighted at the sight of the raven feasting on a discarded fish head near a vendor's stall in the street not far from Madam's house.

"Look, Darius." She tugged at the sleeve of the big Persian's tunic. "Isn't he wonderful? His wings shine like a newly minted coin."

Darius, temporarily relieved of his own wings, turned away from perusing the fish vendor's silvery-scaled wares to look in the direction of the avian scavenger.

"We had lots of ravens in the country," Berta went on excitedly. "They used to call from the pines at sunrise, I recall, when I was just a girl."

"You can't get better fish than this!" interrupted the raucous cry of the vendor. "Buy my freshly landed fish, and feast better than Justinian!"

"They look a bit old to me," Darius told him.

The raven took wing, apparently disturbed by a scrap of a woman who seemed to be scanning the ground for something lost. Berta watched as the raven rose above the crosses on the rooftops with a few beats of its powerful wings, fish head clutched securely in its talons.

Then she looked back at the fish hawker, who looked offended as he waved away the droning flies settling on his wares. "Fresh as country ladies, these fish are!" he protested. "Cheap at half the price. What you complaining about?"

A few of the other shoppers near his stall had begun to move away. Berta hoped Darius would also finish soon. Market place haggling didn't interest her this morning. She wished she could run off on her own to explore the city without the ever watchful Darius at her side, wished she didn't have to see a world whose colors were muted by the flimsy veil over her face. But then again, as Madam had pointed out to her only yesterday, she was lucky to be allowed out into the streets at all.

Darius finally grunted and began to move toward the next stall, a few more of the vendor's potential customers turning to follow in his wake.

"You, girl!" the vendor barked, causing Berta to turn in surprise. But he was addressing the thin, raggedly dressed woman who had inadvertently frightened away the crow. "How'd you like a free fish or two?" The man continued, "You won't find the likes of these fine wares laying about on the cobbles."

"Sir?" The ragged woman sounded bewildered at her sudden good fortune. She was clutching some soiled crusts of bread.

"Yes, you," the man said gruffly. "Being as there's some think my fish is no good, I'd rather give it away to some poor soul who deserved it than offend their dainty nostrils. Here, my good woman, take this."

To the watching Berta's amazement, the vendor handed the woman one of his larger fish, waving away her tearful gratitude. She was even more amazed when, seemingly impressed by the generous gesture, several hitherto reluctant customers suddenly decided to buy, pressing coins into the kind vendor's hands.

Darius put his big hand on Berta's shoulder, urging her to follow him to the next stall, but she ignored him. "Wait! Can you believe it? They're paying twice as much as he was asking in the first place, and they haven't even looked at the wares!"

Darius nodded, smiling, and the pair moved on to the next stall. Looking back, Berta watched the woman who had been searching the ground a few

moments earlier for scraps to eat had remained by the
man's stall, staring at the fish she'd been handed, as if
mesmerized by her good fortune.

Thus she heard the vendor's low growling "You!",
addressed to the woman after his last satisfied customer
had moved well away out of earshot. "I'll have that
back or the Prefects will hear about it!" he threatened.

"But sir," she protested, "you just gave it to me!"

Her voice was so weak Berta could barely
distinguish what she said. But there was no difficulty
hearing what the vendor told her. "It was just for show,
you fool. Now hand it over or it'll be trouble for you."

Berta looked on in distress, her delight in seeing
the raven forgotten, as the woman surrendered the
fish and turned away. Weeping as she walked away
aimlessly, she bumped into Berta.

"Watch out!" Darius warned the woman, in a
kindly enough tone.

Berta pulled away from his restraining hand,
directing language at the vendor which was as ripe as
his fish.

The man laughed. "So now I should be taking
advice from a little whore? You've no right to talk! I'll
come over tonight and then we'll see if you won't take
twice what you're worth when I offer it!"

"Don't mind him, lady. How can there be such
coarse people in a Christian city?" The raggedly dressed
woman's voice shook as she stood beside Berta, her
worn clothing a contrast to Berta's fine green tunic.
"A lady like you shouldn't be walking about in this
part of the city, even if you have brought your servant."
She put her hands up to her veiled face and began to
sob again.

Berta put her arm around the woman's shoulder,
feeling how thin she was, and steered her away from
the jeering fish vendor. Darius followed, watching his

charge carefully from a slight distance.

"You can't let bastards like that see you weep. It just makes them all the happier, the filth that they are." Berta spat on the cobbles, none too expertly. "Why are you scavenging for food, anyway? Don't you have a friend, a lover?"

"I have a husband, lady.".

"But where is he? Doesn't he work?"

"Of course he works. He works very hard, only a few days ago, he was injured and now – well – I have prayed to our Lord day and night, yet they say my Sabas might not live."

The woman began to sob more loudly. Berta impetuously tore off her veil and, pulling up the woman's veil, used it to wipe dry her tears. Gray, very sunken, and red-rimmed eyes gave mute thanks. Berta was surprised to see the woman wasn't much older than herself.

"Sabas? That is your husband's name?" she continued, "And what's yours, my dear?"

"Maera."

"I am Berta. And so, Maera, you have no money and now you must beg?"

"Yes, as your ladyship says." Maera pulled her veil back down to conceal her gaunt face, as was considered proper in public places.

"I think I can find you work."

"Work? For you, lady?"

"Well, actually I am not exactly a lady," Berta admitted, somewhat reluctantly, "At least not the sort you seem to mean. And this work, it would be the same sort that I do."

"I am not afraid of any work the Lord might send. However hard it is."

Berta giggled, her spirits restored by the prospect of helping the woman. "Oh, it isn't really hard work, at all. And you get to meet some really nice people, people from the palace, even. Some of the tales they tell would make a monkey laugh."

"This work you speak of, what exactly is it?"

Berta detected the note of caution in the woman's voice. "It's very respectable actually, despite what some people say. Nothing to be ashamed of. I've been assured as much by men who work for the Emperor himself."

"The man was just telling the truth, wasn't he?" The woman was horrified. "You work in one of those— those houses!" Maera clutched the crusts she had managed to scavenge closer to her, as if she were afraid Berta would attempt to steal them.

"I work at Madam's, yes, just as I have since I came to the city. And a good life it's been, too."

"But you are only a child! Have you no family?"

Berta paused. Hadn't she asked this poor woman the same question a moment earlier? "The girls I work with are my family," she finally said. She remembered then what she had not remembered for a long time, how it had seemed to her then, in the old days, after Madam had struck the bargain.

"I know that it seems unthinkable right now," Berta continued, "but I could introduce you to Madam, and perhaps she would offer you work."

Maera shrugged off the comforting hand Berta tried to place on her thin shoulder. "Never! I would rather be dead!"

"We all say that, but in the end we would rather live. It's not so bad, really. An occasional rough visitor, of course, but we have nothing to worry about. There are guards, we are safe. It's not like being on the street, at the mercy of any passerby. Why don't you at least come along with me and meet Madam, see what you think when you have spoken to her? She's a real lady. You'd be a pretty thing, with a little makeup. You'd do well, I'm sure."

The woman shook her head and stepped away.

"And what of your husband? Sabas, you say his name is. My family was starving too, but my father was able to buy oxen and— "

"Oxen? Your father sold his child for oxen?"

"Well, you can always make more children, but you can't make an ox, just like Madam says."

"Berta," Darius was at her side. "I really do think she does not want to come with us, kind though your offer may be."

"Think about it, then, Maera, my friend. We come to the market often, Darius and I. You can find us here most mornings, if you change your mind."

Maera turned away.

Berta darted after her.

"Here, at least take these." She pressed a few coins into the woman's hand. "It will get you through a day or two."

Maera looked horrified.

"Don't worry," Berta assured her. "There's not two hour's work there. Well, not even that, to tell the truth. The one was but a boy, and much taken with me."

Maera trembled but her fingers closed over the coins.

"I'll see you here tomorrow, then, if you have a change of heart."

Berta's mood was subdued as she returned to Darius' side, but long before they had reached Madam's doorway she had convinced herself that Maera would decide to accept her offer and she would have been able to help her. That raven really had been a harbinger of good news.

❊   ❊   ❊

Maera clutched the coins tightly. They seem to burn, like glowing embers.

The fish vendor, who had been looking on with great interest, called over to her, shamelessly. "Buy my fish, lady? Good for your husband, especially if he is not well. Why, I'll even toss in an extra couple of small ones, just as a thank you for your help. What do you say?"

Maera looked at him. Though without words to express what she felt, her expression was eloquent enough. It seemed to sting the vendor more than Berta's coarse words.

"Yes, well, my fine lady, it won't be too long before you're serving yourself up at some house or other," he jeered, "and then we'll see how fine you stay. I'll be looking for you, and then you'll be singing a different sort of tune, I can tell you. Now take your miserable face away before you scare my customers off."

Gathering her dignity about her, Maera moved slowly away, clutching the coins and her scraps of bread.

She walked home, past stalls filled with fish, barrels of olives, piping hot loaves, poultry of all sorts. With the coins in her hand, on this one morning, she could buy whatever she and Sabas wanted. Then she thought of how they had been earned. Were they a gift from the Lord, or a temptation sent by Satan?

"Oh, God," she prayed as she picked her way across the refuse-strewn cobbles, "show us a way to get out of this terrible situation and away from this disgusting place, where nobody cares for anything but money and people have no shame about selling themselves to strangers." She did not add, "and where whores have more charity than their betters," although, when she thought it, she supposed God must have heard that part anyway.

She was still aware of the weight of the coins in her hand as she passed the last stall in the row and noticed a beggar sitting hunched over at the mouth of an alleyway. At least that was how she characterized the emaciated, ill-clothed man, though he was no thinner or more ragged than she was herself.

She stopped in front of him and his bony hand moved slightly, automatically opening in supplication.

"I could never accept these if I had got them the way they were earned," Maera said, as much to herself as to the beggar, "but I came by them honestly, and so do you." She stooped slightly to place a coin or two into his leathery hand.

Without looking up, the man rasped something. It could have been thanks or a curse. Maera walked away, lighter in spirit, thanking her inscrutable God for giving her the opportunity to help another unfortunate.

Chapter Twelve

More than a century had passed since the Emperor Theodosius had banished all gods but the Christians' heavenly father. Gods, however, are not so easily killed off as common political foes and a few Mithrans still held to their beliefs, even at Justinian's court. However, since Mithra's ever shrinking army was so far outnumbered now, the mithraeum was safely hidden from prying official eyes by being concealed at the back of the network of underground imperial storerooms.

So Anatolius descended toward the ceremony at which he would ascend another rung of his religion's ladder. As elaborately wrought bronze doors gave way to simpler doors of polished wood and finally to crude stone archways, the Emperor's secretary felt himself slipping free of the bonds of palace life. The cuirass he wore concealed beneath his brocaded cloak no longer bowed his shoulders with its unfamiliar weight, and he had almost convinced himself he might come to prefer the uncomplicated blade of the sword to the subtler reed kalamos that he was accustomed to wielding in his official duties.

He was late. However, he was expected to be late.

The others, perhaps fifty in number and all that the mithraeum could hold, were awaiting him. He thought he could hear the murmur of their voices as he turned the last corner of the final damp, stone floored, and poorly lit subterranean corridor.

Two of Felix's excubitors were stationed at a nondescript wooden door, ready to turn away such strangers as might penetrate this far as they would from any imperial granary or treasury. The guards nodded to the young man in recognition. Anatolius handed his heavy cloak to one of them, who took it in a huge fist. Suddenly, Anatolius felt awkward, a fraud, a soft thing in the cuirass he had borrowed from Felix.

The other guard rapped on the stout door and swung it open, allowing Anatolius to enter another world.

Stone steps opening out below him led down to a long nave flanked by pillars, around and between which indistinct figures moved. Sputtering torches set in wall brackets, veiled by their own oily smoke, threw fantastic shadows of the assembly's mask-heads of birds and beasts on the rough hewn walls beyond the pillars and the embedded pottery shards that turned the ceiling into the simulation of a cave's roof.

As Anatolius marched down the steps, the mithraeum fell silent, so silent he could hear the hiss and pop of the torches. In their fitful light, men and shadows jostled each other. The only other illumination was at the far end of the mithraeum. There, a sacred flame on the altar cast light over a white marble bas-relief mounted on the back wall. It showed the powerful and familiar image of the sun god Mithra clothed in a tunic and Phrygian cap. He was in the act of slaying the Great Bull, dagger raised to administer the fatal wound. Contemplation of this sacred scene invariably gripped adepts' imaginations, flooding their minds with exultation.

But this evening Anatolius' gaze went to the white-robed figure who waited for him before the altar. Anatolius, now marching up the nave between double rows of the fantastic throng, was suddenly uncomfortably aware that the borrowed cuirass was too big; its buckles dug into him with each step he took.

He had wanted to savor this ceremony, to burn every detail into his memory. But, as often happened when he tried to grasp time, it slid away faster than usual. Before he realized, he was at the altar and the Father was extending a sword from which hung a narrow gold circlet, offering it to Anatolius.

Anatolius remembered his role. Following the ancient rite, he raised one hand and pushed the sword away. A thread of blood ran down his palm.

"Only my god will be my crown," he declared firmly.

It would not, of course, be too difficult for Anatolius to honor the Mithraic tradition of declining to wear a crown after initiation into the ranks of Soldier since the only crowns worn in the empire other than the imperial were military laurels. And those of martyrs.

Underlining the holiness of the ceremony, the Father poured water over Anatolius' head, sealing his entrance into the new degree. Now a hymn to Mithra rose to mingle with the smoke.

> *Mithra, Lord of Light,*
> *May this new Soldier be worthy of Thee;*
> *Mithra, Lord of Battle,*
> *Give him strength and loyalty;*
> *Mithra, Lord of Heaven,*
> *Guide our feet upon the Ladder;*
> *Lord of all, we worship Thee.*

Anatolius turned to face the masked assembly. He knew he had friends present. John, for one. But he saw only ravens, lions, a Persian: all the Mithraic degrees of rank were represented.

The Emperor's secretary was not a man who thought often of religion, but as he awaited the second stage of the ceremony, the taurobolium, Anatolius felt himself being drawn toward belief. Turning, he faced the marble image of Mithra. It seemed to move in the wavering light. The god had grasped the bull by its nostrils and was pulling back its massive head for the fatal cut. Anatolius' nostrils flared, burning in the acrid smoky miasma of the cavernous room. A scorpion was shown at the bull's genitals. It symbolized evil, seeking to destroy life at its very source. But the ears of grain which sprang from the doomed bull's tail foretold the victory of good over evil.

Yes, clearly, man inhabited a world where the only constant was the endless struggle between good and evil. At this moment Anatolius knew without doubt that this was true, realized it in a way he had, somehow, not grasped before. The marble scene blurred as his eyes filled. It was the smoke—or perhaps it was the water the Father had poured over him.

Even then, caught up as he was in this delirious conviction, Anatolius could not help seeing astride the marble bull not the god Mithra, but a young bull-leaper. The tortured screech of rusty iron on stone shocked this blasphemous image from his mind and brought his thoughts back to the shadowed mithraeum. He recognized Felix by the beard spilling from under his mask as the Captain slid aside the massive grate set in the floor in front of the altar.

A pair of acolytes helped Anatolius disrobe. Painfully tight buckles came loose. The heavy cuirass was lifted over his head and his tunic followed. Cold drafts he had not noticed earlier played over his skin. He felt his scrotum tighten.

In the floor, where the grate had been, yawned an oblong of blackness, a pit like a grave. He stepped forward, placing a bare foot into its dark maw, feeling for the narrow steps he had been told he would find there. Colder air rose around his calves and thighs as he stepped firmly down into the waiting pit.

At the bottom, his feet found icy water. The pit was deeper than a man's height. He looked up as the iron grate was replaced. Was this how the dead felt? Dark shapes obscured the dim oblong overhead, working to secure the grate. When they finally moved away he saw that directly overhead the crushed pottery ceiling was painted to represent the night sky.

Flickering torchlight moved across this frozen sky, wind-blown nets threatening to catch its stars. From a door at the side of the mithraeum, emerging from a maze of passages that led eventually to a well-concealed exit in a remoter part of the palace gardens, came a series of snuffling wheezes. They were mingled with the labored breathing of men who had wrestled a bound and muzzled but still recalcitrant beast through narrow and ill-lit corridors. Anatolius felt the staccato vibration of hooves. He could see only shadows moving against the painted stars, but he knew the bull was being led around the mithraeum prior to its sacrifice.

A grunt of exertion and a heavy thud announced the animal had been thrown on its side. The grid darkened. Only a triangle of light remained and in this, dimly visible against the painted stars, the Father reappeared. He gestured, meaning, Anatolius knew, that the animal was being unmuzzled.

A bellow shook the air. Anatolius caught a glimpse of movement as the Father's dagger sliced down. It was the fiery star Anatolius had seen as a child, blazing for a moment over the Sea of Marmara, so brief he might have imagined it except for the green scar that lingered for moments on his inner vision, and its memory, which never faded.

The bull screamed and Anatolius was bathed in fire.

Hot liquid whipped across his chest and lashed his face as the animal convulsed. Anatolius gasped, choking on a coppery mouthful of blood. Above him the Father was invoking Mithra.

"Accept this sacrifice to your glory, and accept your humble follower Anatolius to serve Thee in the degree of Soldier."

Anatolius wiped his eyes. The shadows writhing above him were red. He had never imagined one animal could have had so much blood. His hands were slick. Blood ran down his stomach and over his groin.

He felt disgust and elation. His heart raced. His ears seemed to ring.

The words above had been soft but exultant. The dying bull bellowed again. Anatolius felt lightheaded. His god had spoken!

The blood dripped more slowly now, draining the life force of the animal just as in Mithra's sacred battle with the Great Bull. The last scarlet streamers trickled through the grid. They were clotting in the young man's curly hair so that bloody rat's-tails fringed his brow and straggled on his neck.

And as strong hands grasped him and pulled him up out of the pit past where the bull lay, its eyes glazing, Anatolius' thoughts again turned, entirely inappropriately, to Europa. He found himself smiling.

❄   ❄   ❄

Standing beside one of the pillars, John, who had ascended to the degree of Runner of the Sun, smiled quietly as he recalled his own mixed feelings when he had undergone the rite Anatolius had just endured: elation, joy, pride, and perhaps a dash of terror. It had reminded him of the last hour before battle in the days when he himself had been a soldier both by occupation and by Mithraic degree. How long ago it seemed. It had been another world, another time.

But for now he rejoiced with the others as the scarlet-bedaubed Anatolius, the new Soldier, was pulled from the pit. Bright red rivulets ran down the young man's body and legs, pooling at his feet. A wide, almost insane, bloody grin had transformed Anatolius' gentle face into one which would have given even a hardened battle veteran pause.

Perhaps Anatolius had found the warrior in himself at last.

Chapter Thirteen

The ceremony in the mithraeum had ended and several more torches had been lit. It was hard to say whether the extra flames threw more light than their smoke obscured.

Several acolytes had led the bloodied Anatolius away to a corner and poured water over him. It was a practical cleansing rather than a holy baptism. Others were preparing to remove the dead bull. The exultation of the secret rite was spent and there now remained the prosaic task of cleaning away all traces of it. It was rather like the aftermath of an illicit meeting between two lovers, thought John.

"It is good to see Anatolius advance," Felix offered, settling his stocky frame next to John on the step where he was sitting, looking down into the mithraeum.

"Yes, this is an important day for him. I expect you will be going to his celebration tonight?" It was a politely phrased inquiry, for John knew how the two men regarded each other.

Somewhat to his surprise, Felix nodded. "Yes, I will."

"Anatolius will be a better Soldier than some might imagine."

"He had a keen eye, just now. Blood will bring it out." Felix lowered his voice. "John, I'm going around to Isis' house, and I'd like you to accompany me."

John looked puzzled.

Felix lowered his voice even further. "I'd like you to help me." He looked around before leaning toward John. "I'm going to make an offer for Berta. I'm not one for business. What does a soldier know about contracts? I'd like your assistance."

Berta? She was the little blonde at Isis' house, John recalled. It was not the sort of request John would have expected from such a proud and fiercely self-sufficient man as Felix. But on the other hand hadn't they all just reaffirmed their brotherhood in Mithra in a particularly moving manner?

"You need a man of law to advise you, Felix."

Felix shook his shaggy head vehemently. "I have no use for them. Men who fight with words, they're worse than poets."

"Well, Isis drives a hard bargain, and I hear Berta is quite popular...."

"I know you're a good friend to Isis, and I thought she might drop the price for Berta if you asked her as a favor."

"Well, yes, she might. On the other hand, the girl might not be for sale."

"She is. I made inquiries when I was last there." John noted Felix's straightforward manner of dealing with sexual matters, perhaps not surprising given the other's practice of dealing squarely and bluntly with problems. It was a good trait in a commander, but sometimes difficult to accommodate in a court as complex as Justinian's.

"What I want to do is, well, marry Berta," confessed Felix. "We are both from Germania, you know. I have always thought, were I to take a wife, I should wish for one from my homeland."

"I can understand that, Felix. May I say felicitations to you both? This seems to be a night for
celebrations." John smiled, tapping the other's chest
lightly. "Of course I would be glad to assist. Shall we
go now before our courage fails us? For I must tell you
that Isis is, before anything else, a terror of a business-
woman."

＊　　＊　　＊

Berta smoothed the last of the kohl into her eyebrows,
pursed the full lips she had reddened with wine dregs—
the customers enjoyed that—and evaluated her efforts
in her hand mirror. Yes, it was a passable job even if
the chalk on her cheeks was a little uneven. She was
almost ready for the first of the night's visitors.

She glanced at the small urn sitting unobtrusively
in the corner. It was a water clock. She smiled when
she recollected that according to Madam it had once
graced a Roman court of law, ensuring that repre-
sentatives for both sides were given an equal but
reasonable length of time for their orations. At least
Berta, unlike men of law, could guarantee her clients
satisfaction by the time the water ran out.

Berta plaited her hair quickly, thinking how much
she enjoyed her life in the city. Perhaps after all her
father had been correct when he had told her, as she
clung sobbing to him before he left her at Madam's
house, that she would enjoy her new life. It was
certainly much more exciting then the countryside
from which he had brought her only a year or so
before.

Her thoughts turned to the woman she had met
in the market place. She had not seen her again, and
perhaps never would. But the woman was a fool to
turn down the chance to save herself and her husband

by working at such a fine house as Madam's. But then again, perhaps they had managed to return to the countryside after all, dull though such a life would be. For what exciting events ever happened beyond Constantinople's walls? Oh, things grew, and died, and grew again. It rained. Or the sun shone. It was always the same.

But in the city, well, in the city anything was possible. Of course, it was true that she was not permitted to go out onto the streets unescorted, but then again at one time or another the whole world passed through Madam's house, didn't it? And as for her men... they had seen the world. Such tales they told. And the gifts they brought her. Cosmetics, perfumes. Wonderful jewelry, as beautiful as anything worn by all those fine ladies she had entertained the other night.

Remembering, she reached into the small tear in her mattress and pulled out the pendant the old man at the palace had given her. She dangled it in front of her. Its fine gold chain flashed enticingly in the orange lamplight. Dimmer points of light flickered within its flecked central stone like stars on a winter's night. She wondered how much she would receive when she sold it.

She smiled as she recalled the palace celebration, how she'd danced, so gracefully, across the table. The handsome young men had all desired her—and the not so handsome old men as well. She liked being desired. It had given her an easier life than having to toil in rocky fields, or chase goats up and down the hillside, or clean out the pens of the swine, just as her father had said. Not but what she still sometimes dealt with swine.

But, as she had recently realized, the career she had chosen for herself was a short one. Applying liberal dabs of perfume to her wrists, she weighed the recent offers she had received from some of her regular clients. One or two were rich men. But not young men. Still, a rich lady such as she would soon become could still enjoy her slim, young men as well as her husband, or so the other girls at Madam's house had told her.

She put the bauble back into its hiding place. A determined look crossed her face. When the time came, she thought, she would be the one to choose her husband. Not Madam.

She glanced around. All was in order. A tray of sweetmeats sat on a low table next to her bed. Soon she would be free of this place, she resolved, arranging cushions. But she would not make a hasty decision. It was too important. She certainly would not leave to live with Felix, even though he'd been cajoling her to marry him for weeks. She had been as plain with him about that as she could be without actually discouraging him from returning. He was too old for her. And what did a soldier earn anyway, even if he did live on the palace grounds?

Yes, when she married, she intended to marry into a noble family. And a wealthy one. Then she would live in a fine house in the city, and spend the hottest summer days at a beautiful villa in the countryside. Her houses would have marble floors and wall mosaics and statues. There would be well tended gardens, with shady trees and flowers and many pools. She would spend her days being waited on hand and foot, with nothing to do but wear lovely clothes and jewelry. Yes, she decided, I shall wear emeralds every day. And all the rich ladies at the palace who think they are better than me will want to come to the wonderful dinners I shall give. They'll envy me, because of my youth, my beauty. She smiled to herself. No, I will never have to entertain men again, well, not unless I want to. And then they'll be young men, muscular, smooth faced, clean. Yet still, she found herself thinking again about Felix. The big bearded captain who made her smile. He was nice enough. Nicer than the fat man. Hope I won't see the fat man again tonight, she thought. Ah, but on the other hand, perhaps the one who called himself a knight would return and ask for her. He had certainly lived up to the promise of his fiery red hair. A barbarian, to be sure. Not as cultured or, by the look of his clothes, as rich as some of her other clients. But yet there was something very attractive about him....

Footsteps in the hallway interrupted her musings. There was a soft knock at her door. It was time to get to work.

"Just a moment," she called, filling the water clock in the corner. The liquid, less than an hour's worth, began to drip steadily from the spout in the bottom of the urn into the holding bowl.

"Come in, my dear," she said softly, opening the door.

❊   ❊   ❊

Madam would be able to grant John and Felix an audience immediately the doorkeeper Darius informed them after inquiring on their behalf.

"And thank Zurvan for that," he added in an undertone, invoking his god of infinite time. "She's been driving us mad trying to play that accursed hydra. I'm surprised the Night Watch hasn't had complaints about the noise. Not but what—hope to see you again, sir!" he broke off to address a departing client as he added the weapons belonging to Felix and John to the pile in the alcove. "Yes, as I was saying, we should be used to it. She's been torturing us with it for days. Go right in, gentlemen."

Isis greeted them with enthusiasm, seating them on the couch next to her. John noticed that the room had been rearranged since his previous visit, the better to display the ungainly musical instrument.

"I seem to be getting somewhat more skilled at playing," Isis claimed, noting the direction of John's glance. "Perhaps Euterpe has smiled on me at last. And what can I do for you?" She poured wine and settled back against the cushions. Her own goblet remained untouched.

John glanced at Felix, who shrugged, looking uneasy. He had no knack for the subtleties of commerce.

"Well," John began, "we are here, or actually Felix is here, on a business matter, although of a somewhat different nature than usual."

Isis leaned forward. "Yes. It's about young Berta, is it not?" She smiled at Felix's expression. "Well now, Berta, like many of my girls, has a loose tongue on occasion, especially when it concerns herself. She's already mentioned your matrimonial intentions to me."

"Well, at least we won't have to haggle too much?" Felix was as blunt as the madam. John chuckled.

"I take it your role is to act as intermediary, John?" Isis was severe. "However, apparently that won't be necessary."

"I think I might still be able to...."

"No, no, no need for you to get involved, John. I've already made a firm decision about Berta. I really don't want to sell, but I'd be willing to sell her to you, Felix. Forty-five nomismata."

"Felix," John put in quickly, "Let Isis and me have a private word. You could buy a scribe for that."

"You'll get more pleasure from Berta than a scribe, Felix," Isis pointed out.

"You aren't selling her," stated Felix, "You're holding her for ransom. But I can meet your price."

"The chariot races must have treated you well

lately! But I'm only doing this because I'll be glad to see her settled," Isis declared airily. "Berta's getting rather old to be working here. At her age I had already saved up enough to buy my freedom and was in business for myself. But Berta spends everything she earns before the coins are cooled. Where do you think all that jewelry comes from?"

"I don't inquire too closely," Felix admitted. "But I can meet your price. Let's get on with it."

John felt he should sound a note of caution. "Excuse me, Isis, but perhaps Felix shouldn't charge in without weighing the... uh... situation a little more closely." He spoke in Egyptian, sparing Felix embarrassment while allowing Isis to comment privately on the proposed transaction.

She took the opportunity, replying in her native tongue. "John, I fear it is impossible to act as friend to both sides. I'll return the money as a gift when they marry. Berta seems have some affection for this unlikely rogue, and I think he will treat her well." Switching back to Greek, she continued. "Now, Felix, you are right to insist on deciding now, for I must warn you, more than one man has his eye on Berta." She rose and opened the door to summon Darius.

Felix's face darkened angrily. "It's that foreign knight. He was... was... with her!"

John tactfully refrained from pointing out that the same might be said of a large number of men. But, of course, Thomas was a man Felix knew, or at least had met. "We really should come back tomorrow," he urged the other.

"Nonsense!" interrupted Isis. "The sealing wax will be melted by now."

As if in confirmation of the madam's words, Darius showed in a balding man who reminded John, for a painful moment, of Leukos. He was carrying a salver bearing wax, seal, and parchment. Apparently a traditionalist, Isis proposed settling the Curse of the 318 Fathers of the Council of Nicea upon the document of sale.

"Are you certain about this, Felix?" John asked one last time.

Felix gave a curt nod.

"Very well." John stood. "Isis, while your secretary is drawing up the contract, would you permit me to talk to Darius? There are some questions I'd like to ask him, if I may."

The woman waved her soft, beringed hand. "Of course, John. Come back for a chat when you're done. And have him send one of the girls upstairs to tell Berta of her good fortune."

* * *

Darius was sitting on a marble bench in the entrance hall. When John sat down next to him, he felt dwarfed.

"Tell me, Darius, did you hear anything unusual or strange the night Leukos was found in the alley?"

"More than the usual odd noises, you mean?" Darius smiled at his feeble jest. He looked tired. "To tell you the truth, John, with Madam torturing that hydra night and day you can't hear a thing. We had a party of Greens last night. Rowdy bunch. I had to subdue a couple of them after they made disparaging remarks about my appearance. Not that I blame them, you know. But they behaved themselves after that."

John, familiar with Darius' methods of restoring order, ventured an estimate of the sum of broken limbs involved.

"Only two this time," the other countered, only to be interrupted by a shriek from upstairs.

Darius leapt up, an erupting volcano. "Someone's hurting one of the girls!" He pounded for the stairs, but had barely set sandal to step when a terrified, half-dressed girl flung herself downstairs into his arms. She clung to him, sobbing.

"There, now, Helena." His voice was surprisingly tender. "Show him to me and I'll... "

"No," wailed the girl louder. "It's not me. It's Berta!"

❋   ❋   ❋

When John reached the second floor cubicle that reeked of perfume, he saw Berta reclining languidly on her pallet, her short tunic hiked up teasingly. Half leaning against the wall, she stared wide eyed, as if surprised by the girls who crowded around her doorway, whimpering and exclaiming over the discovery.

Berta could no longer be anyone's wife, and she was no longer worth forty-five nomismata. She was dead.

John pushed through the spectators clustered around the doorway. He could see the mark of a powerful hand on Berta's slim neck. A bluish tinge showed through the girl's white chalk makeup.

"Strangled," he muttered to Darius.

Darius began to snarl a string of oaths, biting them back as Isis arrived from downstairs.

"Who would do this to one of my girls?" the madam wailed, "He had no right! She was mine!"

The room contained little, John thought as he glanced around. Little except perhaps the dreams any young girl might have had. There was only the pallet, its coverings rumpled. Berta had been a slight girl, and obviously unable to put up much of a struggle against her attacker. On a table near the bed, the wine and sweetmeats awaiting visitors were undisturbed beside a few pots of makeup and a jar of perfume. The water clock in the corner, John noted, was still nearly full.

Had she filled it in anticipation of a client?

He was shoved aside.

"Felix! Stay back!" Darius warned the newcomer.

The excubitor's Captain stood over the girl's body. He was silent but tears streamed down his bearded face. He was familiar with the death of fighting men on the field of battle, but this was a much more terrible scene to contemplate.

"Mithra," he entreated his god softly, "so this is what you do while I am busy at worship, you send a stealthy murderer to my lover? I wonder, would the Christian's God be so cruel?"

"Zurvan!" Darius exclaimed with belated caution. "Who is guarding the front door?"

John heard him pound away, but he did not follow.

There was something unnatural in Felix's strangely calm tone, as if his lips were forming words of their own volition while his brain ignored their content.

"I will have compensation for this," Madam was saying, through great, heaving sobs.

John laid his hand on her arm in silent comfort.

Then Felix howled. It was a wolf's howl, a battle cry, the shriek of a dying soldier who sees his entrails on his foe's blade. It did not stop. The girls clustered around the doorway began to scream, thinly and shrilly. A few of them fled hysterically down the hall to their rooms.

Felix stopped then, turned away from the bed and left the room in grim-faced silence, having paused just long enough to gently adjust Berta's immodestly displaced tunic to cover her decently.

Chapter Fourteen

wo deaths in four days. In overcrowded Constantinople, it was not unusual for death to brush past. But two murders, both involving Isis' house, one in the alley outside, the other inside—could there be some connection, apart from their unfortunate proximity?

The Lord Chamberlain's study was lit by wavering lamplight but when a paler light flickered across its walls, John turned toward the open window, half expecting to see the unsteady glow from one of the fires that so often raged in Constantinople. He was relieved to see a flash of distant lightning from a storm moving in over the sea.

He drank more wine from his cracked cup. Zoe, the girl in the mosaic, seemed to be looking at him, reproach in her big eyes. Why was she chiding him?

"No, my child, I haven't forgotten you now that I have a real daughter," he muttered. The mosaic girl seemed unappeased. If he were unable to deal with a child of glass and imagination how could he deal with one of flesh and blood?

"Perhaps it isn't that," John continued to think aloud. "Do you imagine I have spent too much time thinking about Cornelia and Europa and too little unraveling Leukos' death? I assure you, I have explored many possibilities."

Why then was he no nearer to his destination, his solution?

"And now there has been another murder. But you don't understand," John told the girl. "You are only a child."

He recalled his dream of running tirelessly across fields, from which he had been awakened by the Emperor's messenger, young Hektor. Was the dream perhaps prophetic, or merely wishful thinking?

Surely not. It could be more readily explained as an imbalance in the humors. Or a reflection of his waking experiences. Seeing Cornelia, and seeing her—their—daughter in the Hippodrome had brought back to him the feelings of his youth.

The cup rose to his lips again and John was surprised to find it empty.

As empty as his thoughts.

A well-dressed palace official unadvisedly turns down a dark alley during a celebration and is stabbed to death. A young prostitute is strangled.

These were not unusual occurrences. Perhaps he was trying to find some meaning in them that simply was not there. Thunder began to approach, rumbling over the walls of the city as the storm moved inland. John rose abruptly from his stool.

"Peter," he called. "I'm going out."

❋　　❋　　❋

When he had secured the house door behind his master, Peter returned to the study. Keeping his watery eyes averted from the blasphemous mosaics, he retrieved John's cracked cup. Why did the Lord Chamberlain insist upon using a thing so time worn?

Sometimes it seemed to Peter that John was like one of those holy hermits who denounce every worldly pleasure. Except, of course, that John was a pagan.

More puzzling yet to the old servant was why his master had been speaking to himself, or rather to the wall of his study. Not that Peter eavesdropped, but in the course of his duties he had passed the study more than once, observing John gazing at the mosaic as he spoke. That had frightened Peter. Holy men often went mad, it was true. But surely the Lord Chamberlain was a man of this world?

On impulse Peter sat down on John's chair. His heart raced, although there was no reason he should not rest his old bones for a moment. Certainly his master would not object. He forced his gaze toward the shadowy mosaic, to see what John would see. He found himself looking into the dark eyes of a young girl. Eyes of glass that appeared to look back at him. That would in an instant, blink. He was certain of it.

Peter jumped up, crossing himself, and was out of the room in two strides, droning a familiar hymn as he hurried down the hall. He did not look back because he knew the girl's expression had changed, and he knew that was a vision he did not dare to look upon.

※　　※　　※

John made his way to the Mese. Rather than following the wider, torchlit thoroughfares, however, he soon veered into the alleys that snaked, twisting and turning, up to the wall around the palace grounds, trying to find their way in but being continually forced back on to themselves. A fitful wind snapped his cloak, whipping drops of rain into his face.

From his swift, purposeful stride, his unhesitating turns into obscure byways, an observer would have supposed the Lord Chamberlain was hurrying to some important destination. In fact, John's movements were unplanned, his speed merely a reflection of the frantic pace of his thoughts. Although his mercenary days were long past, when some knotty problem arose to snare him in its serpent's coils there always came a time when John's body insisted on action. Since he was no longer soldiering, and since battling with a blade would not in any case pierce the demons of the mind, at such times he invariably went out and walked.

Yet who could say for certain that John's feet did not, sometimes, carry him to the truth?

Noticing a tradesman, an idea occurred to him. The vendor was on his knees in front of a cramped niche, mending the rickety wooden table on which he displayed his wares during the day. The man looked up, startled, at the sound of John's approach. He was a ragged, rat-like creature.

"Do you have any fruit? Vegetables?"

The shopkeeper eyed John's expensive robes and boots warily. The lamp by which he had been working projected John's shadow, supernaturally large, against the blank wall of the tenement on the other side of the narrow street.

The shopkeeper scrambled to his feet. "None that one of your position would find suitable, great one."

"Anything you have would be acceptable. I shall also need a basket."

The man's gaze darted back and forth in the lamplight, his mind alert for a trap. "I could sell you a basket, but the fruit's sat in the heat all day." he finally offered.

"I assure you, it will be satisfactory." A coin flashed in the dim light.

"The fruit out here's probably spoiled, like I said, but I might be able to find some that'd be edible."

"Believe me, I don't need anything fit for the

Emperor's table." John turned his hand slightly so that the light caught the coin again. The shopkeeper's eyes gleamed as brightly as the currency.

Rummaging noisily through the baskets and boxes in his niche, the rat-faced fellow sounded relieved as he replied. "Well, then, I can promise something that will suit you. That I most certainly can do."

John traded the nominal weight of the coin for the considerably heavier basket of fruit and continued on toward the square at the end of the street. The wind howling through narrow spaces between the buildings on each side pushed at his back as if attempting to thrust him bodily out into the square. When it stopped abruptly, he heard raindrops splattering against the overhanging balconies which nearly met above his head. Seconds later, their staccato beat was engulfed in a formless roar as the storm which had been gathering burst violently.

Under the balconies it had been relatively sheltered, but when John stepped out into the square he was soaked as immediately as if he had plunged fully dressed into a pool at the baths. He paused, wiping water out of his eyes.

At the other side of the square, a marble column rose into the night to a height just above the two-story buildings all around. John hurried forward.

Reaching the column, he leaned his head back, hand protecting his eyes, trying to look through the rain toward its top. A lightning flash illuminated a low railing there, and a motionless figure.

"I am here to pay you a visit, my friend," John called up. "I have brought some fruit. I mean you no harm."

The figure, which might have been a statue since it did not move, refused to reply. Another flash of lightning illuminated a wooden ladder. John reached up to grasp a greasy rung. Thunder shook the column and a foul odor wafted down. Catching his breath, John began to haul himself upwards.

It was a relatively short journey, but not an easy one. The ladder was slippery, the rising wind yanked at his water-sodden cloak, and the downpour seemed to bear down on his shoulders with a tangible weight.

Truth to Mithra, John thought, he was not afraid of Zeus' thunderbolts. It was not that the Lord Chamberlain had more courage, or was more foolhardy, than most; rather he firmly believed that the Lord of Light he followed would not allow him to perish at the hands of a weaker god.

When he reached the top John remained leaning on the ladder, clinging to the railing with one hand. He had no wish to step out onto the tiny space atop the column. There was, he judged, not enough room for him and the stylite unless the man were to move to one side, and John suspected that the stylite's legs had, years since, become locked in their habitual position. Intermittent lightning revealed them to be withered, descending stick-like from a few rotted rags of clothing. The rags squirmed with life. The stench was unbearable, even to John who had helped bury former comrades on battlefields days after victory.

"There is fruit in this basket," he informed the stylite, carefully setting it down near the sticks of legs.

"The Lord in His wisdom announces thunder with the lightning bolt," intoned the holy man in a surprisingly firm voice, without looking at John. "Bless you, my son," he added as an afterthought.

"I have a question."

The stylite nodded, ropy-veined neck moving, while from his shoulders down his body remained motionless. "The fire," he muttered. "God's house is consumed. The evils of mankind will be turned to ashes."

John thought he glimpsed something nomisma-sized emerge from the stylite's tangled beard and scuttle in the direction of the holy man's jaw.

He looked past the stylite toward where Justinian's new church was rising. It was certainly a different sort of tribute to God than the one offered up by this holy man. Was the stylite remembering the fire which had destroyed the old Church of the Holy Wisdom?

"There was a man, a friend of mine, murdered not far from here." From his precarious vantage point John looked out over the city. Here and there a few smoldering torches not yet doused by the torrent shone dimly, like spent charcoal in the bottom of a brazier. Crosses rose starkly from the roofs of many houses. Some crosses were wooden, others more elaborate, alerting both God and men to the faith of those who slept beneath them.

"There," John pointed, trying to direct the stylite's gaze. "In that alley. That is where it happened. Did you chance to see anything?"

The holy man chuckled softly. For a terrible instant, a lightning bolt linked the city to the heavens. It was followed by a wave of thunder. John could feel its vibration in his back teeth and at the base of his skull. Some house close by had surely been struck.

The stylite began to laugh. "Can that be the finger of God seeking out a sinner?"

John felt a sudden wave of anger. How could any god be served by a man choosing to stand perpetually in his own filth?

"What do you have to do but look down into the streets?" John demanded. "You must have seen something. Consider my question, at least. I'm looking for one who is guilty of murder. Doesn't your god care about finding those who are guilty?"

The stylite laughed again. "No man is guilty but one who sets down his cross."

John began to ask the stylite about the guilt of a man who would plunge a dagger into another's ribs but stopped himself. There was no point. The stylite was obviously mad.

He scanned the scene below which was illuminated by torchlight and the intermittant flickering of lightning. The alley he had tried to bring to the stylite's attention ran between a tall tenement and Isis' house, where Berta had died. Further on lay the inn in which he had interviewed Ahasuerus, and where Thomas was staying. The narrow alley continued on toward the Mese and the Church of the Holy Wisdom with patriarchal and imperial palaces close by. The city pressed in all around, a jumble of houses and humanity.

He suddenly realized that his climb had not been wasted after all. Looking down from the stylite's column, John was reminded of what he knew so well as to take for granted, that the city, for all its winding alleyways and assorted squares and forums, its magnificent architecture and obscene hovels, was a small place. Though the world of the palace might seem far removed from Madam's and the alley where Leukos had died, it was not, and although the murderer might be lost among the crowd, if he was still in the city, he was not far away.

The stylite was still laughing. John, growing even angrier, demanded to know why.

The holy man stopped abruptly. "Is it not humorous?" he asked. "Even the holders of the highest offices have sinned, and all of them are but wayward children before the Lord. Even you. Even the Emperor himself." He laughed again.

John began to rebuke him but was distracted when

he felt a feathery brush on the hand clutching the railing. Looking down, he saw something squirming across his knuckles.

"Mithra!"

His hand rose automatically to shake the disgusting thing off it. For a shocking instant, John felt himself fall backwards, his grip on the railing gone. There was a breathstopping lightness in his chest. Like flying. Then his other hand had grasped the side of the ladder.

The shifting wind slapped a sheet of rain across his face, bringing more strongly to his nostrils the putrid stench from the platform. He climbed back down to the street, ears ringing with the stylite's laughter, which began to turn into shrieks. John was hardly aware of the change. Flying. He had felt as if he had been flying. But he had never flown, except in his dreams.

Chapter Fifteen

Elsewhere in the storm-shrouded city, a small group had gathered to consult another sort of oracle. The small room in the palace was as gloomy as the night outside. One of the indistinct figures squatting in the semi-darkness tended to the lantern. It had been kept nearly covered. Now it was all but extinguished and acrid smoke filled the air.

What light escaped was not sufficient to illuminate most of the room, but struck dimly on the white of an eye, a moist lip, the blade of a sword.

"Hold it still! Watch your hand, will you?"

"There! Now! Do it!"

"You won't! You can't do it!"

"Talk, that's all you do, talk!"

"Shut up! Where is it?"

"Hurry up, will you?"

"Crack the lantern, and when I tell you, move your hands out of the way."

"You won't do it!"

"Move! Now!"

The blade flashed. A pathetic gurgle and spurting blood hit Hektor's face, scalding his skin.

Justinian's young page struck with the sword again

and again until the noise stopped.

Then the room was very quiet, except for a child's sobbing. Hektor licked the blood off his lips, its coppery flavor cutting through the waxy taste of his lip-color. Another boy slapped the crier, a resounding crack in the darkened room. "Baby!"

The crier hiccoughed and was silent.

Hektor was aware that his head was aching. "Shhhh," he cautioned his companions. "Is there anyone in the hall?"

They listened until the rushing of blood in their ears seemed loud enough to drown out any other sound.

"More light," he eventually instructed.

The knot of pages huddled around the bloody corpse of a chicken. They were still in the heavy make-up they wore while gracing the court, but aside from that they were entirely naked. It was obvious they were still no more than boys.

Hektor giggled nervously at his handiwork as it was laid out on the tiled floor.

"Said I wouldn't do it, didn't you, Tarquin? Well, there's your proof."

The boy Hektor had addressed reached forward tentatively, fingering the bird's blood. He drew his reddened finger down the concavity of his smooth chest to his narrow navel.

"You're just jealous because the Master of the Offices prefers me," he riposted. His kohl-surrounded eyes glittered in the shadowy room.

"You weren't at the Empress' celebration, were you, chicken-brain? You didn't see the fortune-teller reading entrails for the Empress, did you?" sneered Hektor.

"What did he tell her, then, if you really saw it?"

"Tell us," another boy piped up.

"I don't dare repeat it. It's too horrible. A terrible fate. Now, who wants his fortune told? How about you, Tarquin?"

The dark-eyed boy drew back. "You'd just make up a lie."

"Swear on the True Cross, I wouldn't," Hektor made the Christian sign. It passed through his mind that crucifying a chicken might be an enlightening experience. Unfortunately, this particular bird was beyond feeling pain. "Here," he offered. "You can pull out its entrails yourself."

"Tarquin's all pulled out," observed one of the others, to a chorus of snickering.

"I'll do it myself, then." Hektor grabbed the limp chicken by the neck and held it up so its feet dangled down to the floor. He waggled its head from side to side, making its milky eyes appear to regard each boy in turn.

"Ah, my pretty Tarquin," Hektor leered, in what was supposed to be a basso profundo. "Come and visit your master, boy."

Tarquin shrank back.

"What do you want, poor little Tarquin?" Hektor continued, taking on the fancied voice of the dead chicken in a much more convincing falsetto.

The feathered corpse was whirled around by its feet. Then Hektor, gritting his teeth, rammed the sword savagely into its nether regions.

The boys were about to break into laughter, but when the blade emerged from the fowl, then sliced into the chest and, yanked sharply down, spilled intestines onto the floor, there was little sound in the room.

One of the boys jumped up, preparing to run. "Stay there," Hektor commanded. "Don't alert the guards."

The boy dropped back down, leaned over and vomited where he sat.

Hektor flung the gutted chicken at the boy. It missed, thudding against a wall. Placing the sword carefully on the floor next to his bare thigh, he grabbed the heaped intestines in both hands, raising them level with his nose. Unexpectedly he gagged. He let the intestines flop to the floor. They slithered across the tiles.

"By Jupiter and Cybele and the Emperor of the Toads," Hektor swallowed a sickening lump of bile which had risen in his throat. "By the left arm of John the Baptist and the talisman of all healing, in the names of Justinian and Our Lord Jesus Christ, show us what fate waits for the boy Tarquin!"

He was lightheaded. The floor appeared to be tilting. Perhaps there was something in this soothsaying business, he suddenly thought desperately. Perhaps one of those fearsome entities he'd invoked had actually heard him and had responded. His heart leapt in sudden panic.

The naked boys, spattered with blood, looked savage in the lamplight, startled eyes wide in their garishly rouged and powdered faces.

"More light!" Hektor demanded.

He peered down at the bloody intestines. They seemed to squirm, as if they still lived. It was impossible, of course. Surely it must be an effect of the smoke-induced tears welling in his eyes.

"What do you see?"

"Go on, you can't see nothing in some chicken guts."

"Be quiet!" Hektor' voice was quavering. "It's like listening to thunder to foretell the future.... Look there, see, waves."

He suddenly felt a powerful presence. Someone

or something was looking down at him from a great height. He hadn't meant any harm. It had all been a joke. He hadn't even remembered exactly what the old soothsayer had chanted. Or had he? The uneasy feeling that he was being watched grew stronger. The coils of intestines formed shapes. There, a face... a familiar face... it was... no... it couldn't be... and yet... it was....

"Hektor!"

He leapt up wildly at the sound of his name. Startled boys were screaming. A hand grabbed his bare shoulder, spinning him around as easily as he'd spun the dead chicken.

Hektor gasped. He was looking up into the scowling face of the Lord Chamberlain who, without benefit of chicken entrails, well knew the destiny of pretty powdered boys who dared to grow into manhood, but was too kind to reveal it.

❊   ❊   ❊

By the time Hektor had washed all the blood and some of the make-up from his face, and dressed, his fright had faded. He was now slumping down bonelessly on a couch in the nearby sitting room where John had led him. He regarded the Lord Chamberlain with sullen contempt. His look reminded John that while most court pages left imperial service upon attaining manhood, a number stayed on in other employment at the palace. He wondered briefly if Hektor might take that path, and if he had already made a bitter enemy of him.

"What do you need me in here for?" the boy snarled. "I know it's not the usual reason. Not you!"

John shut the door. The room was simply furnished with the couch, a stool, a low table on which a lamp burned, and a wooden cross on one wall. There were no windows. John pulled the stool to the couch and sat down. The rain had soaked him to the skin. He tried to suppress a shiver.

"Were you at the Empress' gathering the other night, Hektor?"

"All of us were."

"I thought so."

"I'll tell Theodora you've been asking about her."

"I'm sure you will." John ignored the boy's insolence. "But it isn't the Empress I'm interested in. Tell me, what went on that night?"

Hektor shrugged. "Nothing much. The usual things."

"Dining, entertainment?"

"Are you sure I can't do something for you, Lord Chamberlain? I'm very obliging. Is there anything anyone can do for someone like you?" Hektor reached out and stroked John's knee.

John felt his face redden as he brushed the boy's hand aside. He felt anger at himself for allowing a mere child to discomfit him. Hektor permitted himself a faint smirk.

"I've been told there was a soothsayer there," John continued, keeping his voice even. "Is that true?"

"Perhaps. I don't remember."

John forced himself to lean forward. The boy still reeked of perfume despite his recent ablutions. "You will remember to whom you are speaking. No doubt there are powerful men at court who would protect you to conceal their secrets. Unless, of course, you are merely silenced, for a dead tongue can tell no tales. But I advise Justinian, who has condemned the sort of services you provide, and I am afraid your friends, if that is what you call them, won't dare to defy their Emperor if he decides to grant me your pretty little head on a stake."

Hektor' dainty fists clenched. His mouth tightened into a line of pure hatred, but he said nothing.

"Now," John continued, "I want you to tell me about the soothsayer."

Hektor glared, but answered immediately. "The charlatan? For one thing, the smelly old goat had his wrinkled paws all over one of the whores there."

"You mean he didn't prefer little boys? What about his readings? Did he tell anyone's future?"

"Theodora wanted her fortune told."

"Using a chicken's entrails?"

Hektor nodded. John wondered if the high-born lady for whom Ahasuerus had mentioned providing such a reading had been the Empress herself. He would have to speak to the soothsayer again. He asked Hektor about the chicken used for the Empress' reading.

"Theodora sent one of the guards to the kitchens for a chicken, and a knife as well. It must have been quite blunt, since the chicken squawked a lot." Hektor smiled at the memory.

"I presume the reading was conducted in a more decorous manner than your own?"

"If you mean were Theodora and her guests naked...."

John's warning look stopped Hektor in mid-sentence.

"Do you remember her fortune?"

"The old goat told her she would be rich. Some prediction, her being an Empress."

John's attention was drawn to the room's closed door. There was muted shuffling outside; the other pages were probably taking turns, eavesdropping.

"Who else was there? Did you see the Captain of the Excubitors?"

"He was there, making sure the guards were watching out for enemies, not ogling the women. Or the men."

"Who else?"

Hektor shrugged again. "Just the usual people. Men and women of the court, pages. And a flock of whores. Some of them were dressed like virgins!"

"What about the entertainment?"

"Jugglers, mimes, some poor whiny poet, dwarves. The usual rubbish. Then there were two women, acrobats. One was an old hag, but the other was younger. They were doing handstands and cartwheels, things like that."

John frowned. "Two women?"

"Bull-leapers was what they said they were."

It seemed then that Cornelia and Europa had attended Theodora's party. John suddenly felt cold. Perhaps it was just his soaked clothing that clung uncomfortably to his back and shoulders.

Lounging even lower on the couch, Hektor was beginning to regain his courage. "Perhaps you should get out of those wet clothes?" he suggested sweetly.

John got to his feet instead, pushing the stool away more violently than he had intended. It crashed against the wall. The wooden cross, jarred loose, fell to the floor. Hektor clamped his hand over his mouth to hide his smile.

John walked out quickly, ignoring the cluster of pages gathered across the corridor in an all-too-obviously innocent game of knuckle bones. He hoped the rain was still pouring down. He needed cleansing.

Chapter Sixteen

In the first light of morning, the Inn of the Centaurs lay quiet save for a repetitive dripping, a reminder of the previous night's storms and the rickety roof's woeful lack of repair. So it was that Mistress Kaloethes, polishing silver in the kitchen, was immediately alerted by the creak of leather and heavy footsteps to the passing of someone down the hallway. She looked out.

"Thomas!"

Caught at the door of the inn, he turned with apparent reluctance, his face growing as red as his hair.

"Mistress Kaloethes! I thought everyone would be sleeping this early. I was trying to leave quietly. Not permanently, of course," he added, flustered. "I haven't got my baggage. I... I'll pay you in advance." He fumbled at the pouch on his belt.

The innkeeper's wife emitted a piercing laugh. Her chubby face was as red as Thomas' beard. Her bright color stemmed not from embarrassment but from her usual liberal application of rouge.

"Your word is good here, Thomas. It's a pleasure to have a guest of your quality. An emissary from a king's court. Some of our other guests, well, they're not really the sort I prefer, I must say. But I hope you can draw your sword more quickly than coins from your pouch!" She gave another loud laugh, like the rasping jubilation of a raven spotting carrion.

"I hope so, for I am trained in war, not commerce, lady."

"Lady? Well, well, you are a silver-tongued rogue!"

"My apologies, but I really must be on my way."

"Always out and about, aren't you?"

"Constantinople is a most interesting city."

"Have you seen the old soothsayer in your travels?"

"Ahasuerus? Not this morning. Is he causing you some trouble?"

Mistress Kaloethes, forgetting her manners, waggled a fat finger in Thomas' face. "I'm not the sort who would disparage my guests, Thomas. Let's just say he eats like a winning horse at the Hippodrome, but pays like a loser."

"He's an old man. Just forgetful. If I see him I'll remind him about his debts." Thomas backed out of the door, making his way hastily across the courtyard where puddles gleamed in increasing sunlight.

Admiring the newly-washed sky, Thomas almost collided with the innkeeper who was staggering in, burdened like a mule with a large sack. As soon as he was indoors, his wife, who had come to the door to see Thomas away, fell into his wake like a plump dolphin pacing a trireme. She did not, however, emulate the dolphin's traditional bestowal of good fortune.

"How did it go? A good night?"

Master Kaloethes dropped his sack down on the kitchen table next to an array of half-polished silver.

"Well?" His wife persisted, shrilly. "I expect that swindler of a tax collector will be back with his hand out again today."

"People have been celebrating. They've spent a lot. There's not much left." The innkeeper wiped away the sweat on his forehead with his meaty hand. New beads popped out immediately. His sack, which had not lightened during his rounds, was exceedingly heavy, stuffed with everything from saints' bones to kitchen utensils, not to mention a few vessels of wine.

"So? You spoke to a lot of people?"

"People are tired after the celebrations. They have headaches, bellyaches. Give 's some wine."

She ignored his request. "They were interested in your wares, though?"

"No. Probably more interested in examining their privates for signs of disease," he snapped back, wearily sitting on, or rather engulfing, a stool beside the kitchen's one open window.

"You fool, you missed your chance! You could have offered them all the cure. The powdered thigh bone of a celibate saint staves off the pox, so they say."

"People say a lot of things, but when it comes to parting with good money, that's a different matter."

"Well, I hope those ruffians you pay to help out have better luck selling to the gullible otherwise you can have the pleasure of talking to the tax collector." The woman hovered over him, a thunder cloud that, unlike those of the previous night, offered no prospect of relief after its downpour.

Inspiration struck her husband. "The collector's new to this quarter, isn't he? Do you think he'd accept a, uh, gift?"

"He might. On the other hand. he might tell the Eparch to knock out a wall or two in the prison to make a big enough space to accommodate you."

The innkeeper was suddenly aware of a spreading wetness on the inside of his thigh. He looked down and saw the folds of his breeches were soaked. A fat droplet of water passed through his line of vision and plopped onto his leg. Looking up, he saw the source, a leak in the ceiling.

"The place is falling to ruin," his wife scolded him. "And now we have guests who don't pay. I don't know what you expect me to do."

"Keep fewer silks in your chest, for a start."

Mistress Kaloethes' porcine eyes glared. "Those are necessary to me, necessary, do you hear? If you aspire to deal with the better classes—not that you could, of course—you must dress to their standards. There's a meeting of the guilds next week. Do you expect me to go in rags? With my hand out? 'Oh, please, lady, a few pieces of copper. My husband's too poor to patch the hole in the roof.' I don't intend to attend as a beggar, you bastard!"

Kaloethes was too exhausted to escape either the maddening drip of water or the equally insistent onslaught of his wife's insults. He shifted slightly, considering the vexed question of his household's lack of finances. Finally he spoke. "I still say we should keep a few girls upstairs. There's always a market for the natural pleasures."

"I wouldn't call what some of them get up to natural. I'd never stoop to that kind of business, anyway."

"I wouldn't expect it of you personally, naturally."

"I should think not! I left the theater a long time ago. And besides, how do you think you'd compete with the Whore of Babylon next door?"

"She isn't next door."

"Well, she's near enough so I can hear that dreadful contraption of hers moaning all hours."

"Anyway, as it happens, I've been exploring possibilities with a couple of her girls."

"Exploring possibilities? A nice phrase to use to

your wife. You ought to plead in the courts of law. I suppose you think I don't know you've been over there?"

"As I just told you, I've been talking to several of the girls about moving here."

"It is out of the question!" Mistress Kaloethes theatrically stamped her surprisingly dainty foot. Her husband winced. From long and bitter experience, he knew a squall was about to break over him. He was correct.

"You miserable excuse for a dog!" she screamed, loosing a string of ripe oaths. "How dare you insult me by even considering bringing those disgusting whores to live under our roof! You'll ruin what little reputation I have left, you bastard!"

Her husband tried unsuccessfully to divert the flow of words raining on his head, but she stormed on, shrill voice rising even louder.

"And that reminds me! Someone complained to the Night Watch about the noise the other evening. If I find out who it was, I will personally wring their miserable necks!" The possibility evidently cheered the woman, for she burst into a barking laugh. He breathed a sigh of relief.

"Now," she concluded, glaring at him, "if you don't have anything better to do like earning a living, get out and find that old charlatan who calls himself a soothsayer and ask him if he can predict when he's going to pay his debts."

Thankful to escape her wrath, Kaloethes hastened to do her bidding.

※　　※　　※

Outside, cat-like, John stepped carefully around the puddles in the inn's courtyard. As he crossed, a yawning man emerged from the building. It was the charioteer whom he and Anatolius had interrupted beating Felix at micatio. John greeted him.

"Good weather now, but much hotter later," remarked the charioteer. He was hefting a large satchel.

"Yes, it might not be a very pleasant day for travel. Much better to lounge in front of the fountain here."

"I've seen enough of it," the charioteer laughed. "Not that I didn't deserve the dunking I got."

He hitched the satchel over his shoulder as if it weighed nothing, but the muscles in his powerful arms bulged momentarily with the effort.

John realized the young man must have been the celebrant he had seen being restored to sobriety in the fountain. "How did you fare at the races?" he inquired, recalling the man's boast to Felix.

"Well enough. My name's Gregorius, by the way."

"I happen to know the Greens' head charioteer, but I don't follow the races as closely as Felix. Celebrations and feast days are busy times for me."

"It's a pity the races aren't held as regularly as they once were. Then you might be able to attend more often. But my services are in demand. I'm off to Thessalonika now. There's a new Eparch taking office, so public games are to be held." John noticed that the charioteer's gaze had moved to their reflections in the fountain. The young man brushed a stray strand of hair off his forehead. Vain, like so many young men, John surmised.

"How well do you know Felix?"

"I wouldn't say I know him that well, but he loves to wager."

"And you wager also?"

"I'm a charioteer. I like taking chances." He shrugged. "And others like to take a chance on my racing."

"Do you indulge them?"

The charioteer smiled knowingly. "Well, you say you know the Greens' head charioteer. You must know we do."

"I know you can't win betting on races against a charioteer. After all, they usually have knowledge which we do not. If a horse is running slower than usual, which charioteer has been up all night carousing, that sort of thing."

"Does everyone wager just to win? I've heard people at court brag about how much they lost on a famous charioteer."

"Did Felix have much to brag about in that regard?"

"How famous am I?" The smile Gregorius flashed was not returned. His face darkened. "I don't know who you are. "

"My name is John. I am Lord Chamberlain to Justinian."

The young man sucked in a deep breath. "You should have said so right away, my lord. If you're asking whether Felix placed wagers with me, the answer is yes. And no, he didn't fare very well, or at least not these last few times. But I wouldn't have guessed he was in any financial difficulties. He didn't ask to defer payment."

"I didn't say he was in financial difficulties." John corrected him sharply.

"Well, if you don't mind," the other said abruptly, "I have a long journey ahead of me."

"Good luck."

The young man strode away, powerful tread propelling him quickly out into the street.

John stood looking down into the fountain basin. His reflected face floated as lightly as a leaf on the surface of the water, wavering slightly where it was rippled by a breeze he could not feel. Then, abruptly, his reflection appeared to be underwater, staring up at him. Almost immediately his attention was drawn away by an outburst of noise from the inn.

❅   ❅   ❅

Following the loud sounds, John sprinted up to the second floor. Oaths from along its corridor resounded on the narrow stairs. There was a crash and a rusty brazier rolled out of a doorway. He peered somewhat cautiously into the room.

The ample girths of the innkeeper and his wife diminished the small space. The man stood still, a fleshy Mount Athos of despair, while his yelling wife stamped about looking for items to throw but finding little since the room had not been well furnished originally.

"He's disappeared in the night," raged the woman, apparently holding her husband personally responsible. "The cheating old fraud! If I catch him, I'll tell his fortune with his own gizzard, and it won't be a pleasant fortune either, nor a long one!"

In her anger she ignored John's sudden appearance, until he stepped forward. "What has happened here?" he asked quietly.

"The miserable old vulture has gone without paying me a single coin," the woman retorted. "And with all the rich folk who came up to listen to his lies, he must have made a fortune. Money up their arses, they have." Her business sense asserted itself. "And what is it I can do for you? Are you looking for a room? It'll be payment in advance, no argument."

John waved her back. "How do you know he's not returning?"

"He's taken all his possessions, such as they were. A few things in a moth-eaten sack he had. Tools of his trade, I suppose," the innkeeper offered.

"Tools!" The woman spat out. "Some colored rocks and his fancy chicken-splitter. You call those tools?"

"When did you see him last?" John's gaze scoured the room. There was little enough to see beyond a verminous looking straw pallet and a cracked clay lamp which had somehow escaped the woman's wrath.

"At the evening meal yesterday, of course. Christ himself couldn't have broken enough loaves!"

"Excuse us," Master Kaloethes put in belatedly, apparently having now recognized that John held a high position. "We run an honest inn here. We don't even employ women of the lower sort, which is the case at some of our rival establishments. Never mind the money, we say, it's better to do what's right in the eyes of Our Lord."

Warming to his theme, the innkeeper nodded at John. "Yes, as my good wife will agree, here we would rather eat plain bread bought by honest labor than lark's tongues purchased with the coin of sin. So, your honor, when we are so badly used...."

"I understand," John said mildly. "I'm looking for him myself. I may be able to assist you."

The woman took an enraged step toward the window, perhaps intending to see if the villain might still somehow be lurking in the courtyard below. She winced as her bare foot came down on something. She picked the object up. John recognized the round, green stone as one of the keepsakes Ahasuerus gave to his clients. A brief search garnered several similar stones. Had they fallen from the old man's sack? Why hadn't he gathered them up before leaving? Could he have been in such a hurry?

Rage temporarily spent, Mistress Kaloethes leaned on the rotted windowsill, composing herself. A low gasp escaped her. She was looking down into the courtyard again.

"What is it?" John's immediate thought was that Ahasuerus had returned.

The woman directed her glare at her husband. "There are men down there, and by the look of them, they're here on official business!"

The innkeeper paled, but remained silent.

Four men wearing military cuirasses, swords drawn, entered the inn on the run. John had barely reached the stairs before they came pounding up. Seeing the Lord Chamberlain, they halted.

"What is your business here?" John demanded.

"We've come for the one who calls himself Ahasuerus. A soothsayer, or so he claims," the man in command replied.

"What leads you to think he is here?"

"Certain information has been received."

"I see. Unfortunately, he is gone," John informed him.

The man pushed by to peer into the room.

"I suggest you not question my word. It is not wise." The commander's lips tightened at the reprimand as John continued. "Under whose authority do you seek this man?"

The commander hesitated. Then his eyes narrowed defiantly. "We are here in the name of the Patriarch of Constantinople."

Chapter Seventeen

The Patriarch's palace was not far from the Inn of the Centaurs and John, striding through the puddled streets, covered the distance quickly, determined that the Patriarch would reveal to him more than his commander had dared to say. However the Patriarch, John was told, was not available at that hour. Nor was he available at the next hour, or the next.

It was afternoon when John decided to seek Epiphanios out at the Church of the Holy Wisdom. The great domed building was still under construction and it was common knowledge the Patriarch was fond of inspecting the work in progress.

John had not had reason to set foot in the church before. Anatolius had joked that the Lord Chamberlain would have visited long since had vast sums been expended on a temple to Mithra. In fact, John doubted that any gods could be propitiated with gold and silver. Even so, as he stepped into the enormous nave, he felt a momentary lightness in his chest, that visceral reaction to the shock of unbearable horror or beauty.

His first thought was that Justinian had unknowingly erected a tribute to Mithra, Lord of Light, because the overwhelming impression was one of light. The enormous dome curved upwards gradually, as if the sky itself had been pulled earthwards and brought close enough for its true immensity to be grasped. The partially completed dome and walls were pierced with numerous, blindingly bright openings through which sunlight flooded, filling the vast space beneath with the other-worldly light that presages a violent storm.

John's second thought was that the events of the past few days, the deaths of his friend and of Berta, the reappearance of his old love, must have upset his humors, rendering him dangerously susceptible to emotional overreaction. He became aware of the smell of wet plaster and the echoing of laborers' hammers.

"Lord Chamberlain! You have finally graced my church with your presence."

John turned toward the querulous voice. Scaffolding clustered on all sides. Laborers were ill-defined shadows flickering against the brilliant openings in the dome. The air was filled with dust. It was a moment before John could distinguish the bent figure dressed in simple white robes. As he had hoped, the elusive Patriarch Epiphanios was here. He walked over to the old man.

"It is as magnificent as everyone claims," complimented John.

"High praise, from you." The voice was forced and thin. A whisper from a sickbed.

"I notice also that you have the building well guarded."

The Patriarch shrugged bent shoulders. "There are forty thousand pounds of silver decorating the sanctuary alone. Each seat will have silver revetments."

"An impressive tribute to one who lived among beggars."

"It is a measure of our Lord's power, is it not, that

man must spend a fortune in silver and gold to achieve merely the palest imitation of the glory found in the poorest part of His creation?"

"Some of the guards detailed here, were they diverted to other ends this morning?"

The Patriarch looked at John but said nothing. His eyes were red and watery. Perhaps it was the dust.

"Over there, we are already installing the reliquaries." The skin of the bony hand that gestured toward the shadows at the base of the wall behind the columns and scaffolding was ancient parchment through which John could see the faded writing of veins. "The fragment of the True Cross will be set in that spot, for example. One day all of the most holy relics of the city will be gathered in this one magnificent place. And we are in the process of obtaining even more, both minor and major."

John, who believed a saint's bones to be indistinguishable from the bones of any other man, changed the subject. "The effect of the light is quite remarkable," he said, truthfully. The quality of the light, insubstantial as it might be, struck him more forcibly than any supposed physical manifestations of the Patriarch's religion.

"Wait until the lamps are lit, Lord Chamberlain. There will be hundreds, suspended from the dome, fastened to the columns, set in wall sconces. The architects have been instructed to leave not a single shadowed place. The whole of the interior must be bathed in light."

"Surely a man passing by a lamp will cast a shadow?"

The Patriarch allowed himself a weak chuckle that turned into a rasping cough. "You are a theologian. But then, in Constantinople, who is not?"

They walked out into the center of the nave. Beams

of light, given tangible shape by the dust clouds filling the air, appeared from this vantage point more substantial than the dust-obscured pillars along the aisles.

"You were at Leukos' funeral?" asked the Patriarch suddenly.

"Yes."

"How was it?"

"A simple ceremony, conducted inside the city walls. It might well have been out in the countryside. Birds were singing."

"It was a dignified burial, then?"

"Very much so."

"Excellent. I had opportunity to deal with Leukos frequently. He looked after some of our reliquaries, ceremonial goblets, and such like. After the last fire, much of what would usually be stored in the church treasury was placed temporarily in his care. He was a good Christian, unlike many in the palace."

John followed the old man until he came to a halt near a partially disassembled scaffold leaning against a pillar. The Patriarch looked up at the dome.

"It may surprise you, but I am as puzzled as the poorest peasant by the ways of Our Lord."

John, in fact, was not surprised, but remained silent.

The Patriarch continued, "Just a few days ago, a young laborer, a country boy, fell to his death right where I am standing. I am given to understand that part of the scaffolding gave way. And so he fell through that glorious light down to these beautifully laid tiles. He must have died instantly. But he was serving the Lord. And when I heard about it I thought of Leukos, dying in the darkness of a filthy alley. So different an end."

"Leukos was the Lord's servant as well." John was

not sure what point the Patriarch intended. He wondered if the old man was losing his mental powers.

"Yes," agreed the other. He began to add more, but lapsed into a wheezing cough instead.

John realized his chance to question the Patriarch was slipping away. Perhaps that was what the old man had intended. "I did come here with a question. As I understand it, several of the guards detailed to you were pursuing an old soothsayer who had vanished from an inn. Did they find him?" He half expected a reproach.

"I ordered the arrest of the self-styled fortune-teller, the man Ahasuerus," the Patriarch replied calmly. "He had not vanished, I assure you. My guards found him at the docks. Seeking transport, no doubt."

"He is in custody, then?"

"He is drowned. He flung himself into the sea to escape capture."

John felt disappointment settle with the dust in the back of his throat. "This is certain?"

"The undertow pulled him down immediately, I am told. You look distressed, Lord Chamberlain."

For an instant giddiness washed over John. The golden air, pierced by shafts of light, took on an underwater aspect.

"I sympathize with your distress," the Patriarch continued. "Drowning cannot be a pleasant death. The mouth opening for air, finding only brine. A quick descent from a height would be preferable. On the other hand, drowning can be no worse than a knife in the ribs. Or am I wrong? I have no experience of these things."

"For what reason were you having him pursued?" asked John, barely managing to control the quaver in his voice.

The Patriarch, surprisingly, took no offense at the

blunt question. "You recall the distinctive weapon used in Leukos' murder? It was identified as belonging to Ahasuerus."

Chapter Eighteen

Anatolius gave no thought to Leukos' murder or John's investigation as he strolled down the Mese with Europa.

He had been bold enough to call on her at the *Anubis* and the moment she agreed to accompany him on a tour of the city the unpleasant thoughts which had been competing for his attention the past few days were, temporarily at least, banished. He hoped her ready acceptance of his offer indicated something more than just curiosity about the sights of the capital.

Anatolius thought they made a striking couple, he in his finest brocaded cloak announcing his status as a member of court, she in a plain, modest tunic, but with her tanned features uncovered in contrast to the few women they passed. Anatolius imagined their unpainted lips drawing tight in disapproval behind their veils. Did they envy this young foreigner's freedom?

The eerie light of an impending thunderstorm was caught between the seven hills of the city and the heavy gray clouds scudding overhead. In the still air, the rumbling of passing carts sounded far off.

At the base of a marble obelisk, a crone sat

surrounded by birds in wicker cages. She plucked boldly at Anatolius' cloak. "Buy one of my pretties for your lady," she wheezed, "for I see she has traveled far and will appreciate my beautiful birds." She waved a withered hand toward the cages.

Europa glanced down at the bedraggled birds. Her mouth set firmly in a thin line, and Anatolius saw, suddenly shocked, how she favored her father in mannerisms as well as in looks. Grasping his chance to impress his guest, he picked up a cage to examine its occupant.

"A partridge," he remarked softly. "Some keep them as house pets."

"It's a pity to see a free creature caged."

"Shall I buy one for you?"

"Only if you let it go!" came a deep voice behind them. It was a large, redheaded man Anatolius did not recognize. "You must be the Lord Chamberlain's friend Anatolius," continued the stranger. "I've seen you at the palace. I am Thomas."

Anatolius set the birdcage down carefully. "Oh yes, the emissary from Bretania. John mentioned speaking with you," he responded politely, concealing his annoyance. "May I introduce you to Europa? She is one of the bull-leapers currently performing at the Hippodrome. I am showing her the sights of Constantinople."

"Indeed? I am glad to make your acquaintance." Thomas bowed to the slim girl, ignoring the crone's "Hippodrome? No lady she!" at the revelation of the girl's occupation.

"We call this the Milion." Anatolius indicated the marble obelisk beside them. "It measures the distance from Constantinople to all the major cities of the empire."

Europa studied the structure for a moment. "Well,

Thomas, a quick glance reveals no mention of your great land." Her ready smile took the sting from her words.

"That is because, my lady, Bretania is no longer under Roman rule. Besides, Constantinople would suffer by comparison!"

Anatolius, with a youth's hot temper, stiffened his back in outrage.

"Nay, lad!" Thomas grinned, clapping a beefy hand on the young man's shoulder. "You must take the humor of us barbarians with a grain of salt. If you can afford a grain of salt, that is." He guffawed loudly.

"You will not, being a guest, realize that over-familiarity is not encouraged here," Anatolius gently pointed out. Turning back to the birdseller, he dropped several coins into her dirty palm. "How many of your poor captives will this ransom?"

The old woman gazed at the coins in amazement. "In truth, these would free every partridge in Constantinople."

"Be quick about it, then."

She began opening the doors of the cages, her withered hand making her clumsy. The dispirited birds seemed not to notice their chance for freedom, remaining perched or huddled where they were.

Europa brushed past Anatolius and removed one of the partridges. Cradling it in her hands she drew it up to her face. "Have you forgotten the sky?" she asked it.

She tossed the bird high into the air. For an instant the poor creature seemed about to fall back to the ground, but its wings flapped weakly, then picked up a stronger beat. And suddenly it had cleared the top of the Milion.

Its escape seemed to rouse its former companions. For a moment the air around the obelisk was alive, then only a few floating feathers remained as partridges scattered up into the sky above the glittering domes and roofs.

The old woman seemed unimpressed. "If you keep spending all your money on pretty faces," she scolded Anatolius, "you'll end up with less than fifty nomismata. And then you'll have officially joined the ranks of the poor!" She cackled, finding something humorous in her legalese. "But then you can come and visit me. There's always a warm corner at the Cistern of Hermes."

Thomas, puzzled, asked Anatolius what the woman meant.

"You've probably noticed cisterns here and there," replied Anatolius, glaring at the crone who had so rudely spoilt his generous gesture. "But there are others hidden beneath buildings and forums. The one she's talking about is under a storehouse that used to be a law court. Some wit named it after an old Greek statue that's on it. The forum it graces isn't much, especially now it's been turned into a sort of repository for old statues." He turned to Europa. "But I could take you to see them, if you wish?"

"I'd much rather continue along the Mese and see the sights and the people than look at a collection of old statues," the girl replied, still looking toward the sky. A thought struck her and she glanced at Thomas. "But since Anatolius is showing me around," she added, "why don't you accompany us?"

Her invitation struck Anatolius as much too eagerly offered. "John tells me you are on an important mission of state, Thomas. I'm sure you have no time for sightseeing," he remarked pointedly.

"There is always time for beauty," was the other man's reply.

Anatolius noted that Thomas' gaze was not

directed at the busy street. It was with a heavy heart that he lead his two guests away, across the Forum of Constantine and on up the Mese toward the Forum Tauri.

As they neared it, Europa stopped to stare raptly at a bronze pyramid. "By the bull's horns!" the young woman exclaimed, "What is this manner of thing?"

Grateful for a chance to display his knowledge, Anatolius pointed out the various animals, plants, and birds decorating the monument. "The ornaments symbolize spring," he lectured. "It was erected by the order of Theodosius, the Second, that is. They say some of the figures came from a pagan shrine in Dyracchion."

Thomas leaned back, hair cascading past the nape of his neck, and squinted up at the female figure pivoting back and forth atop the pyramid. "The wind's moving the woman to and fro, I see. Do the people here believe a woman is so fickle as to change direction with every breeze?"

"Not so," denied Anatolius, leaping to the defense of his fellow residents of Constantinople. "The decorations, as I was saying, represent spring, when all the world renews itself. The female, then, must be the Mother of All."

"I see. Well, still, it is true that there are many women who are fickle. I remember one time when I was in Crete...."

"You know Crete?" Europa looked up at Thomas' ruddy features with the exile's hungering look. "You have been there in recent times?"

"Well, my dear, I was there some months ago, some time after I left Cyrenaica and before I journeyed to Syria. Not much to see in the former, I recall, and too much in the latter. But as for your fair island, I also lived there for a time some years ago when you were but a child."

Anatolius sensed the redheaded visitor was bent upon passing him in the race for Europa like a charioteer wielding his whip on the final circuit of the Hippodrome. "Yes, it is a lovely island," he put in, quickly, "or so I hear. However, if you will just follow me, I have something I think will be of interest to you both. It's in the Forum Bovis. A little surprise, you might say. It's a particular favorite of John's, by the way. He often walks there from the palace."

Thomas glanced at the younger man, his green eyes alive with interest. "He is an interesting man, is he not, the Lord Chamberlain? You have known him a long time?"

"Indeed I have," said Anatolius readily, relieved at the chance to divert attention from Europa with a few tales about his friend. But before he could say more three men embroiled in a noisy argument erupted from an alley.

Two of the brawlers were squat men whose flour-bedaubed tunics proclaimed them bakers. The third was a poorly dressed man with the knee-high white boots of a laborer. Anatolius stopped short, preparing to call for assistance. Hadn't they just passed a Prefect? Thomas' beefy hand went to his sword hilt. Europa, however, simply skipped nimbly around the melee, hardly glancing at the three men.

It was momentarily apparent that the trio were a danger only to themselves, but, as he carefully sidestepped them, Anatolius felt renewed admiration for the slim self-possessed girl. But, of course, on consideration he shouldn't have been surprised that one who dealt with charging bulls would not be intimidated by an acrimonious public discussion.

"So what was that about?" growled Thomas, as they continued down the Mese. "Their Greek was too fast for me to follow. Not to mention too coarse."

"Well," Anatolius began, "the younger man...."

"The fellow in the white boots?"

"'Krepides,' they're called. Yes, well, he is a laborer. He says he did not travel all the way to Constantinople to work on the Great Church only to be sold barley bread at wheat loaf prices. He was also quizzing the bakers concerning their ancestry and their religious beliefs."

"I've noticed the good folk of Constantinople have elevated invective to a fine art," Thomas said with a soldier's admiration for inventive cursing when he heard it. "And now tell me, Anatolius, what is it you will show us?"

"Ah yes. Europa, if you will cover your eyes?"

The girl obliged. It gave Anatolius an excuse to take her by the arm. Trailed by the redheaded foreigner, he steered her carefully past a knot of hagglers at a grocer's stand, under an archway, and into the Forum Bovis. The rising wind swirled debris about their feet, whipping and tugging at Anatolius' cloak. The clouds were getting lower, daylight fading into an early twilight. Around them statues and columns and porticos leaned into shadows. Anatolius led the girl to the foot of an enormous bronze set near the center of the forum.

"Now you can look," he instructed, hand lingering on her arm.

She did. A broad smile settled on her face as her dark gaze wandered over the huge bull's head which gave the forum its name.

"How beautiful! You must bring mother to see this too!"

"Perhaps John will," mused Thomas. "But it is indeed a beautiful beast. It must surely have once adorned a great temple of Mithra." His admiration was not merely politeness or that of one interested in history.

Anatolius glanced at him with renewed interest. It was beginning to dawn on him that the supposed plain barbarian had hidden depths which might reveal strange aspects. He wondered when Thomas had seen him at the palace. Was this meeting a coincidence or could Thomas be following him for some reason? Surely not.

Instincts honed by his long residence at court, Anatolius did not sense the other was a danger to him. But Thomas seemed oddly interested in John. Resolving to express his unease to the Lord Chamberlain at his first opportunity, Anatolius devoted his attention to enjoying the delighted reaction to the bull head of the young and undeniably attractive bull-leaper who looked so much like her father, especially when she smiled.

※　　※　　※

John waited for Cornelia and Europa in the cramped cabin of the *Anubis*. He had hurried to the docks immediately after his conversation with the Patriarch. If the soothsayer were dead that made two now who had died after attending Theodora's celebration because Berta had also been there. Did that mean that Cornelia and Europa, who like Berta, had been summoned to entertain, were in danger as well?

John wanted to speak with them about that celebration, warn them. While he waited he pondered why the Patriarch's own guard should have been pursuing a murderer but found no satisifactory explanation.

He waited for a long time and when he finally left the cramped cabin for a breath of air, he found that Europa had already returned. Rather than going inside, she was sitting on the rail of the bow looking out over the darkening harbor where the wavering reflections of countless ship-borne torches formed unfamiliar constellations on the water. He walked over to her and placed his hand on the smooth rail.

"Lord Chamberlain," said the girl, swiveling effortlessly to face him.

Her formal mode of address sounded wrong to John, but then "father" would have sounded just as strange.

"Europa... I had hoped to talk to Cornelia."

"Mother's probably with the troupe. I'm not certain. I just returned myself."

"I trust you haven't ventured into the city on your own?"

"I'm old enough to take care of myself. But, as it happens, Anatolius showed me around. We met a knight. A fascinating man."

Staring out at the scattered lights in the harbor, John was brushed by a touch of vertigo. It was as if the dome of heaven had been inverted and the *Anubis* was bobbing upon its endless depths. His hand tightened on the rail.

"Isn't that a dangerous perch?" he asked Europa.

"Not compared to the back of a bull," she replied. "Besides, there's water below to catch me, not hard earth." Torchlight glinted in her dark eyes as the ship moved on a swell. She seemed to be studying John. "You're afraid of the water, aren't you?"

John ignored her comment, but it made him uneasy. He was accustomed to reading others, not to being read himself. In the dusk Europa had a remarkable resemblance to the woman he had fallen in love with so long ago. Cornelia had been little more than a girl herself then, not much older than their daughter was now.

"What did you want with my mother, anyway?"

"I had some questions concerning Theodora's celebration and some of the other guests."

"It's about the murder of that friend of yours, isn't it? Anatolius told me all about it."

"Anatolius has a bad habit of talking about things that are dangerous for him to reveal, and just as dangerous for others to hear."

"I am sorry about Leukos. Was he a good friend?"

"A very good friend, Europa."

"Did he have a wife, a family?"

"None that I know of. He never talked about his family."

"Where was he from?"

"I do not know."

The girl was silent for a moment. John could hear the wash of waves against the dock. "A strange friend, one you know nothing about," she finally said.

"You wouldn't understand, Europa. That is just the way it is at the palace."

"I don't think I would like the palace, if it is truly a place where your friends are strangers. And what about daughters? Are they usually strangers, too?"

"Europa, I had no idea you existed until...."

"You knew my mother existed." The girl had turned away to him to stare out across the harbor. "You never sought her out."

"The world is vast."

"And how many troupes of bull-leapers does it contain?"

"I am a different man. I would not have wanted your mother to see me as I am now."

"Was that for you to choose?"

"I am sorry, Europa, but when I knew your mother it was in another life. A life that ended. It was an ending that was not my choice."

"Well, that life may have ended for you, but here I am. A wonder, isn't it?"

"Europa, I will do my best for you, you have my

word. I'm not used to the thought of being a father...."

The girl turned back, swinging gracefully down from the rail to land surefootedly on deck. "Father? You've killed my father! He was a mercenary, a soldier. My mother used to talk to me about him. A good man. Brave. Something terrible must have happened to him, she always said. He must have been carried down to the underworld, because nothing in this world would have kept him from returning to her. To us. And now, here you are. A rich man, who didn't care!"

For a second, in the dim, dancing reflections of torchlit water she was her mother's daughter, with Cornelia's pride and fierce temper. Then tears began to flow, and the woman's face dissolved into that of a child.

John stepped forward, reaching out awkwardly to draw her toward him. She shrugged away, half-heartedly John thought, then turned and leaned her head on his shoulder. As she sobbed quietly, John became aware of stealthy movement behind them.

"Europa," he whispered, "don't look, but is there a watchman on this ship?"

"Watchman?" Europa quickly collected her thoughts. "There should be, but the crew's an idle lot. The watchman's probably asleep inside, or else gone ashore with the others now that everything's been unloaded."

A shadow moved again at the other end of the vessel. John could distinguish the sound of stealthy feet on planks, sufficiently different from the random sounds caused by the gentle motion of the ship on the water to be noticeable. His dagger was suddenly in his hand.

"You may be in danger," he whispered to Europa. "Stay here. If need be, get ashore and run."

His soldier's instincts taking over, John crouched

low and moved away to investigate. The deck shifted under his boots, each movement bringing a different patchwork of shadow and reflected light. But there now seemed no sign of the intruder.

As he reached the cabin's dark doorway, the vessel dipped in a sudden plunge. Caught off balance, he was forced to grab the doorframe to maintain his footing.

A coarse oath came from inside, but before John could enter, a dark figure burst out, knocking him down. Footsteps clattered hastily away across the dark deck as the intruder escaped. A boyish voice shouted belatedly from within; the watchman had been awakened.

"Whoever that was must have crept aboard while we were talking. Are you unharmed?" Europa was staring down at him.

John climbed back to his feet, embarrassed, but grateful that the anonymous intruder had not met him at the cabin doorway with sword at the ready.

"Yes," he sighed ruefully. "I'm unharmed. Just badly out of practice."

Chapter Nineteen

"Two ladies, coming to stay?"

Peter had been caught off guard when the Lord Chamberlain sought him out as he was cleaning dishes after the morning meal and instructed him to prepare the smaller bedroom for guests.

He was even more surprised when John told him the ladies would be his assistants. He bristled at the idea. "I am certain I'm not too old to handle the household duties on my own."

"Of course. They are here to assist you. Officially. You understand?"

The old man nodded, puzzled. Deception was a common palace tool but one John normally did not employ. It was worrying.

"Excellent," said John. "They will be escorted here by Anatolius. Please prepare something welcoming, something special, for this evening's meal."

Peter beamed, putting aside his concerns for the moment. John's austere tastes seldom tested the old cook's skills. "I shall go directly to the market, then, my lord. Perhaps a duck? And to go with it?"

"I leave that to your good judgment."

❋　　❋　　❋

John, leaning on the windowsill of his study, observed his servant departing the house. Although Peter's gait often betrayed the age in his joints, he was managing a particularly brisk pace this morning. John sighed. At some point the strong-willed servant would really need assistance with his duties. For all his diplomatic skills, the Lord Chamberlain was not looking forward to dealing with him when that day came.

John looked further afield. That part of the palace grounds visible from his window was not busy. The guards in the barracks across the cobbled square would be eating their morning meal, although certainly nothing as elegant as duck, he thought, recalling his own days in the field. Unless, that was, his fellow mercenaries had happened to plunder ducks from farms along their way.

The women would surely be safer here than on a ship in the harbor.

Beyond the military quarters, John could see a row of trees marking one of the many gardens in the palace grounds, more roofs, a clump of trees around a church, and in the distance the bright swell of the Sea of Marmara. In a month or two the breeze would bring with it the sweet soul-scent of summer flowers.

Suddenly he regretted that he had not instructed Peter to look for roses at the market. They were probably not yet available. A pity. They always brought to mind his friend Lady Anna, whose death had caused him much grief but as if in compensation had brought him the services of her freed man, Peter. Or had it obligated him to Peter? No sooner had the thought formed than the man in question reappeared, accompanying Anatolius and two cloaked figures to the door below.

John pulled in a quick breath at the sound of their murmuring voices in the hall below. In a moment Peter ushered Anatolius, along with Cornelia and Europa, into the study.

"I met them as I was nearing the palace gate," Peter informed his employer in a somewhat reproachful tone. "So I returned to announce them properly."

"A man who observes the proprieties, I am glad to see," Cornelia complimented the old man.

"Or one who can't control his curiosity," commented Anatolius.

Peter directed a look of outrage at the young man.

"These are the ladies I was telling you about, Peter," said John. "This is Cornelia, who will assist you in the kitchen, in case the wag-tongues at the market ask you. I know you prefer not to have anyone present while you cook. And the young lady, Europa," he continued, "will help with the linen. Now, let's sit down. If you will fetch wine, Peter, then you can be off to the market before all the best and plumpest ducks are gone to grace other tables!"

After Peter finally departed, John noticed the women eyeing the scandalous wall mosaics.

"The previous owner's," John mentioned with a slight smile.

Smothering a grin, Anatolius raised a goblet of John's favored wine and drank deeply. He coughed. Wiping his mouth with the back of his hand, he complained bitterly about his host's choice. "By Mithra," he choked, "you certainly like your wine raw. You take your pleasure and do your penance in a single gulp." He took another swallow.

"I got the taste for it when I lived in Alexandria."

"You seem to have lived in many places, John, although I would venture to say you do not belong to any in particular." Anatolius turned to the two women. "Well, ladies, it seems that you have come to a spartan household despite the luxurious edifice in which it is housed." The glance he directed at the mosaics spoke volumes.

Cornelia chuckled. "John was never one with a taste for luxury," she said, then added, quietly, "For himself, at least."

"I'm sure you won't have to sleep on the floor," the young man smiled over his wine at Europa, who was sitting quietly by her mother. The girl's dark eyes, he noticed, were both watchful and serene. Perhaps this curious combination had been born of bull-leaping. She might be a difficult person to surprise, not a bad thing in this complex and dangerous city to which the womens' wanderings had brought them. He gave a slight sigh. It was not difficult to forget a whole world existed outside the palace, outside the city.

Cornelia sat as watchfully still as her daughter, her gaze locked on John's face. His expression was unreadable.

Noting this, Anatolius realized that behind the events through which he was moving, other, different scenes were unfolding. Or perhaps, he thought, the whole situation was clouding his brain. Then again, perhaps it was the harsh wine burning his throat, but leaving a lingering sweetish after-taste from its bitter passage like memories of a long lost love never seen again. He must write a poem about it, he thought.

But there was more pressing business to hand. "John," he said, "presumably the ladies will be safely out of sight and notice here?"

The other shrugged. "Probably by now most of the palace gossips know that two women are visiting me. Fortunately I have no reputation to ruin, at least in the romantic arena. But it may be remarked upon in the wrong places. Nothing goes unnoticed."

"They will certainly have marked these new arrivals," Anatolius nodded. "But I know you can rely on Peter."

"Yes, he is discreet and can be trusted completely. He would not, otherwise, live here. But there are many other eyes. A whole barracks full of them over the way, for example. They will certainly have noted the ladies."

"Well, at least if there is any, let us say, difficulty, help will not be far away," Anatolius pointed out.

"If it were a case of force of arms, perhaps," sighed John. "Unfortunately, often it is not. Poison, a stealthy knife in the ribs, these are the commonest dangers."

"So much darkness in such a bright city." Europa spoke without apparent irony. "It almost makes me wish for the true brightness of Crete."

Anatolius lifted his eyebrows in inquiry. "Almost?"

The girl colored, glancing down at her sandals.

John, watching this exchange, was set adrift on a sea of emotions. Cornelia, looking sideways at her daughter, had a slight smile. The curve of her cheek against the colorful riot of mosaics behind her was uncomplicated, clean. John, suddenly weary, longed for sunwashed walls, blue vaulted skies, open fields. His life then had been new, uncomplicated. Regretfully, he pulled his thoughts back from the long-ago to say reassuringly, "Ladies, to reach you, it would be necessary to get past us. And, let me assure you, despite youth in Anatolius' case, and a somewhat sedentary occupation in mine, we are upon occasion quite handy with the iron, as someone recently remarked in a quite different context."

Noticing Europa's look of skepticism he added, "Now that I've had at least a little practice, of course."

Cornelia frowned. "Why do you imagine the intruder on the *Anubis* was looking for Europa and myself? The city is filled with common thieves."

John briefly explained what he had learned during his investigations. "A girl who was at that accursed celebration of Theodora's is now dead, and another person who was there, an old soothsayer, is said to have drowned. What's more, Leukos had visited the same soothsayer, and was later found with the soothsayer's very distinctive knife in him. I am not sure what the connection between them all is, if indeed there is one, but I intend to find out without further loss of life."

"But, John," Cornelia protested, "surely the soothsayer's dagger proves it was he who killed Leukos, just as the Patriarch told you. Surely that is an end to it?"

John shook his head. "I don't believe it, though I couldn't tell you exactly why. "

"I don't believe he was a murderer either," put in Anatolius. "Ahasuerus struck me as an honorable man with a real gift for prophecy, judging by what he foresaw in my future." Saying this, he looked over toward Europa. However, she did not return his fond gaze.

John gave his young friend a sharp look. "Anatolius and I have been neglecting our official duties," he said, getting up from his chair. "I hope you will not consider me a bad host if I leave you to amuse yourselves for the rest of the day. We shall see you this evening."

❋ ❋ ❋

Anatolius' portion of Peter's honey-glazed duck went uneaten. Justinian, heedless of time's passage either for himself or his secretary, had innumerable epistles to be dealt with: exhortations to less than zealous tax collectors, hints on theology for several bishops, notes of appreciation to architects, not to mention replies to a number of prominent Persians in the never-ending negotiations which saw the cost of border warfare sometimes exceed, and at other times fall below, the price of tribute.

The Lord Chamberlain's duties kept him elsewhere in the palace, which was why a tired and hungry Anatolius was left with the burden of carrying the Emperor's final message of the day back to John at home.

As Peter closed the door behind him, Anatolius noticed a single lamp had been lit in the entrance hall of John's house, less to combat the early twilight, he supposed, than as a courtesy to guests unfamiliar with the rooms.

"The master is in the garden," said Peter, in answer to Anatolius' question. "When you are ready, I've saved your portion of the duck."

As he crossed the hall, Anatolius thought he detected a hint of Europa's perfume, more exotic than the scent of any flower.

John sat on a marble bench in a corner of the garden. A few rays of dying sunlight straggled down over the roof to coruscate off a pool fed by a soothing trickle from the mouth of some unidentifiable, time-worn creature.

"I have a message from the Emperor, John. He thanks you for your efforts on Leukos' behalf and advises that you may now turn your attention back to state affairs."

John made no reply for a moment, but Anatolius saw his eyes narrow and his lips tighten. "That cannot be!" John said at last. "Leukos is unavenged. Justinian was so anxious to find the culprit that he summoned me in the middle of the night. Why would he now wish to stop my investigations?"

Anatolius sat on the smooth edge of the fountain basin. He pointed out that Justinian often acted on a whim.

John directed his gaze toward the eroded creature in the middle of the fountain. "Look at that poor beast," he mused. "The elements are sending him back to the lump of stone from which the sculptor coaxed him."

"Are you unwell, John?"

"Tired. I'm just tired. My mind wanders when I'm tired."

"Mine just lies down and sleeps," Anatolius said, but his attempt at levity was apparently lost on John.

"Anatolius, you remember I mentioned I had visited a stylite a couple of evenings ago? I haven't had the opportunity to tell you much about that, so I'll take it now.

"It was harrowing enough to be out in a storm," he continued, "but worse still trying to climb up an exceedingly narrow and remarkably slippery ladder in order to converse with a taciturn holy man not in the best of tempers. And especially with the wind plucking at my cloak and plunging cold fingers into my tunic."

"Reminds me of some wild actresses of my acquaintance," Anatolius remarked, still hoping to elicit some sign of good humor from his friend.

John simply frowned. "I think one of the oddest aspects of this younger and gentler religion is the strange encrustations it seems to have acquired. Look at all those monophysites in Egypt, for example."

"I would rather not travel so far to see such things, nor do I need to, considering the strangeness at our own house fronts. Besides, it isn't wise for palace dignitaries to be too close to such heresies, or at least heresies according to the Patriarch. And I had better not say that too loudly, either." Anatolius looked around with exaggerated caution. "Mind you, Theodora has monophysites living in the palace grounds. I wonder what the Patriarch says about that in the privacy of his chambers?"

"Probably he says a lot worse about the stylite established scarcely a stone's throw from that huge church of his, a holy beggar sitting up there on his crow's nest of a column, communing with his Lord and himself and the occasional charitable visitor."

"If he had good eyesight, a less holy stylite might enjoy such a good view of the chariot races."

John smiled at last, albeit begrudgingly.

"I've only seen the stylite from the ground. What was he actually like?" asked Anatolius.

John wrinkled his nose at the recollection. "It would be difficult to guess his age. He is bearded, and dressed in rags. At least he isn't the sort who goes semi-naked, wearing just chains."

"You make him sound like someone who's managed to get on the bad side of the Empress. Or perhaps the good side."

John shook his head in mock disapproval. "You must watch your tongue, my friend."

Anatolius made an even more scurrilous joke.

"You shock me," John was stern-faced but faint lines of amusement were blossoming around his mouth and eyes. "I hope you will not be a bad influence upon Europa." The admonition went home.

"No, of course not. But after all that effort, did you learn anything?"

"I learned that Constantinople is a small city full of twisting alleys. We live here in such close proximity, each to all, that we are often closer than we realize. The Prefect considers Leukos' murder the sort of thing that happens in the poorer byways of the city all the time, but that alley is practically as close to the palace as to the tenements."

"But surely you already knew that?"

John ignored the comment. "And as for you, my

friend, this morning you told me that you thought Ahasuerus to be an honorable man."

Anatolius looked uneasy. "Well, Justinian did say that the Patriarch's men had found witnesses who identified the dagger used to murder Leukos as belonging to Ahasuerus. We know they met. Leukos had that green pebble in his pouch, just like the one the soothsayer gave me." A look of alarm crossed Anatolius' face. "It occurs to me that I'm fortunate the soothsayer didn't follow me into an alley instead."

"You change your opinion easily, my friend."

"The Emperor is convincing. And, then too... well... about what I said this morning. I wanted to believe what the old man told me." He couldn't help recalling how he had, perhaps foolishly, told Europa about the soothsayer's prediction that he would be lucky in love. "I suppose I wanted Europa to believe it also," he concluded.

"Do you mean because a young lady is not likely to accept a fate decreed to her by a murderer?"

Anatolius flushed but was silent.

"But at least you are being honest now," John continued. "So, do you imagine the soothsayer followed Leukos?"

"I don't know if he followed him. Perhaps they arranged to meet later for some reason. A longer reading, for example. Or Leukos might have been talking too freely about the valuable imperial plate in his charge, or perhaps the old man got the notion he was carrying a lot of money. Perhaps he just happened to see Leukos on his way to somewhere else." Anatolius was becoming exasperated. Although he knew it was unfair, he was angry at John whose doubts were beginning to dampen his own good spirits.

"Why did Leukos seem so distracted at the Hippodrome?"

"Well, I supose he was anticipating his visit with the soothsayer. It wasn't the kind of thing he did every day."

"And what about Berta's death? Do you suppose that was unrelated? The alley where Leukos was murdered runs behind Isis' house. And Berta was at the same palace celebration that Ahasuerus attended. And now I fear that Europa and Cornelia are in danger. After all, they were at the same accursed gathering, were they not?"

"You think too much, John. It's just coincidence. And after all, in Berta's line of work, those things happen. As for Leukos, he visited the soothsayer. A few hours later the old man's dagger is in Leukos' ribs. Even a theologian would have to agree it was the soothsayer. Then Ahasuerus was drowned when he tried to flee, pulled to the bottom of the sea. What better vengeance could you want?"

"You're right about one thing, Anatolius. I do want revenge. I admit it. But drowning… no, I wouldn't wish that."

John fell silent for a moment. The setting sun had disappeared behind the roof.

"You are wrong about one thing, though," he said finally. "It isn't reason that leads me to believe the soothsayer wasn't the murderer. It is a feeling. If Leukos' murderer were dead, it would be gone. If he were really avenged, this black creature inside me would have taken wing. But it has not, and I feel that if I don't bring his murderer to justice, it will gnaw at me for the rest of my life."

"But, John, what has happened has happened. It was unfair, but will finding the murderer make it any fairer?"

John glanced at the younger man. "But more than that, Anatolius," he said, "I can't help feeling even so that Cornelia and Europa are in some way involved, and that makes it is even more imperative that this mystery is unraveled. Until it is their lives are in danger. And we can't even guess which direction the danger will be coming from."

Anatolius was silent. In the gathering darkness the scent of spring flowers in the garden seemed stronger. He wondered what went on in his maimed friend's mind when he lay alone at night. What other demons that could never be exorcised raged inside John? What agonies that dared not be remembered hammered at the flimsy door of suppression? And it occurred to Anatolius, perhaps only because he was of a poetic turn of mind, that John's controlled and rational exterior might be no more than a thin varnish over madness and despair.

Chapter Twenty

Alerted by a shrill squeal, John looked away from the Armenian ambassador, straight into the eyes of a wild boar. The sharp tusks of the charging beast were a foot from John's face. The animal's tiny eyes were glazed with death. It was an expression John had seen before.

"There's another who aspired to sit at the Emperor's table but now regrets it." John remarked. He was restless. He should have spent the day searching for the murderer of Leukos, who might well be Berta's murderer as well, and who had already threatened Cornelia and Europa once and seemed almost certain to try again.

Instead he had wasted the day fretting over this infernal banquet, unable to leave final preparations in the hands of an assistant thanks to a direct order from Justinian. Yet, the Emperor had ordered him to find Leukos' killer, a task he could hardly perform while preparing for a banquet. Did that mean Justinian, too, believed the killer was the soothsayer?

The ambassador, a large, soft man on the verge of old age, laughed too heartily. John suspected this ambassadorship to the empire's capital was the man's reward for a lifetime of administrative service.

"Lord Chamberlain," said the ambassador, "please excuse the ignorance of a foreigner, but in Armenia we associate with your title one named Narses, a native son. Indeed, we have heard that he assisted in putting down those unfortunate riots in Constantinople some years back."

"Yes, Narses is well known outside the city. But the organization of the palace is complex indeed. Theodora has her own Lord Chamberlain, for example. Has his name reached Armenia?"

The ambassador looked puzzled.

Before John could continue, the pulley arrangement at the end of the long table squealed again and the immense silver platter on which the artfully posed and thoroughly roasted boar lay inched forward as it was pulled along by ropes running under the gilded ceiling. A few places distant the carver awaited the beast's arrival. John had prudently positioned him at the opposite end of the table from the Emperor and Empress.

"Certainly whets the appetite," remarked Anatolius, sarcasm in his tone. "I think Justinian has them posed like that on purpose." It was not clear if he meant the departed boar or the imperial couple.

John shot him a look that was meant as a caution but which Anatolius seemed to take as a question. "Perhaps it amuses him," he mused. "Since Justinian doesn't eat flesh, he has decided to make the rest of us uncomfortable. Well, after all, it's his imperial right, isn't it? Just look at that animal. You can't delude yourself that you're not eating something that once breathed. It still looks like a living creature. In fact, it makes me feel a little ill."

John suspected it was not the roasted boar but the quantity of wine Anatolius had drunk that was making him ill. "Justinian doesn't drink wine either," he pointed out. "But he's free enough serving it. Besides, it is the Empress who orders particular 'embellishments', is it not?"

"Perhaps Theodora intends it as a joke at Justinian's expense?"

The Armenian ambassador laughed again.

John shifted uncomfortably on the couch, an anachronism now, except at banquets. His thoughts were with Cornelia and Europa. He had left Peter with strict instructions to look after them.

He noted that the ambassador was beginning to look flushed and uncomfortable. Fortunately he seemed to have turned his attention to the senator on his left, allowing John a respite.

Anatolius leaned over to John. "Seeing all this fancy dress, I'm reminded of the Picts. They go into battle with blue paint on their faces, the better to frighten their foes."

"I've seen them myself, when I was in Bretania," John reminded him.

"Is it really true, they fight naked as well? Less to encourage valor than to promote comfort, I suppose." He wiped his perspiring face with a heavy sleeve.

"I suppose, when you consider the question, in the end we all fight our personal battles naked." John spoke absently, his thoughts elsewhere.

He had been distracted all day and now he wondered suddenly if he had completed the arrangements properly. Where should he seat the ambassador in relation to Justinian's other guests? Should the Eparch of the city, who ranked only eighteenth in prestige among the sixty highest officials but whom many considered second in importance to the Emperor in civic administration, be seated nearer to Justinian than the ambassador given that this banquet celebrated the empire's relations with Armenia?

He glanced around. Several couches down the table the Patriarch was dining frugally, as was his wont, on bread and red wine. The Mithran in the Lord Chamberlain would have admired a man whose religious sensibilities did not allow him to partake of the world's wealth, even an arm's length from the Emperor in the imperial banquet hall. Then again, the old cleric's lack of appetite here might be plain common sense, for at court even members of the church were not immune from political machinations and assassination attempts. John didn't trust the man. Why should he evince such interest in Leukos? Clearly he had been trying to distract John, to gain his trust. To what end?

By the fitful light of lamps and candles, away from the ethereal radiance of his magnificent church, the Patriarch looked even paler and more gaunt than during their recent conversation. John wondered whether the old man's professional interest in eternal salvation was becoming more of a matter of personal concern.

The Lord Chamberlain grimaced, pushing aside his burnished silver plate. Not so long ago it had been in Leukos' charge.

Two of the kitchen servants approached their earthly lord carrying a large salver displaying piles of darkly browned roast fowls, each bird glazed to perfection and surrounded by preserved peaches on a bed of saffron-colored rice. Conscious of their master's eye on them, the two sturdy slaves presented their aromatic burden to the imperial couple.

Theodora leaned forward, spearing one bird expertly on the point of her knife. It would, John mused, be difficult to say whether the Empress was an attractive woman without rouge and powder and out of her bejeweled robes. The abstemious Justinian, he noticed, regarded her with an expression of fond indulgence even as she bit daintily into the bird's flesh with her small carnivore's teeth.

For no apparent reason, John found himself recalling the saying about ravens by which Thomas set such store. His attention wandered to the pile of epistles awaiting attention in his study. It occurred to him that it was probable that more than one of those communications carried ill news. John glanced around the room again, automatically noting how many goblets of wine were being consumed and by whom.

The banquet ended. Patriarch Epiphanios muttered the closing grace, rose with the assistance of a guard, and then, as custom demanded, was escorted out. Only then did the music begin. John looked toward an arched doorway. Its heavy draperies, embroidered with representations of the wisdom of Solomon, were parted by two slaves. Through its shadowy width streamed a line of girls, clad in white from shoulder to thigh. Their scanty clothing shimmering in the lamplight that flickered across the mosaic floor, the troupe danced toward the head of the table.

Their youth reminded John of Berta with whom Felix and Thomas had been so taken. What was her connection with Leukos' death?

At last it was over. Or almost.

It was Justinian's practice to mingle informally with those who had been near him at table. His apparent amiability was much remarked upon at court. But despite John's close professional relationship with Justinian, he still could not judge with certainty whether the Emperor's geniality was real or an artfully designed mask.

But now he must continue in his own role. He made his way to Justinian's side. The Emperor's round face beamed at him. "All was perfect, as usual, dear Lord Chamberlain."

"Thank you, Caesar." He bowed.

Justinian waved a beringed hand. "And that reminds me. I have not thanked you for your efforts, my friend, in the matter of the death of the Keeper of the Plate. I understand you took great pains investigating. I am confident you would have apprehended the old fortune-teller soon enough, but luckily for all of us the hand of the divine exacted its own punishment. Our minds are all easier now."

John's stomach knotted. He had hoped the Emperor had not kept abreast of events and had not yet been informed of the supposed solution to the crime. "My own mind, Caesar, is not settled. I am not certain that the old man was the murderer."

Justinian's smile deepened, even as his gaze grew icy. "But the facts presented to me by Patriarch Epiphanios clearly implicate the soothsayer, Lord Chamberlain. Everyone in the palace agrees that he was the murderer."

"You have yet to hear my report."

"Do not trouble yourself further with this matter, my friend." Justinian turned away, with an abruptness that would have been characterized as rude in anyone other than the Emperor.

John knew he had been dismissed and dared say nothing further. He turned to look for Anatolius, but found, instead, the Empress standing beside him.

"Lord Chamberlain, my husband is too kind. I am not always so pleased with your efforts. You might, in the future, keep that in mind."

"Of course. And speaking of the future, I hear that you met the soothsayer? Did he strike you as a murderer?"

Theodora's heavily painted features betrayed no

surprise at John's knowledge. It was commonly said she had not been a very good actress in her youth; if that were true, John guessed her knowledge of the craft had deepened during her years as Empress. "I fear I did not speak with him long," she said. "He seemed to prefer little girls. An unpleasant man."

"One not taken by your charms?"

"In that respect, one much like yourself, Lord Chamberlain."

John stared pointedly at a drop of grease shining at the corner of the Empress' mouth. She licked away the tiny gobbet.

"A word of caution, Lord Chamberlain. Being too observant can be dangerous."

Chapter Twenty-one

Isis' private chambers were not quite so sumptuous as the Emperor's banquet room, and the gathering hosted within this evening was smaller, consisting of Isis herself and Felix and Thomas, who had arrived separately to offer their condolences for the death of Berta.

Felix, looking dazed, sat next to Isis, gulping wine as tears streamed down his face. The madam was uncharacteristically quiet, refilling his goblet as fast as it was emptied. Thomas sat opposite, hands folded.

Isis, having offered her condolences to Felix, was now fumbling for some words of praise for the dead girl. Without any apparent irony, she mentioned how popular Berta had been with her clients.

"Except for the misbegotten bastard who strangled her!" Felix tossed down another mouthful of wine.

Isis' tone was cold, her house having been insulted. "We have never had such a thing happen here before, Felix. And what I can't understand is who it could have been. So far as I know, only our regular guests were here." Her dark eyes were somber. It was rare that the dangers inherent in her profession impinged so closely upon her and her girls, and the ugliness of the event which had so recently transpired upstairs was thus doubly shocking to one who prided herself on being professionally unshakable. "Is no one to be trusted these days? I do believe I shall have some wine myself. Thomas?"

The knight shook his head. Felix banged down his goblet. Isis sighed. She was well enough acquainted with the emotional tumults of the male, but usually met the sweeter side of their passions. Anger, in her house, led to a swift and oft-times undignified exit aided by the brawny Darius. But murder was another matter. She had had to ask the clients to leave, refunding their money. Now, for the first time in the years since she had arrived from Alexandria alone and afraid, she felt unsafe.

Shuddering, she poured more wine, returning her attention from the past to Felix, who was now holding forth to Thomas in a monologue concerning Berta's last rites.

"She had a fine funeral, my Berta. I paid for it myself." Despite the wine he had imbibed, his words were carefully formed and clearly spoken, but shaped by that terrible frozen grief of the newly and suddenly bereaved.

The madam sighed. "Poor Berta. Only a few days ago, dancing at the palace, and now, alas, the only people she will be dancing for are the dead, and that after her heart is balanced on the scales against the feather of truth."

"I spit upon your feathers!" Felix snarled.

Thomas, who had been largely silent since arriving to find the morose Felix with Isis, inquired about the feather, less from real interest than to calm a situation which might turn ugly.

"Oh, yes," Isis replied, "yes, when we die, our hearts are weighed against the feather of truth. It is an ostrich feather, such as is worn by our goddess Maat. She represents truth and justice, you know. If the scales of judgment balance evenly, then the departed are judged worthy. If not, they are destroyed."

Felix rose ponderously from the couch. "That may well be, Isis. But Mithra will surely aid me, and a veritable tribunal of judges of the dead, a whole milling herd of ostriches, none of these things will hide the truth of it, for I shall find out who did this thing, and I shall...." He paused, wiping tears from his face. "Let me repeat this, as Mithra is my lord, I shall personally ensure that justice is meted out. I shall take great pleasure in squeezing the miserable dregs of life out of the bastard who took my Berta away from me. But slowly, very slowly, you understand? I want his agony to be long, and when he dies, the only prayer over his body will be mine, that Mithra will continue that agony in the next life, for all of eternity." His words were the more terrible for being spoken in a gently conversational tone of voice. "And now, I must go."

✻   ✻   ✻

Neither foreigner nor madam spoke for a few moments after the bereaved man staggered out. Finally, Thomas broke the heavy silence by wondering if Felix would ever find the man he sought.

"It is possible," Isis opined, "for in certain circles every person knows every other person, and thus quite often a fair amount about their affairs. Although if I were one to lay wagers, I would not give Felix odds on finding the culprit."

"Perhaps Felix would like a momento of Berta," mused Thomas. "Didn't she have some jewelry? I recollect some barbaric bracelets. I would be happy to deliver them to him if you would trust me."

"As it happens, I have already given him some of

her small pieces as remembrances."

Thomas nodded. "Excellent, excellent. She was very fond of green, wasn't she?" He sounded wistful.

Isis stared at him with surprise. "You were quite fond of her yourself, Thomas, I think?"

He blushed. "Yes," he admitted, "she had a lively mind, as well as a lively body, if I may say so. She was really quite interested in my travels, you know."

The madam did not point out that in her trade interest in a client's concerns was sound business practice. In fact, she herself was quite interested for other reasons in Thomas' travels and said so, noting that since she was from Alexandria she also had traveled a long way from home.

"Didn't John live in Alexandria for a while?"

The madam confirmed that he had. "In fact," she went on, "he speaks the language passably well, especially when cursing!" A soft smile briefly illuminated her plump face. "You know, he is a good man. He has suffered much, and yet remains kind."

Thomas smiled. "No higher praise can any man, or woman for that matter, have bestowed upon them. I would be proud to have that said of me."

"I think, Thomas, that your heart is true and you need not fear the weighing of it when the time comes. What a strange and terrible city this is! I shall be glad enough to return home eventually. I daresay that you feel the same way? Do you think it will be a long time before you return home?"

He shrugged. "It is a long time since I've walked under the gray skies of Bretania, and I really cannot say when it will be that I shall feel its kindly rain on my face again."

"You are quite the poet, Thomas!"

"All men wax poetical about that which they love."

"And there is no doubt that Felix loved Berta." Isis had forsaken the wine and was now neatly peeling a small apple. "If only we knew who murdered her. Here is an apple for knowledge, as the Christians say. Perhaps it will work for you."

Thomas chewed the proffered fruit thoughtfully. "In the part of Bretania where I was born, the north, apple-cores are called gowks. Yet you could put apples in huge piles and ask a man from the south to find the gowks, and he would look forever. They would be there, in plain view right in front of him, yet hidden, so that he would not find them. Well, not unless he asked someone from the north, I suppose!"

"It seems that the moral of your tale is that with good will and many eyes the hidden cannot remain so forever."

"Let us hope so, for I fear Felix is going to be a dangerous man until he exacts his revenge for Berta."

The madam agreed, adding gloomily: "Perhaps someone can assist him with some information, some pointers, something that might show the way."

"And the Night Watch? Surely they will be making inquiries also?"

"A prostitute murdered by a client? I doubt much effort will be expended. This is a city where those who are powerless take such justice as they may find. And whatever justice is meted out will be brought about more by our own efforts than by those of the ones in power. Or most of them."

Thomas shifted his weight slightly, stretching out his legs and wincing. "It strikes me," he yawned, "that more people than one might suppose are interested in finding out who murdered Berta, including you, Isis."

The other smiled stonily. "Indeed? I was very fond of Berta, yes. She reminded me very much of myself when I was her age, only she remained very childlike in some ways. No business sense at all. And yet there she was, so close to freedom, to marriage, to a respectable life.

"And beyond liking the girl, Thomas, it must not be overlooked that she was still, after all, my property. If nothing else, I intend to get the compensation to which I am entitled."

❊   ❊   ❊

"Berta. What about Berta?"

John was momentarily blinded as he stepped out of the imperial dining hall's fitful torchlight into the darkened garden. He could not see the source of the voice.

"What about Berta?" it repeated.

Outlines of trees and buildings coalesced out of the faint glow of the sky. John tried to blink away the darkness that remained below the line of the horizon.

"They killed Berta too."

The words were slurred by wine, the accent pronounced. John began to turn, his hand moving to the dagger he customarily wore at his belt. The dagger he now remembered he had been careful to remove before attending Justinian's banquet.

Just as his hand found nothing where a hilt should have been, a heavy figure bulled into him. He smelled soured wine and sweat. John tried to twist away, but large hands had fastened claw-like to his robes.

John had retained his military instincts and agility, but he no longer had the strength to match the brute who now seemed intent on pulling him to the ground.

As John staggered backwards, his attacker began to emit gasping, inarticulate noises. John recognized first, that the man was sobbing, and second, that it was his friend Felix, his accent thickened by wine.

"Captain!"

The big man's grip loosened. "Berta," he mumbled as his legs buckled and he fell forward. John helped him to a nearby bench.

"What have you been doing, Felix? In your condition, it's fortunate you ran into me rather than one of your own men or some administrative troublemaker."

"Berta is dead."

"I know that. I was with you when she was found, remember?"

"But you've been looking for Leukos' murderer. And even though the old soothsayer's dead, the bastard, you're still looking."

"Who told you that? Anatolius? Have you waylaid him tonight also?"

The burly captain let his head drop against John's shoulder and began to sob. John hoped the man was intoxicated enough so as not to remember in the morning. Of those three things that relieve men of their senses and dignity—wine, religion and women—wine, John thought, offers the least recompense. There are those who insist it brings out the true man, but isn't a man's true character what he chooses to make of himself?

Still, Felix was right. Berta was dead, too. He must not forget there were two murders to avenge.

"We have to get you home, my friend. Can you stand?"

Felix grunted, clambering unsteadily to his feet.

John steered his friend deeper into the garden. Who at court hadn't taken too much wine on some occasion? Yet there was no misstep so slight that it would not be noted and used at an opportune moment.

Distracted by his efforts to keep Felix upright, John

left the path. Suddenly there was soft grass beneath his feet. Felix lurched into shrubbery, dragging John with him.

There was a muffled oath, movement in the dark, a transitory gleam of naked flesh, rounded, a knee, or breast.

"Zeus take you!" came a hoarse male voice. "Find your own spot, you two!"

Summoning all his strength John pulled Felix back to the path. Muted giggles, faint as a memory, pursued him out of the thicket. The night closed in like dark water.

John was sweating with exertion by the time he coaxed, coerced and dragged his drunken friend back to his, that is to say Felix's, house. He managed to prop Felix up with his back resting against the front wall and rapped at the door to alert a servant to their arrival. The door, unsecured, swung open.

Felix was too intoxicated to protest as John armed himself by slipping the Captain's sword from its scabbard. Perhaps Felix had over-imbibed before he left home and forgot to secure the house, and perhaps his servants hadn't noticed. It seemed unlikely.

John entered the house warily. The atrium was dark. From somewhere, perhaps the colonnade surrounding the garden, enough torchlight filtered in to reveal the rough outline of the holding basin in the atrium. John took a few steps toward the gray rectangle of a doorway just visible across it.

Felix's sword was far heavier than any John would have chosen. He paused, listening. A cricket trilled from some nearby crevice. Did he hear breathing? Just his own, he realized. Nevertheless he had the distinct sense that the darkness enclosed something more solid than the cricket's repetitive song.

He heard movement behind him and when he

turned he could see a dim patch of light on the tiles, escaping from a covered lantern. So it seemed that, despite his protestations, his military skills remained woefully rusty.

"Home at last, Captain?" The voice was muffled. John could discern no more than the outline of the speaker, who appeared to be a huge man. Felix's visitor could no doubt in his turn distinguish John only as a shadowy figure.

As the muffled voice continued it became apparent that the intruder assumed he was speaking to Felix. "I hope Fortune has treated you more kindly tonight, my friend, than it did when last we spoke. If not, however, I have been authorized to offer you, shall we say, the usual arrangement? But we must know by tomorrow at the second hour. By the way, you should have wagered against your marriage. I put ten nomismata against it and made a killing!"

The words were loud enough to penetrate Felix's befuddled haze. "No. I'll take no more of your dirty money!" Felix's slurred shout echoed. "Tell your master to find someone else!"

In his wrath the captain lurched forward, his shambling figure filling the doorway for only a second. Then he lost his precarious balance and toppled forward. By the time John reached the door, the mysterious visitor was gone.

❅   ❅   ❅

Kaloethes' fears pounded in his head like a creditor at the door. He had awakened in a panic, only a moment after falling asleep, or so it seemed. He woke to the familiar thought. All his bills were falling due at once. It was an impossible situation.

The innkeeper crept out of the suffocating room he shared with his wife, half expecting the woman to awake and thunder down the hall after him, demanding to know what he was up to. He escaped down the stairs and into the open air of the courtyard safely, but his accounts did not add up there, either.

Half asleep, tatters of nightmare still clinging to his mind, his eye was drawn by the glimmer of the water in the fountain, the only hint of light in the courtyard. For an instant he contemplated throwing himself into it, but then realized even that dramatic gesture would be doomed to failure for the basin was too shallow.

He was saved from whatever more practical solution might have occurred to him by the sound of a footstep.

"Who is it?" he demanded.

The figure that solidified from the darkness was the big redhead, Thomas. He should have guessed.

"Ah, innkeeper. Taking in some of the night breezes too, I see? I find the city most pleasant before dawn. Quieter."

Kaloethes was fully awake now but his black mood remained. "You would know. I suppose this mysterious wandering in and out at odd hours is what you Bretans call a 'quest'?"

"I hope I haven't disturbed anyone. I wasn't trying to run off without paying my bill, by the way. As I told your wife just... "

"Yes, she keeps pointing out to me how fortunate we are to enjoy your good credit. If only my own creditors could enjoy it as well." Given a target, Kaloethes' worry over his financial difficulties had transmuted easily into anger.

"But Master Kaloethes, if there's been some misunderstanding, well, I'll pay on the instant."

This was a chance the innkeeper could not let pass, whatever the hour. Cautioning Thomas to tread quietly, he led him through the kitchen and into a cramped cell of an office, striking a light to the small clay lamp he kept beside the door.

"There," he said, tapping a meaty finger on the figures in the codex under Thomas account. "You're in arrears to a sum of almost... well, see for yourself."

"I'm afraid I must leave that task to you. But my purse is open."

Kaloethes opinion of Thomas soared upwards as the coins fell into his hand. Perhaps he had been too sharp tongued with the man.

"Look, come and share some our excellent wine. I can't sell the stuff, anyway, so we might as well enjoy it."

They sat down at the long table in the kitchen. The trembling lamp light struck sparks of gold off Thomas' beard and accentuated the concavities around the innkeeper's squinty eyes.

"I am sorry if I gave the impression I mistrusted you, friend," the innkeeper confessed. "But you have been in this damnable city long enough now to know its ways. A nomisma to take a drink, two to take a breath. Endless legions of officials with a limitless armory of rules and regulations, taxes and license fees."

Thomas nodded silently in hearty agreement.

"I am besieged by an army demanding a ransom an honest man could never have," the innkeeper concluded with a heavy sigh.

"Indeed, it is not a good situation, although in my experience the besiegers always carried swords."

"Swords? What can a sword do but rip out your guts? A pen, now, applied to the right scrap of official parchment can rend you to your very soul! I tell you, I'd rather they came at me with swords, the bastards, rather than sitting fat and wealthy and smug in their offices. It would be a fair fight then, and one I'd relish!"

"There isn't much fairness in this city, I agree with

you there. Though I have rarely been offered wine so freely. In fact, my visit here has taught me to hold my wine, if nothing else."

Kaloethes studied Thomas' shadowed face, wondering how many more coins Thomas had and how he had come by them. Kaloethes always wondered how people came by what they had.

"You've made no secret about this quest of yours. But what exactly are you looking for? Something of value, from what I hear."

"You are safer not knowing."

"I see. An object of very great value then. Perhaps I could help? I do have certain business contacts, including some at the palace." Kaloethes drew his bulk up straighter, causing the wooden bench to creak loudly. "I am familiar with danger myself."

Thomas coughed, releasing a spray of wine. "I don't doubt it, having met your wife."

Kaloethes grinned and poured Thomas more wine. You couldn't hold it against a man, what he said when his tongue was loosened by drink. He'd seen babes in arms who could hold their wine better than Thomas. "My wife has large ambitions, Thomas."

"Indeed, everything about her is large."

Kaloethes felt the need for some more wine himself. "Can you believe, when I met her she was a wood nymph?"

"As easily I could believe the girls at Madam's were once husky charioteers."

"Well, it is true. And now? I can see that beautiful young girl in my mind but there is nothing else left of her, nothing of what she was that I could show a doubter like you." Kaloethes felt his eyes stinging. "She is gone, Thomas. Dead. That young girl I once loved is dead."

"And yet she commands you still."

Kaloethes nodded morosely. Did he harbor some vague feeling that if only her wishes were satisfied that girl would return to him?

"But what of these contacts you have at the palace?" wondered Thomas. "I have been attempting to see the Patriarch, without much success."

Kaloethes sighed. "If my acquaintances reached that high level, I would not be in the straits I'm in."

"Then there is the question of who has been appointed to deputize for the unfortunate Keeper of the Plate. It might be useful if an interview there could be arranged."

"That might not be out of the question, although gold would almost probably have to pass hands. But I thought it was some sort of relic you sought, not palace treasures?"

"As I said, it is better for you not to know. Excuse me now, I must at least be in bed before dawn. I have some appointments this afternoon." Thomas rose unsteadily, banging into the table. Kaloethes was afraid the noise of the redhead's muffled curses might rouse his sleeping wife.

"Let me reimburse you for the wine, innkeeper."

The suggestion roused Kaloethes to action. "Before you're off, there's something you must see."

Taking the lamp, he persuaded Thomas to follow him back into the kitchen, where he lifted a trapdoor in one corner, and descended a rickety ladder into a musty smelling catacomb. Large rats and assorted smaller vermin scuttled away from the flickering light.

"We keep our stores down here," explained Kaloethes.

He could see Thomas' eyes widen with surprise as he looked around at the crates and boxes piled to the ceiling. Several were close enough to ascertain that what was stored was largely unfashionable clothing, pottery that had sustained a chip, kitchen utensils that were no longer adequate and other domestic bric a brac. Balanced precariously on and among the boxes were various items of furniture, ornate tables and decorated chests that had evidently fallen from favor.

The innkeeper motioned Thomas to follow him through a winding gorge, almost too narrow for the bulky innkeeper, which was the only clear passage through the storeroom.

Kaloethes ducked through a low portal, leading to another chamber. He couldn't help thinking, fleetingly, that he was alone, in the dark, with an apparently inebriated man who was carrying a large amount of money. On the other hand, he saw, the drunken man also had a hand on his sword.

"Selling off a few of your stores might solve your financial problems," suggested Thomas.

"These are my wife's things. It's more than my life's worth to even suggest selling them," the innkeeper replied curtly. "But, look, here is what I have brought you to see." Reaching into the shadowed depths of a scarred wooden box he drew out into the feeble lamplight a large, yellowish bone.

"An authentic relic of Saint Prokopios. Not just a knuckle or a finger. The very thigh bone which bore his blessed weight."

"Martyred by being thrown into a pit of rats and devoured, by all appearances."

"It is somewhat distressed, I agree, but that is no doubt why it was offered to me for a very reasonable price. I can assure you it is no less potent."

"That would explain the well fed rodents I saw being drawn bodily up to heaven a few days ago." Thomas chuckled. "But no, my friend, this is not the type of relic I am seeking."

Kaloethes tossed the bone back into the box.

Perhaps Thomas held his wine better than it seemed. "Well, I was told it was authentic and I have no reason to distrust the rag seller's nephew," he grumbled.

"At least not yet?" Thomas yawned. "And now it truly is time that I retired, if you will be kind enough as to lead me out of your subterranean treasure house." He stooped to pick up a scrap of shredded fabric lying at his feet. "Your vermin at least live well, with nests of silk." He paused, looking around.

"I know I am not alone in taking some comfort at Madam's," he continued, pitching his voice lower. "If you have a favorite there, I am sure she would appreciate some of these things. And your wife would never notice they were gone."

"Ah, but she would," Kaloethes sighed. "Believe me, she would."

They climbed back up the ladder, Kaloethes breathing hard with the exertion and frustrated by his inability to persuade Thomas to part with some of his remaining coins. His opportunity was passing.

"Look, Thomas. I know you are on a quest, but even one on a quest has to pay the bills. You strike me as a man who would dare much. I might be able to offer you some tasks which could benefit both of us financially."

"I fear not, friend. The task I have is enough for now."

On their way back upstairs, Kaloethes noticed gray light creeping into the courtyard, as dawn arrived to reanimate his besieging army of creditors.

"Think about my offer, Thomas," he whispered as they crept up the stairs. "At least think about it."

Chapter Twenty-two

John suppressed a yawn while the elderly Quaestor worked his way through the complicated legal preliminaries to reading Leukos' simple will with the patient determination, but none of the artistry, of a spider spinning its web.

It had been a late night.

Felix had to be assisted to bed. He kept repeating Berta's name. John found it distressing, less because of Felix's emotion than because of the humiliation he knew the man would feel later if he remembered the night clearly.

John stifled another yawn, this time tensing his jaw painfully. The reading had been scheduled for a cramped hearing room near the courts. There were no windows. Apparently the reality of the outside world was considered an unwanted intrusion.

John had brought with him the pouch Leukos had been carrying when he died. Not because of the value of its contents; the few trinkets it contained were worth little. But it was, after all, part of Leukos' estate, and John was hoping that someone from Leukos' family would be there to claim it.

The Lord Chamberlain glanced around at the

handful of people seated in the stuffy room. No one he recognized. A few men who appeared to be minor officials, professional acquaintances of Leukos, perhaps. Several others might have been hangers-on, present just in case they were mentioned in the will.

It had been foolish of him to hope that some family member might attend, someone who might shed some light on Leukos' past, perhaps even on the recent past, and on what may have caused his death.

And quite apart from John's investigation, it would have been comforting to know that his friend had not been as alone as he had seemed, that the tree from which he had sprung still grew. But if Leukos had had a family they remained as absent at his death as from his life.

There were more yawns. A fly explored the wall behind the droning Quaestor, and in the end, those assembled learned that Leukos, Keeper of the Plate, had granted manumission to his slaves and placed the bulk of his estate in the hands of John, Lord Chamberlain, to dispose of as he saw fit. John signed and swore out the required documents before the Quaestor. When he was done he allowed himself a sigh.

❊   ❊   ❊

John returned to Leukos' house. He thought he must have missed some pointer to the truth during his first visit. Certainly a person's house should reveal something about its inhabitant. But Leukos' residence seemed barren of the man's personality. And now it had the air of a building to which no one would return. The water clock was still dry. The kitchen walls retained the odor of meats that had been boiled there. In the reception hall this suggestion of recently consumed meals was fainter and mingled with the cloying perfume used when preparing Leukos for burial.

Someone, presumably Euphemia, had thrown open cupboards and chests, preparatory to packing their contents into the crates strewn about the tiled floor. John paused, examining a few plates, an ornamental lamp. Compared to the treasures with which he had dealt at the palace, Leukos' own possessions were simple. A suspicious person would not have had to examine his belongings for the palace mark to know that the Keeper of the Plate had not been in the habit of bringing his work home. But didn't Christians pray not to be tempted? Leukos' mysterious god had granted his request in that regard, at least.

John found Euphemia in Leukos' bedroom, carefully removing clothes from the chest at the foot of the bed and smoothing out their wrinkles one last time.

"I'm happy to see you're still here," John told the girl. "I wanted to ask you a few more questions."

Euphemia turned her gaze to the robe draped over one arm. Her finger traced the gold embroidery along the hem.

"If it's about my master's visitors, or his doings, I can't say more. I've thought about it, since we talked. But I've told you all I know."

"And the other servants?"

"I asked them. They know less than I do."

"You are certain you didn't know your master better?"

The girl reddened. Her fingers worked, plucking a loose thread from the hem of the robe. "Oh, never, Lord Chamberlain. He wasn't the kind who would take advantage."

"No. He wasn't. He was a good man." John wished her answer could have been different. He would have liked to have thought Leukos had enjoyed more companionship than a few visitors in the late hours and associating with high court officials.

"He spoke highly of you." The girl seemed to read his thoughts.

John took Leukos' pouch from his belt, emptying its familiar contents onto the bed.

"Do you recognize any of these things?"

Euphemia looked puzzled. "No. But the necklace is lovely."

John picked it up. "I wonder if this was for a new love, or is it a remembrance of an old one?"

"Truly, I've never seen it before."

"Did Leukos trust you?"

"Trust me?"

"Did you take care of his personal belongings? Keep the cupboards in order, look after his jewelry?"

"Oh, the master didn't have much jewelry. Just a few rings. I would have seen the necklace if he'd had it, I'm sure. He must have bought it just before he died."

John looked thoughtful. "So, you are returning to the countryside where the mice are friendlier?"

The girl looked startled. "Did I tell you how I hate the mice here, Lord Chamberlain? I don't remember."

"I miss very little," John said, with a laugh, convinced he was missing something very important.

✻   ✻   ✻

It was late afternoon when John, carrying a basket containing a few small cakes, set off along the Mese toward the cemetery where Leukos was buried. Despite the somber purpose of the walk, John was enjoying the mild exertion and the warmth of the sun against his face.

Peter had been happy enough to prepare the cakes. "Kollyba? Of course, I know all the ingredients. Raisins, pomegranate seeds... things that represent life."

John had seen the question in the old man's eyes, although Peter hadn't dared to ask. "Leukos seems to have no family to hold the graveside meal," John had commented.

"But, if you'll pardon me, this is not the correct day. Traditionally it would be the... "

"Of course, Peter, you know better than I, but I hope your god will take my tribute for what it is intended to be and not hold me to the letter of the law."

Peter had looked less than happy, but said nothing more.

John had now left the city's inner wall behind and reached the cemetery. It had been Leukos' wish to be buried in a simple manner. His tomb was marked by what appeared to be the top of a vault but was only a thin layer of plaster over a mound of dirt. There was a lamp on a low pedestal beside the grave and, unlike most of the other lamps in the cemetery, it still burned. Perhaps these matters were taken care of for a decent amount of time following burials.

John set the basket down in the grass beside the pedestal and removed a cake. Suddenly he felt more awkward than he ever had in directing court rituals for the Emperor and Empress.

"Will it help or hurt you, my friend, to have a pagan eat kollyba before a god he doesn't believe in?"

His voice sounded much louder in the open air than it did when he spoke to Zoe, the mosaic girl in his study. Was Leukos now, like the girl, no more than a vision in his imagination?

He reminded himself that Christians believed in the immortality of the soul just as Mithrans did. But was it huddled amongst Leukos' bones in the earth, waiting for his Lord's return, or had it, as Mithrans believed, already escaped its crumbling body and begun its ascent toward the eighth rung of the ladder? And if it had, how would Leukos, good man, good Christian, pass by the fierce guardians along the way? Leukos had not had the benefit of learning the mysteries in which John was initiated.

When faced by such troublesome questions, John realized that he obeyed Mithra as a good soldier obeys his commander, equally ready to polish a buckle or go forth and die, all unthinking. Or at least unquestioning.

"I am sorry I didn't share meals with you more often in life." John addressed the earthen mound. As he raised the cake to his lips there was a pitiful mewl, and glancing toward a nearby stele he saw the large black cat he had glimpsed after Leukos' funeral. He broke off a piece of the kollyba and threw it to the animal, watching as the cat pounced on it as if it were a living thing.

John was so preoccupied he did not notice the man until he felt the sharp tip of a sword prodding his side.

He turned slowly, knowing a sudden move would only mean death. He was surprised to find himself staring into a face as gaunt-looking, he imagined, as many beneath his feet.

The skeletal man laughed with a wheezing sound, as if some of his breath were escaping through the rents in the loose tunic flapping on his thin frame. "You've picked the right grave, you have. The Keeper of the Plate himself. Some fine things he must have carried down with him. But you've not been careful enough. So I've got you at last."

"You're mistaken. I'm not a grave-robber. I've come to pay tribute to my friend." John held out the piece of kollyba, and even that movement was enough to elicit a cut from a harder prod from the cemetery keeper's sword.

"They generally don't come alone, who come to feast the dead."

"I'm not of my friend's faith. I am, however, a servant of the Emperor."

"Ah, so you're a liar as well as a grave-robber."

"Can't you see?" In the stratified society of Constantinople the less fortunate recognized the powerful by their rich clothing.

Another death-bed laugh issued from the man's thin, colorless lips. The sword point bit more deeply and John felt a warm trickle of blood down his side.

"Can't you see?" he repeated, and as he did so John noticed with consternation that his captor's eyes were milky. He was half blind.

"You've sported with me for months. Now it's my turn." The gaunt man took a long jerky step forward, forcing John back a step. "Plenty of room for the likes of you around here," he added. And John, looking carefully in the direction the man indicated, saw that they were standing not far from one of many fresh graves.

"You would follow me into the earth before the sun sets again. I am Justinian's Lord Chamberlain."

"Well, that makes it clearer," wheezed the man. "You're a very, very bad liar. And as I'm not one for lies, or a man of many words like your advocati with their legal talk, I'm afraid I'll have to draw things to a close."

John, armed only with the kollyba in his hand, suddenly remembered the cat which had been scavenging nearby. Praying to Mithra that the animal was still lurking about, he dropped the morsel of kollyba.

Just as he'd hoped, a black shape erupted from the long grass and pounced onto the cake like a demon springing at a damned soul.

John's captor, confronted unexpectedly by what must have appeared to him only as a terrible black specter, gasped, tottering backwards for a second on thin legs. Then he was lying on his back, John's knee digging into his ribs, dagger hovering over the other's bulging Adam's apple.

The cat stood nearby, eyes alert for danger or more largesse, but refusing to retreat as it desperately attempted to swallow the remains of the kollyba in a single gulp.

Perhaps, John thought, this ally had not been sent by Mithra. Perhaps he had appeased the old Egyptian gods who had given him an opportunity to gain the advantage. He remembered now that in that far-off country the cat was sacred.

"Fortunately for you," John told the cemetery keeper, "I really do serve the Emperor. I am his Lord Chamberlain. Were I a common grave-robber, you'd be dead by now." John let the man climb clumsily to his feet.

"Spare me, excellency." The man cringed, hunching over in terror until his head was almost level with John's knees.

The Lord Chamberlain wondered whether the man was actually convinced of his identity or simply recognized who now held the sword in the upper hand. It was not the tribute he'd planned for Leukos. Then there was the question of his friend's remains being disturbed. "You've had trouble here?"

"Terrible, terrible, sacrilege."

"What are they carrying off? Grave goods?"

"Who's to say? Gold and silver jewelry. The skull of John the Baptist. Leg bones of martyrs, saints' knuckles."

"You make it seem as if all the apostles and fathers of the church were buried here."

"You'd think so, seeing what's been dug up and put on display." The man lowered his voice. "Years ago, I was digging a grave and, God forgive me, I came too close to someone who'd already been here a while. Not that we don't allow for plenty of room, you understand. Anyway, I accidentally sliced into his side. 'Course, he was just rotten cloth and bone by then. No complaint there.

"But not long afterwards, I was in a church, I won't say which one, but what do you think was there, displayed in a reliquary? It was our poor Lord's rib, the very one they say was damaged when his side was pierced by the centurion's spear. Well, excellency, I could see better in those days, and so I can assure you that the only problem with that relic was that the nick in the rib was identical to the outline of the edge of my spade."

"I can well believe it."

Night had begun to creep in among the steles and mounds and small mausoleums that crowded the cemetery. Here and there, lamps flared in the encroaching gloom.

"This place is so large and you are but one man. How did you notice me?" John was suddenly reluctant to leave his departed friend under the care of a man who was nearly blind.

"I heard you talking. My ears are better than my eyes. And then I saw a shape coming out of the field right where the aqueduct cuts through."

"But I came from the road."

The cemetery keeper frowned. He straightened to his full height and turned his head to one side, then the other. "I thought there was something. Yes. Listen."

John could discern only insects heralding the approaching night.

"A spade. I hear a spade!"

He bolted away into the growing darkness.

John followed. It was hard work. The man's long, ungainly stride ate up the ground. Though he was half blind even in daylight, the cemetery keeper dodged around grave markers and mounds in the gathering dusk as if he possessed some extra sense or had ingrained the topography of the place in his mind as a blind man memorizes the rooms of his home. John cursed as he banged his shins on low memorial stones and stumbled over mounds and raised slabs. Ahead, the cemetery keeper gasped and wheezed as he loped along.

The intruder, alerted by the noise of their approach, had vanished by the time the two reached where he had been digging. It was at a grave in the corner of the cemetery, even more nondescript than Leukos'. A pile of dirt lay on one edge of a hole that reached down to the tile-lined crypt where a partially exhumed body lay.

John and the gaunt man knelt by the graveside, staring down as the remnants of day slid into the tomb of the night.

"It doesn't appear as if he had the opportunity to take anything," observed John.

"She's fortunate." The other man was curt. It would be his task to refill the grave.

Fortunate. It was a word John would not have chosen. In a sense, he supposed, the guardian of the graves spoke truly. But John could feel no sense of relief that the slumber of the departed had not been further violated. He felt only shock when he saw blonde hair and green silk robes.

It was Berta.

Chapter Twenty-three

"Are the women safe? Is everything all right?" John's fears had raced back to his house much faster than his legs could carry him. If the murderer had sought out poor Berta again, even after her death, surely he might be expected to come after Cornelia and Europa a second time, after being thwarted on the *Anubis*.

With no explicable reason, John nevertheless found himself believing that the same person must be involved in all these incidents.

Now he arrived, late and in a state of agitation that clearly alarmed Peter.

"They are well, Lord Chamberlain. And too well guarded, in my opinion. That knight, as he calls himself, has been here half the evening visiting Europa. I can't get rid of him." He drew his lips tightly together in disapproval. "I kept hoping you'd return."

John explained, very briefly, why he had been delayed and Peter's shoulders sagged. "Evil is abroad, master."

"You may retire now," John instructed. "I'll attend to Thomas."

John found the girl and her visitor in his study.

Thomas leapt up.

"Lord Chamberlain! We were beginning to worry!"

"What are you doing here, Thomas?" John cut in, his voice curt.

"Oh, I've just been telling...."

"I mean, here in my study?"

Europa began to explain. "As I told Thomas, I was informed by Peter that in Constantinople men are not allowed to visit women in their rooms. So I suggested that we talk here. The mosaics are beautiful."

John hoped that the girl had not noticed the obscene animation which the flickering lamplight lent to the cut-glass country scenes.

"The previous owner commissioned them, as I mentioned. I would have preferred something less elaborate."

"I don't agree. I think they're wonderful. Except for that little girl." Europa's large eyes glanced at the even larger, darker eyes of the portrait of Zoe. "She frightens me. Watching all the time. And listening. She could tell you everything she's heard."

Did Europa dart a glance at Thomas? Was that a raised eyebrow, a flash of a smile? In the fitful light John could not be sure.

Thomas cleared his throat. "She would only have heard about my travels and the wonders of my country," he claimed. He tugged at his ginger mustache. "No wonder her eyes are glazed."

"Really, Thomas, you're too modest. I could listen to your tales until dawn."

"And you nearly have," pointed out John. He felt uneasy, uncertain of his role. This young woman was, after all, his daughter. But how could he be a father to someone he had never known as a child? He felt an irrational anger at Thomas. But was it fatherly concern or rather from jealousy over this almost stranger who reminded him so much of a young Cornelia? "I think you'd better leave us now, Europa. If your mother wakes and finds you gone she will be worried."

Europa stood. She was graceful even rising from a chair. "Yes," she said, "yes...."

And for an instant John thought she was going to say "father", but she did not.

She paused in front of Thomas, leaned close and gazed up into his ruddy face. "You'll come back another time and finish your wonderful tales for me?"

Thomas grew even redder. He appeared to be struck dumb.

When she had gone John nodded toward the half-full bowl of the water clock in one corner.

"Why are you here at this hour, Thomas?"

The knight frowned. "As I said, we were talking."

"You were not concerned about getting back to the inn rather late?"

"Well, I didn't plan it. You're back late yourself," Thomas pointed out.

"For one not native to this dangerous city, you seem to keep odd hours."

"Do I?"

"And I seem to be running into you with remarkable frequency."

"Not surprising, when I'm visiting a guest in your household, John."

"But on the street, at the dock, in the palace gardens in the middle of the night?"

"Constantinople is small."

"To a traveler such as yourself, perhaps."

"Something's upset you, my friend?"

"Some beast dug up poor Berta's grave."

Thomas said nothing, but he sat down as abruptly as if he'd been clubbed. "But this isn't wild country."

"I don't mean an animal," snapped John. "I meant

some two-legged beast."

Thomas looked stricken. "That is unmanly."

John felt a momentary softening toward the big redhead. Thomas had understood John's horror. They were both soldiers and soldiers were most solicitous of the dead.

"Why, John?"

"Grave robbing is common enough."

"Not in my country."

"Is this truly a surprise to you, Thomas? Are you really so horrified?"

The other looked up, his eyes glistening. "I did know Berta. Only briefly, but better than you." He caught himself. "I'm sorry."

"Yes, you knew her much better than I could." John sat down. His eyes burned and he felt slightly lightheaded. His lack of sleep the previous night was catching up to him. "You visited Leukos too before he died, didn't you?"

Thomas said nothing for a moment. He appeared surprised, as if he hadn't thought of it before. "Yes, that's so."

"You have had an eventful visit to this city, all in all," John remarked.

Thomas' usual frank gaze wavered. His green eyes veiled, his look strayed from John's face to the mosaic walls. He appeared to be considering his answer with some care. Finally, he spoke. "I'm ashamed to admit I haven't been entirely honest with you, Lord Chamberlain, although I suppose I could argue that my duty to my king is greater than my duty to the truth."

"So you have indeed been following me?"

"No. Not you. The old soothsayer."

"Ahasuerus?"

"Yes, I followed him here, after nearly catching up with him in Antioch."

"I don't understand."

Thomas smiled weakly. "It is a long story, but I will be brief. I've talked enough for one evening. Could I trouble you for some of your excellent wine?"

"There is a jug on the table. Help yourself."

Thomas rose heavily, brought the jug back to his chair and set it on the floor at his feet. He smiled again, even more weakly than before. "My throat is dry."

John remarked that he did not doubt it.

"As I told you," began Thomas, "I am an emissary from the court of Arthur, High King of Bretania."

"That was indeed the truth?"

"Oh, yes. And my quest for the Grail, that too is the truth. You see, the king, and the kingdom itself, they are both in need of the Grail's healing power."

"Is it wise to offer such information to someone who reports to the Emperor?"

"Does Justinian's ambition range that far west?"

"I do not know the limit of the Emperor's ambitions, nor does any man."

"Well, at any rate, the Emperor's ambitions are of no consequence to my tale. Briefly, I set off last year. Superstition pointed me to the east. I started searching in Jerusalem. From there certain stories directed me to Antioch. It was in the Kerateion, the Jewish quarter near the southern gate, that I heard of the soothsayer known as Ahasuerus." Thomas took a gulp of wine before continuing. "Now, you are aware of the story of the crucified god, Jesus?"

John pointed out that he did, after all, serve in a Christian court.

"Of course, as do I. Well, as you know, Jesus was forced to drag his cross, the instrument of his death, through the streets to his execution."

"That is so. A barbaric thing. We do not crucify criminals any longer. Not even pagans."

"A terrible spectacle it must have been." Thomas shook his head sorrowfully. "And yet there were those who, seeing it, laughed and mocked him. One in particular urged him to hurry, following the condemned man through those dusty streets, shouting at him to make more haste toward his death. At last Jesus could tolerate this brutality no longer, for even though he was the son of God, he was also a man."

"Much blood has been spilled over that question," John remarked.

"I forget, even the laborers here are theologians. And so Jesus finally spoke. This was one who had performed miracles, raised the dead. Now he struck out with a terrible curse. The torments of flesh scourged and beaten had driven even him to despair."

John nodded wordlessly.

Thomas continued. "Thus it was that he foretold that the man who had so mocked him must wander the earth until the end of the world. And then he staggered on to his terrible death. And as for the man. His name was Ahasuerus."

A lamp flame leapt and sizzled, guttering in a draft. The mosaics on the wall squirmed. John could almost imagine that Zoe had blinked.

"That was almost five hundred years ago, Thomas." he pointed out. "Surely you don't believe the soothsayer Ahasuerus is the man you just mentioned?"

"I do. And what is more, if the stories I've heard are true, he is the keeper of the Grail. That too was part of his fate."

"Well, by all reports, the soothsayer has drowned."

"You believe that?"

"The Patriarch does."

Thomas took a deep draft of wine, then shook his head. "He cannot drown, John. He is doomed to live until the end of the world. But is he now beyond my reach, along with this precious Grail? Yes, that, alas, is certainly possible."

"But you say you followed him to Constantinople?"

"Yes. As I said, I almost caught him in Antioch. He had done readings there, and become well-known. I learned of his whereabouts from a barber who regularly trimmed the beard of a night watchman. This watchman reported he had seen the man I sought pass through the city gates before dawn that very morning, sitting in the back of a rag seller's cart, it seemed. On this chance information, I purchased a horse and set off, expecting to catch up by nightfall. But just outside Antioch the road passes through a swampy region along the river. I don't believe that road could have been constructed by Romans, the stones were so badly laid, but I whipped the horse on, Mithra forgive me.

"Well, the poor beast caught a hoof in a hole and its leg snapped like a dry stick. I was thrown and ended up in the river. Nearly drowned, I did, and broke my own leg besides. I recuperated for weeks in a nearby hostel, nursed with lepers and dying flagellants and others of a religious nature. As you see, I still have a limp."

"But you were able to follow his trail here, even after all that time?"

Thomas nodded. "Yes, I was informed that the rag seller was actually smuggling silks. The head of the hostel was a customer, you see. He told me the rag seller had gone to Constantinople. Again, I took a chance, hoping that I would find the soothsayer had come here too."

"Constantinople is a favored destination for silks and soothsayers alike," remarked John. He inquired if the rest of Thomas' journey had been uneventful.

"Well, the ship I took passage on was boarded by

Isaurian pirates," he replied. A crooked smile curved his mouth. "By then, I was glad to encounter a situation I could actually come to grips with."

John said nothing. He felt the urge to help himself from the jug of wine at Thomas' feet but controlled the impulse, remembering the results of his last overindulgence.

"A fantastic story, Thomas," he finally observed. "It has the sound of some poet's concoction."

"I wouldn't know. I am not a learned man."

"Which is not to say you lack imagination. What do you know of this Grail?"

"It is the most powerful of all relics."

"Here in Constantinople we have several fragments of that very cross which Jesus dragged through the streets, the pillar to which he was tied while scourged, and the crown of thorns, to name but a few. Not to mention several heads of John the Baptist. We also set great store in the Virgin's girdle. These holy relics are said to protect Constantinople. I would prefer to face a Persian with a sword rather than a relic but then, as you know, I am not a Christian. And neither are you, or so you have claimed. So why quest for this Grail? Could you not serve your king in other ways?"

"The world has seen many religions and many miracles. What one person might attribute to one god, another might credit to some different deity. It is all a mystery to us mortals, anyway. But if the edge of my sword draws blood when the need arises, does it matter what forge it came from?"

"True enough. What does this Grail look like?"

Thomas admitted he was not certain.

"That complicates the finding of it, then."

"Oh, there are many tales. Some say it is a cup, others insist it takes the form of a plate. Still others believe it is a magical stone."

"A stone?"

"Yes. A small, round stone. It isn't the form that is important. Jesus manifested himself in human flesh, after all."

John took Leukos' pouch from his belt. Opening it, he drew out the green stone.

"Could it look like this? It belonged to Leukos."

Thomas' eyes widened and John wondered if he had been given a more detailed description of the Grail than he had just revealed.

"The soothsayer was in the habit of giving such stones to all of his clients," John explained. "But they can't all be Grails. Anatolius had one, too. May I remind you there was also a monk who reportedly sold fifteen hands of Saint Prokopios?"

"Yes, the stones couldn't all be… but… don't you think it shows… ?"

The knight's hand twitched and John wondered if he was thinking of reaching for the stone. Thomas watched intently as it was returned to the pouch.

"I can assure you this stone has no healing powers, Thomas. I've carried it at my waist all day and I am still as I was."

Thomas looked distressed. "Berta's pendant had a stone just like that. It was the talisman she tried to use on my leg. If someone thought it was the Grail…. Could that be why she was murdered, and her grave violated?"

"How could that be? So far as I know," John pointed out, "you're the only person in Constantinople searching for this particular relic, Thomas. Tell me, were you at Isis' house at any time the night Berta died?"

The other stood. It was the natural reaction of a military man who felt himself under attack. John stood also.

"I had been to Isis' house that night," Thomas

admitted, "but to the best of my knowledge, I wasn't there when Berta was killed."

"As Lord Chamberlain, I have many men under my command. I can have you arrested. Can you in fact give me the name of anyone who will vouch for your whereabouts for all of that evening?"

Thomas paused. "No, I can't," he finally admitted.

"Why is that? Do you claim you were spending a quiet night in your room at the inn? Or perhaps wandering the streets? You say you visited Isis' house that evening. Then doubtless Darius will recall you?"

"Yes, he should. Otherwise, I was with others. But they would not recognize me."

"How could that be? Were they blind?"

"We were all masked."

Now it was John who was silent for a moment. "Where was this?"

"In the mithraeum. John, remember, I too am a Mithran. Soldiers will talk to their fellows. I heard of your friend's initiation, and borrowed a mask from one who had climbed to another rung. It was a glorious ceremony. Terrible but glorious. The blood reminded me too much of battles and death. Most people don't realize how much blood there can be when a man is killed. The corpse is cold by the time they see it, and the dead don't bleed."

"It was true," thought John. "The dead don't bleed." And didn't that tell him something?

He was groping for the meaning when a flaming projectile burst through the window in an explosion of glass and sparks.

There was fire everywhere. Thomas leapt up with a roar, frantically pawing at his beard. Small rivulets of fire ran down the mosaic wall, past the wide eyed Zoe and onto the tiles. John grabbed the wine jug and emptied its contents on the main source of the flames, revealing a large, heavy torch.

"The villain can't be far," Thomas was saying. "Quick. My sword!" he shouted back over his shoulder as he pounded downstairs, wakening the house.

John stamped out another gout of flame. Europa looked in the door and then ran down the hallway.

"Wait, Europa!" John shouted, "Don't go outside!"

She would have run downstairs blindly, but Peter, on his way to John's study and hearing his master's command, placed himself squarely in front of her. She collided with the old man and they fell to the floor. Though she helped the old man back to his feet, Europa uttered some words that John, familiar enough with the life of a traveling troupe, should not have been surprised his daughter knew.

There was little in John's spartan study on which the flames could feed and by the time Europa and Peter had climbed to their feet, and Cornelia had arrived, the fire was all but out.

Cornelia patted out a smoldering patch on Johns tunic. Thomas returned and Europa made synpathetic noises over the singed breach in his red beard.

"I was too late," Thomas growled.

"I could have caught up with the culprit," said Europa. "You should have let me help Thomas."

John glanced out of the broken window. A few men had emerged from the barracks across the way and were looking about curiously.

"Didn't it occur to you that that was the intent? To lure you outside? You will not leave my house until I've found who's responsible for all this. It is far too dangerous."

Europa glared at him. "I can take care of myself— Lord Chamberlain."

John watched in dismay as she stamped out of the study. So this was what it meant to be a father.

Chapter Twenty-Four

Old habits die slowly, and John, a veteran of many military encampments, still retained his ability to sleep lightly. It was a practice that was useful in Constantinople, where a court official camped as near to his enemies as did any soldier on the Persian border.

In sleep, John remained almost consciously alert for sounds of danger. Thus while the downpour which dowsed the roofs of the city and their many crosses was merely a soothing hymn and the braying complaint of an overburdened and sodden mule went as unnoticed as the creaking of the rafters, a faint rustle in the hall screamed out that someone was making a stealthy approach.

John woke, rose from his bed, and, moving more silently than the intruder, was positioned behind the door by the time it swung open. His visitor paused for a moment. The lamp in the hall had gone out, or been put out, for the opened door admitted no light into John's room. Lightning flickered briefly as the intruder stepped forward, to be greeted with a chokehold.

A chokehold that was quickly released as John felt a woman's soft hip pressed against his thigh and recognized one of his guests.

"Do you usually welcome ladies in this fashion?" Cornelia gasped, rubbing her throat. She turned to face him, but did not step away.

"Ladies who arrive unannounced at this hour are usually not ladies, and more often than not visit with evil intent."

"I could not sleep, after all the excitement. I thought you might be awake too. I was hoping we might talk."

John felt her breath against his face. She was wearing only a thin sleeping tunica, and he was aware of her breasts brushing his chest. Up until then, he had been careful to keep his distance. Except for clasping her hand when they had reunited aboard the *Anubis*, he had avoided touching her.

"Of course. We can talk."

Cornelia closed the door and sat down uninvited on John's bed. The ropes holding up its cotton-filled mattress creaked under her slight weight. He lit the single candle on the chest by the window and sat down next to her as she looked around the dim room.

"Well, John, it seems that despite all your fine gold-embroidered robes and silver goblets and late nights feasting at the palace table, your true tastes remain spartan. Not even a mirror, I see. Or I don't see."

"I know what I look like, so I don't need one," John pointed out.

Cornelia laid a delicate hand along his thin face, and looked into his eyes. Her touch made him catch his breath, as it had on the *Anubis*. "Time works swiftly," she said softly. "Most people who haven't looked in a mirror for a year no longer know what they look like."

"Some don't know what they look like even while they're looking into the mirror."

She ran her fingers down John's sunburnt cheeks and along the line of his jaw. "Sometimes you are too deep for your own good, John. You still look much as you did when I knew you. Remarkably so, in fact."

"When you knew me? Don't you know me any longer?"

"I... can't say."

"So your wish to talk has brought you here at this hour?" John asked, to make conversation, for he knew that Cornelia had always had difficulty sleeping and that when sleep refused to visit, she liked to talk. "You'll ruin my reputation!" John felt inexplicably awkward, a boy from the country again.

Cornelia looked around, lowered her voice, and leaned closer. "There are too many people within earshot during the day." John was aware of the clean smell of her hair. It was achingly familiar.

Cornelia, seeming not to notice the longing look on his face, rushed on. "I see you have a few scars you did not have before." She touched his chest. "Here, and here. And on your back. Was it—was it as unspeakable as they suggest?"

The Lord Chamberlain reddened. He remembered he was wearing only a loincloth. Was Cornelia also wondering about the scars that it hid?

"And did you think of me at all, John, all through those long years?"

"Often, Cornelia, especially on rainy nights like this." It was the truth. But he did not reveal how he had tried not to remember, and how he had cursed his inability to forget.

"On rainy nights, I thought of you, too, and prayed to the Goddess that you were safe and would come home to us soon. Mark you, sometimes I called down demons on your miserable head. But I did not know... I would never have wished this on you, John."

Her voice was almost drowned by the rain splashing hard against the window panes.

"Europa was talking with Thomas," John said abruptly, wishing to change the course of the conversation.

Cornelia laughed quietly. "He is harmless enough, I think. Nothing will come of it. We move around, Europa and I. One day, there may be someone who will keep her from traveling. Not yet, I think."

"I would not keep you here, Cornelia. I am not who I was."

"Nor I."

"To look at you, though...." The candlelight was kind to the few wrinkles at the corners of her eyes and mouth and the threads of gray in her hair. "Why are you really here, Cornelia?"

"Because it was a rainy night, and I wanted to be with you."

John's hands moved to her hair. "Silk. It's just like silk." He was vaguely aware how foolish and trite he sounded.

"They say the Empress sleeps between silk sheets."

"Between silk vendors, more like it!"

They both laughed.

"And I see," Cornelia observed, "you still sleep naked."

"Not quite. Not any longer."

"My poor lover...." There was a catch in her voice.

John grasped her hands in his. He felt a sudden need to protect her, although he realized she was no longer the girl he had known but a woman who had made her way in life, with a daughter to shield from harm. "Don't feel sorry for me, Cornelia. How many die before they ever reach manhood? How many more are ill treated or starved of affection by those they desire? You gave me all the pleasure the gods will allow a man."

The ropes strung across the old wooden bed-frame had allowed the mattress to sag, bringing their hips together. The rising wind lashed rain against the dark diamond panes of the window and sent drafts through cracks around the window frame. In the gathering chill, John could feel the warmth radiating from her body.

"I have some wine here," he said, taking the clay cup from the chest and placing it in her hands.

She took a sip and coughed. "Your taste in wine is still terrible."

"You sweetened it for me once, remember?"

"I still can."

She leaned closer and John again tasted the sweet heat of her mouth. He sank into it, thin hands tracing the still familiar contours of her warmth and softness.

He pulled away. He could see her eyes glinting in the candlelight.

"It is just the same, as in my memory at least." He was afraid she was about to cry. "Do you remember that cup?" She was still holding it. "I don't suppose you would recognize it. A plain clay cup. Peter has wondered aloud on more than occasion why, with that crack in it, I insist on using it when I'm alone. I wonder what he would think if he knew that I had had it made specially?"

Cornelia looked puzzled.

"It is because it is identical to one we had when we were with the troupe," John explained. "Because your lips had touched its twin when I first knew you."

Cornelia smiled. "I do remember, John. And now I think on it, I also remember how you almost broke the original when you knocked it off the table that time when...."

"As I recall, it was you."

Cornelia reached down abruptly and pulled her tunica over her head. She was naked.

"Cornelia, I can't...."

"I know. I just wanted you to see me, John. Move the candle. Just look at me, lover. Or am I hurting you?"

John shook his head.

The rain beating on the window was washing away the sorrows of all the years, leaving only Cornelia. Cornelia of the silken hair, Cornelia of the small, firm breasts.

She looked at the cloth around his hips.

"No," he said. "I cannot. There isn't...."

"I know how it is done."

She rose and blew out the candle. The acrid smell of smoke mixed with her scent. "There, John. I won't look, or touch. I just want us to be together."

He reached down, hesitant even in the darkness, and undid the garment.

She pulled him down on to the mattress and they lay together, joined at thigh, hip, chest and mouth, intersections of warmth in the chilly room.

He tasted her mouth again. She moved against his lean frame, her body forgetting what her mind knew.

Suddenly she rolled to one side, apologizing.

He leaned over her. "Why should you be sorry? It always gave me the most pleasure, knowing you wanted me. But I'm afraid nature makes young men much too impetuous. I loved you then as a boy might, for myself. Now, I can love you as a man. After all, I still have...."

He kissed her deeply again. His slim fingers found that the language of his lover's body had not changed. Rain sheeted rhythmically at the window. His mouth finally left hers and as the rising tides of her senses swept away time and memory, he let himself drown in her secret seas.

By the time Cornelia awoke, the sun had long since risen over the newly-washed city. John was gone, having placed in his spartan room a single lily, the royal flower of Crete. It was balanced precariously in the cracked cup on the chest by the window.

Chapter Twenty-five

Time was running out.

If the murderer knew where Cornelia and Europa were staying and had become bold enough to attack the Lord Chamberlain's own home, he must be desperate indeed.

John had to find him before he claimed another victim.

And if the Emperor discovered John was disobeying his orders? Well, John resolved to deal with that problem if it presented itself.

So it was he returned to his investigations, returned in fact to the beginning, to the alley where he had stumbled on Leukos' body. The first light of day crept cautiously down the alley behind him. It glinted sullenly off puddles left by the storm and nightsoil emptied before dawn from the windows of the surrounding tenements. Even in this sordid place, on such a grim task, John could not keep his thoughts away from Cornelia and what had passed between them during the night.

John followed his long shadow down the narrow alley. The buildings rising on either side seemed to sag inwards. Overhead only a crack of sky showed. A few dark shapes scurried to sanctuary in the shadows. They were the size of cats but squealed like rats.

John paused, looking around. The back door to Isis' house opened directly onto the alley. He recalled that the inn at which Thomas was currently residing, the same lodging place where the soothsayer had stayed and been visited by Leukos, was a short walk away. It was quicker to use the network of alleys to get from one place to the other rather than the main streets, although it was difficult to say why anyone, especially a meticulous man like Leukos, would choose such a route after dark. At best a passerby ran the risk of being relieved of his dignity by the contents of a chamber pot and, at worst, deprived of his life by a lurking thief.

Although, John now realized, that had not been what had happened.

The spot where Leukos had lain was occupied this morning by a reeking puddle. This was not surprising, since the spot was directly below a second story window. What was surprising, John thought, was that Leukos' body had not been befouled as it lay in the darkness.

What was even more surprising was how dry the cobbles under Leukos' body had been. It had occurred to John when Thomas had been recalling, or at least claiming to recall, Anatolius' initiation, that the knight had been all too correct about how much blood there was in a human body. John had suddenly remembered that little, if any, of Leukos' blood was pooled in the alley where he was discovered. But if Leukos had not died there, then where had he been murdered?

A sound above caught his attention. John looked up at the window over the spot where Leukos had lain, but it was closed.

※　　※　　※

Maera pulled the shutters closed as quietly as possible. Her heart was leaping. It seemed it was not even possible to get a breath of morning air any longer. What kind of place had Sabas brought her to, this filthy city where you couldn't even open your own window without some awful shock?

At least it wasn't a corpse this time. But for what good reason would a gentleman—and surely he was a gentleman, judging by his expensive robes and boots, even a country girl could tell that—for what good reason would such a person have to linger in an alley examining the contents of Maera's chamber pot?

It had always made her feel dirty and shamed, having to throw something so... private... yes, that was it, private, out for anyone to come upon. It wasn't like that in the countryside. There was some decency there. Not like Constantinople. A hundred churches, a thousand religious relics, a hundred thousand holy men, but no decency at all.

Sabas, lying sprawled on a pallet by the wall, erupted in a series of gasping snores. There was barely room in the tiny room for him to stretch out. His eyelids fluttered but did not open. It was a fever, perhaps. God forbid that he was getting a fever now. He had slept much of the time since he had been carried back home.

Maera heard a footstep in the hallway and her heart thudded harder.

"No," she pleaded, "No... ," but even as she began to pray there was an imperative knock on the flimsy door. What to do? There was no escape. Again there was a knock. The door had no lock, anyway.

Maera pulled it open a crack. She was trembling. It was the man from the alley. Closer, he looked even more elegant, tall and smooth-skinned. Not one who worked with his hands, that was obvious.

A hundred thoughts began to run through Maera's mind. She had never had so many thoughts before she came to this place. Perhaps he was coming to help Sabas, perhaps he was coming to take him away. Or perhaps they were to be thrown out for not paying their rent.

"May I come in?"

The request was surprising. The voice was less imposing, gentler, than its master. Soft, but not feminine, thought Maera. But didn't the educated always sound like that?

She looked around, unsure of what to say. Sabas' pallet occupied nearly the entire floor space. The close room smelled of sickness. The gentleman stepped inside anyway.

There was gold embroidery at the hem of his robe. Gold. She remembered that she was clothed only in the thin, sweat-stained tunica in which she had slept.

"I'm sorry to disturb you. I am John, Lord Chamberlain to Justinian."

Lord Chamberlain? To the Emperor? In this place? Surely the city had driven her mad. Why should she doubt him, though? His robes were hemmed in gold. He could have been Justinian himself, or the Patriarch. Maera shrunk away, instinctively.

"I want to ask you a few questions," John continued quietly. "Your window overlooks the spot where a body was discovered."

Had he come to accuse her, then? "I don't know anything about it," she stammered.

"Don't worry. This has nothing to do with you or your husband. What is your name?"

"Maera." It stuck in her throat like a stringy scrap of meat.

"And your husband?"

"Sabas."

"Maera, I just wanted to know if you saw anything strange on the night of the festivities?"

Maera's expression must have given her away, because John's eyes narrowed. "You did see something, didn't you?" he pressed.

Maera bit her lip.

"You looked out of the window, didn't you? And you saw something in the alley? What did you see?"

"Oh, sir, it was just as you said. I was going to throw out.... But there was a dead man. Looking right up at me."

Sabas groaned and one big arm slapped bonelessly at John's leg. Maera felt faint, but the gentleman seemed not to notice Sabas.

"Is that all? Did you look out again? I know you didn't befoul the dead man."

Maera felt humiliation. Her shame nearly overwhelmed her fear. "I saw nothing, after I saw him lying there."

"And before? Did you open the window at any time before you saw the dead man?"

Maera nodded. The Lord Chamberlain was looking down at her, his face stern. She forced herself to speak. "It was dark in the alley. At first I thought it must be demons, lurching along, stumbling and falling against the walls. Then I saw it was just two men, drunk, holding each other up. Quiet though, not like most who have drunk too much. And then I wondered again if they were really men or if I'd been right the first time and they were demons, and then I slammed the shutters closed."

"What made you think of demons, Maera?"

"One was masked. It must have been a mask. Some terrible bird-headed thing. It must have been a mask, don't you think? Or else it must have been a demon."

"There's nothing uncommon about masked

drunkards wandering the street during celebrations,"
John reassured her. "I saw quite a few myself that night.
Was your window open during the day?"

"I usually keep it open but I don't look out much.
There's nothing to see that you'd care about. Men using
the back door to that... house. And some beasts that
can't even be bothered to get inside first."

"Did you know there was an... " John hesitated,
considering how best to phrase the question. "An
incident at that house? A girl was murdered there
recently."

Maera paled. "It does not surprise me that
someone working at such a trade would come to grief,
God rest her soul. I shall pray for her. But I saw nothing
then either, sir. I wish I could help you."

"And you are sure you didn't see a well-dressed
man go by on the night of the celebrations?
Completely bald, pale? Older?" John made a final
attempt to refresh the woman's memory.

Maera shook her head. How would she notice such
a thing?

"I saw such a man."

Maera was startled by her husband's voice. He had
not spoken since his fellow workmen had carried him
back to her.

She knelt down beside him, taking his hand in
hers. "Sabas!" For the first time she felt hope. He would
live.

"Where did you see the man?" John bent down
to inquire softly.

"The Great Church." The words came in a hoarse
whisper.

"My husband is a laborer," explained the woman.
"He was hurt. He fell from the scaffolding. They
thought he was as good as dead. They say it was a
miracle he survived. He landed in a pile of straw, you

see, although that shouldn't have been enough to save him."

"Did this man come to see the church?" John bent closer to catch the mumbled answer.

"No. No. I would never have noticed, there's so many people there. But I work a lot. Sometimes late, sometimes early. I usually work high up in the dome, where you can look out through the openings where the light comes in. You can see as far as the city walls, and down into the Patriarch's garden, and into the guarded way that leads to the private entrance of his palace. The bald man used to go in that way. At strange hours."

"To the Patriarch's private quarters?" John persisted. Why would Leukos be visiting the Patriarch? "Was he alone?"

But Sabas' eyes closed, and as suddenly as he had awakened he lapsed back into unconsciousness.

Maera's lips trembled. "Sabas! Sabas...." She turned tear-filled eyes to the Lord Chamberlain and saw compassion for her husband's terrible injuries. "We'll go back to the country when he's healed." she cried wildly. "I'd rather he laid up stone walls than churches, if this is how God rewards poor workmen."

"But he is alive, Maera. That is the important thing. No matter his injuries, he is alive."

Maera saw two gold coins in the Lord Chamberlain's palm. She had never seen even one gold coin before.

"Here. There is a palace physician across from the Chalke. His name is Gaius."

"We are poor people," she protested.

"You are less poor now. Gaius will take one of these and heal your husband. Don't pay more. If he is drunk, however, go back when he's himself again."

Maera was transfixed by the coins. How could she

take them? Weren't they part of the city which had so hurt her husband? She shook her head.

"Take them, Maera," John said gently. "I have many more. More than I can possibly spend in ten lifetimes."

"I can't. I can't take them from you."

"They are not from me. They come through me from your god. Would he have saved your husband so miraculously, only to have him die for lack of a physician's attention? Of course not. This is but the second part of the miracle."

Maera took the coins in trembling hands. When the Lord Chamberlain had departed, she saw that indeed, though they bore the likeness of Justinian on one side, on their reverse they bore a cross.

❋   ❋   ❋

Madam's was but a few steps from the entrance to the tenement where Maera and Sabas lived. As he entered Isis' house, John saw that Darius, the doorkeeper, had not yet been liberated from the incongruous role of an enormous Eros. Noting John's look of inquiry, Darius shrugged, moving the tiny wings attached to his broad shoulders.

"Fortunately, we won't be a Temple of Venus much longer. After Berta was murdered, Madam said we'd have to change."

"To a motif that will suit you better, I trust."

Darius shrugged again. "I doubt it. It won't be a military encampment. I've suggested that more than once."

"I'm afraid I've come to ask more questions, Darius. Do you recall the evening of the celebrations?"

Darius grimaced. "I always recall such nights, only too clearly. But, as I told you already, I didn't see or hear anything out of the ordinary. Except for Madam's accursed hydra."

"Did you have as a guest an ordinary looking man who was completely bald?"

Darius shook his head immediately. "No."

"You'd remember?"

"Oh, yes. I remember people's faces well. It's a useful skill, if only to keep track of who's a regular visitor and who isn't. With the regulars, you know what to expect. Strangers, the first time at least, you keep an eye on them."

"And the night Berta was murdered? You say you didn't notice anyone suspicious?"

Darius shrugged again, the movement causing his stiff little wings to flap delicately.

"No one suspicious. We had a few travelers— pilgrims by the look of them, though they claimed to be traders—except for them, it was just the regulars. You were here that night yourself, with Felix as I recollect."

"What about Thomas?"

"The redhead who claims to be a knight? I'm not sure. He's been here a few times. Not that I stand guard every hour of every day and night. Madam can give you the names of the other guards, if you wish."

"That won't be necessary." He paused. "Tell me, Darius, is there only the one door into the alley?"

"Yes, just that one. Some of our more discreet guests use it. Often those of high rank." Darius raised an eyebrow, creating a somewhat alarming effect for an oversized Eros.

John asked to see the door to the alley. Darius summoned an assistant to take his place at the front entrance, then led the Lord Chamberlain through a beaded curtain, along a wide door-lined corridor and down a narrow hall dimly lit by a smoky torch at each end.

The low, plain wooden door Darius halted before was a stark contrast to the elaborately carved main entrance.

"At our establishment, unlike the palace, the beggars enter in grand style while it is the powerful who often make their way inside in humble fashion." Darius grinned and gave the door a rap with his enormous fist.

John had been scanning the walls and floorboards. "It may be a humble entrance," he remarked, "but Madam evidently has ordered it be kept well scrubbed, I see."

"Madam takes pride in her house."

John bent to examine the floor more closely.

"One thing, Lord Chamberlain," said Darius, abruptly. "You asked about whether a completely bald man was in here the night of the celebrations. I didn't see anyone like that. But then again, it has just occurred to me, more than a few who visited that evening were wearing some sort of fantastic headdress or mask or whatever. A ridiculous-looking bunch, if you ask me."

"Ridiculous, indeed," agreed John. "And by the way, your left wing is crooked. Isis wouldn't appreciate that." He paused. "Could I trouble you to stand aside for a moment, Darius? There is a stain near the bottom of the doorframe."

The big man stood aside as requested. John bent to examine the door. After a moment he straightened.

"It appears to be dried blood," he frowned.

❋   ❋   ❋

Darius escorted John back through the halls to Isis' private chambers. The usually cheerful madam seemed to be in a disagreeable humor.

"You can be certain, John, that if I say your friend Leukos did not set foot in this place that night, then he did not."

"Well," offered John, "he might have used an assumed name."

Isis laughed. "Who doesn't? Believe me, if the Keeper of the Plate was here, I'd know about it."

"Or a bald-headed man?"

"Or a man with a birthmark on his bottom shaped like a bust of Caesar. We had such a guest last week, actually. No, John, if your friend had been here, I would know."

John changed the subject. "I understand from Darius that you've been devoting a lot of time to music?"

She nodded, walked over to the contraption and depressed several keys. The hydra sounded just as ailing as it had when he first heard it. "I'm beginning to understand why the Patriarch won't let these things through church doors. I would have thought something the holy fathers found anathema would have suited me. But perhaps I wasn't blessed with musical ability."

"It takes years of practice."

"I'm sure you're right, John. But, tell me, why are you asking me about Leukos? I never saw the man."

"One of his servants told me he sometimes went out at night at odd hours, and didn't have anything to say about where he was going."

"Mine is only the best house in the city, you know," Isis smiled, "not the only one."

"And something else. Before he showed me in, I asked Darius if I could take a look at the back door, the one that opens into the alley."

"What about it?"

"When I examined that door I found dried blood on the bottom of the doorframe. I'm hoping you'll be able to explain how it got there."

Isis looked thoughtful. "Do you recall the bear trainer who was killed right at my front door? Such a lot of blood to clean up, there was. Evidently Darius was careless in disposing of the rags he used. I shall have to have a word with him."

Chapter Twenty-six

In the evening John sat in his quiet study, trying to make sense of what he had learned, and not succeeding. He thought of what the young man, Sabas, had said. Strange enough, Leukos visiting a soothsayer, but visiting the Patriarch? Of course, there were other bald men in the city. And then again, Sabas had been feverish. Could what he'd said be trusted?

John's gaze fell upon Zoe. He began to ask her opinion but stopped himself this time. What sort of man was it who could talk to a mosaic girl more easily than to his own daughter? Who understood glass but not flesh and blood? But then glass could not grow and change and a mosaic girl could not speak, although it sometimes seemed she did. John turned away.

Outside his newly repaired window the sky was threatening. After the recent dry period, it seemed that the spring rains would never stop. Dark clouds loomed low, and there was that eerie hush that signaled yet another storm would be upon the city within the hour. Gusts of heralding winds swirled about the house. Several large seabirds strutted on the cobbles below, shrilly squawking. Their ghastly cries suggested the screeching of the Harpies tormenting their prey. John shuddered. It was only his imagination, of course. Just as he only imagined he could sense Zoe's disapproval.

"Will you speak to me no more then?" she seemed to whisper. "What will I do with no one to talk to?"

There was a tap on the door.

"Enter!" he commanded in a tone curter than he normally used with Peter. The old servant, looking offended, silently ushered in a cloaked and hooded figure. John recognized the cloak. It was one of his own.

"Who is this?" John was surprised, for Peter never allowed anyone into his master's presence without announcing a name.

Before Peter could answer, the stranger pushed the hood away from his face, which was familiar if somewhat more worn than the last time John had seen it. Concealing his surprise, John indicated to Peter that he was to withdraw. The mystery was solved, although the soothsayer's unheralded reappearance immediately replaced one puzzle with another.

"Your servant lent me this cloak, John. It appears it will be another wet night and he has a kind heart."

John recalled that Ahasuerus' own cloak had been washed up from the sea that, so everyone seemed to assume, had claimed the old man's life. He offered wine, but his visitor shook his head.

"One needs a clear head at all times in this city," he rasped, sinking onto the chair to which John gestured him. "Especially when one reaches my advanced years and becomes easily confused, even when sober."

"Quite so," John replied mildly. "I must confess that I thought that Atropos had cut the thread of your life—the more so because the last time I had news of you, I was reliably informed that you had, shall I say embarked on your journey across the Styx."

"That is a journey that I will not take for a long time, my friend." The old man chuckled hoarsely. "However, I am off on another sort of journey. Did you ever hear that the mantis warns travelers of danger, pointing the way to go to avoid it? Well, I've been hiding. For a while I was over there in the stables debating whether to stay." He gestured vaguely in the direction of the barracks. "When I awoke today what did I see but a mantis. It was pointing toward the sea. Even a soothsayer need not cast pebbles to know that it was urging me to depart."

John could not help thinking of Thomas' extraordinary tale. Surely, though, Ahasuerus was nothing more than an old man, and in fact one whose advanced age might well be clouding his brain.

"You look exhausted. At least eat. Should I ask Peter to bring something?"

"Thank you, but I am not hungry. You do not seem surprised to see me." Ahasuerus sounded hurt, but John noticed how shrewd were the eyes under the brows bridging the old face. "Tell me, Lord Chamberlain, where do you think I have been?"

"As I told you, I had feared you were dead."

A gust of wind rattled at the window, underlining the old man's words as he replied. "I will tell you where I have been, then. I was summoned from the inn somewhat urgently, to see Patriarch Epiphanios. Imagine my surprise at such an honor being extended to one so humble. It seems word of my modest gifts had spread throughout the court."

"Are you a gifted theologian then? I can scarcely believe that the Patriarch wished to have his fortune told."

"You would be surprised to hear which people are interested in having their fortunes told. Or perhaps you would not."

John leaned back wearily. "You are but lately come from Antioch, I believe," he probed, recalling what Thomas had told him. Had some new cult sprung up mushroom-like in that area, as occasionally happened?

"No, not quite. I was born there, yes, but it is years since I last visited. No, I journeyed here from Lazika, near the border."

"Indeed?" John's skin turned cold.

"Not that that is important, unless you are suspicious of those who journey too near the border. There's more than one in the palace." The statement was ambiguous, but the old man's gaze was knowing. John began to understand why the superstitious set such store by the soothsayer and those like him. Was it just a spear's throw into the darkness, he wondered, or did the old man really possess the powers to which he laid claim? "But to return to the Patriarch," the old man continued, "he wished to discuss holy relics."

"I had a similar discussion not long ago in this very room," John mused, recalling his first encounter with Thomas. "However, Patriarch Epiphanios did not figure prominently on that occasion."

Ahasuerus smiled slightly. "Yes, there are many relics in this city, and many who are interested in adding to their number. A holy city indeed, but riddled with much that is unholy."

John immediately thought of the banquet he had recently attended and of the Empress with her scarlet sickle of a smile.

"The learned ecclesiastic wished also to discuss what I might know of the murder of the unfortunate Keeper of the Plate," Ahasuerus continued. "I admit that this interest is more secular in nature, but then I appear to have been the one who saw the murdered man last. Or at least, that's the position so far as could be ascertained by, shall we say, assiduous questioning

"Surely there was no force involved?'

The old man pulled John's cloak closer around his slight frame. "You know the ways of the court, Lord Chamberlain. But I have suffered far worse. At any rate, I know no more of the whole sorry affair than do other men. The Patriarch did, however, instruct me to cast the pebbles for him."

From long training, the Lord Chamberlain spoke evenly despite the shocking revelation.

"The Patriarch? Of all people, why would he consult a soothsayer?" It could hardly be represented as entertainment, not with Leukos hardly buried and the entire palace in a turmoil. And what about the religious ramifications?

"There were only the two of us in the room at the time," Ahasuerus pointed out mildly, apparently not aware that the Patriarch, like all court dignitaries, had armed guards close to hand and within earshot at all times. Whatever had been said would be no secret.

John inquired if the soothsayer had used his gifts to good effect. Ahasuerus confirmed that this had been the case. "I was able to tell the Patriarch that the answer to his question lies in the palace."

John felt some disappointment. The soothsayer hardly needed any supernatural skills to provide that answer. He could have given it after only a few days in Constantinople. Was this unnerving foreigner merely a common trickster after all? He pursued his questioning by asking whether the Patriarch was surprised by the soothsayer's revelation.

"It did not seem so. Perhaps he already had suspicions?"

"We all have those. So you believe that Leukos' murder is somehow connected to something or someone at court?"

"I am as certain of it as I can be. Did not the pebbles

tell me so? And now let me tell you something. You are no doubt wondering, are you not, why the Patriarch is so concerned about the death of a palace servant, one not even under his command? So concerned, in fact, as to go beyond his Christian duty and consult a heathen soothsayer in his own residence? I pose this riddle, while noting that you at least were shrewd enough to come to see me alone rather than announcing your intent to all and sundry by sending armed men to escort me to your presence."

"The Patriarch is not noted for his subtlety, even in his theology." John again found himself wondering why the garrulous old man had come to see him, but from past experience fully expected the reason to meander his way in due course. For the moment, however, he might learn something from this apparent rambling, so was content to wait and listen.

His visitor obliged by taking up his story again. "Tell me, my lord, why are you so interested in this death?"

"Leukos was a friend of mine. A good friend." John did not see any reason to mention that he also had been imperially commanded to do so, or that the command had subsequently been abruptly withdrawn.

"Ah. Then I shall tell you why the Patriarch seeks advice in such strange places. The Keeper of the Plate was his son."

"Of course! I might have guessed!" John leaned back in his chair.

Ahasuerus looked even more hurt than before. "Can I never surprise you, Lord Chamberlain? How could you have known?"

John had no intention of revealing what, in hindsight, pointed to the relationship: the laborer observing Leukos entering the private entrance to the Patriarch's palace, the night visitors mentioned by the dead man's servant, the way Leukos had always maintained secrecy as to the whereabouts of his family. As to how the soothsayer had known... John supposed the shrewd old man could have pieced together rumors and gossip. Or perhaps one of his clients from court had talked too much.

"You should not be too quick to reveal such knowledge, however obtained," he advised the old man.

"Well, even so, in answer to the question no doubt uppermost in your mind, my lord, I did indeed tell the Patriarch the reason why his interest in the unfortunate Leukos was so great."

John said that he thought the soothsayer a more courageous man than most.

"I am constrained always to be truthful," Ahasuerus responded, "even when it is an unwelcome, even dangerous, truth that I must tell."

"And not welcome would be the case most of the time, I imagine." John's tone was dry.

"I told this to the Patriarch, realizing that I would not be in a safe position once I conveyed my knowledge to him."

John noted that he was not certain that he would have revealed such knowledge, especially when by so doing the powerful would inevitably be alienated.

The soothsayer smiled, his brown face wrinkling walnut-like. "And yet, even so, many are placed in harm's way by the most ordinary of actions. Observing something better not seen, for example. I am sure you can think of many such circumstances from your own experience, my lord."

The Lord Chamberlain again felt a frisson of cold chilling his skin. It was obvious why the old man would appear supernaturally gifted to many. "After hearing what you have told me, I confess I am even more surprised to see you alive."

"True enough. So, sensing that my welcome in the city was fast losing its heartiness, I decided to leave forthwith by the first ship which would take me."

Counterpointing his narrative, rain gusted against the window and John got up and closed the shutters.

"So I went immediately to the docks to seek passage on the next tide to wherever it pleased the Lord to send me," Ahasuerus continued.

"You were pursued?" John wondered whether the guards he had encountered at the inn were those sent to escort Ahasuerus to his interview with Patriarch Epiphanios or those dispatched to dispose of the old man after his return from it.

"Well, if not, there are more clumsy ne'er-do-wells in Constantinople than live in most cities, for while I was standing on the dock looking about for a likely ship, something struck me squarely in the shoulder blades and I fell into the water. And, Lord Chamberlain, I cannot swim."

John made no comment. The story he had been told by the Patriarch about the old man's supposed death had differed in the details, but then it had not been revealed that an interview had taken place. He did not trust the Patriarch, or Ahasuerus himself for that matter.

"And so," Ahasuerus continued, "I went down into the sea, plummeting like Icarus to a watery end." He rubbed his face, his shoulders sagging. He was obviously tired to the bone, but it seemed to John that the old man genuinely had had no doubt he would survive. "As I said, however, it is not a journey which I shall take. Not yet, at least. And now, Lord Chamberlain, since you are doubtless wondering why in the circumstances I returned to the palace, I shal' tell you. I have come on this rainy night to cast th pebbles for you."

Chapter Twenty-seven

When John called on Patriarch Epiphanios he was led to the enclosed garden of the patriarchal palace. Pale morning sunlight cast time's faint shadow across the face of a sundial standing at the center.

The Patriarch was bent over, examining a flower bed near the garden's single poplar tree. John could see only a few green shoots. The old man straightened up with obvious difficulty. He looked even frailer than he had at the banquet, John thought.

"The dial reveals the hour, the flowers reveal the season," the Patriarch commented. His skin showed the first hint of the translucence that so often signals the approach of death, as if the body were already giving up its corporeal qualities. "What do you wish to speak to me about, Lord Chamberlain?"

"I don't know that this is the place."

"Some delicate subjects, then? Don't worry. We will not be overheard here. I preferred to be out in the garden today. The walls of my rooms feel much too close. And the Great Church... everyone speaks of the beauty of the light under its dome. It feels much too ereal to me. Come, then. What is it? I don't have time to waste."

"Leukos, the Keeper of the Plate. He was your son."

The Patriarch smiled faintly. "Very few know that, and fewer still dare put the knowledge into words."

"Ahasuerus, the old soothsayer, knew."

"It's hard to believe how that old scoundrel could have such knowledge. Perhaps he simply divined it. Perhaps he did possess the gift he claimed."

"I'm surprised you don't deny this."

"It is a little late for that, Lord Chamberlain. It hardly matters to me at this point." The Patriarch took a few hesitant steps and lowered himself on to a bench. "But I am surprised that you would accept the word of a self-styled soothsayer, Lord Chamberlain," he concluded.

"Leukos was observed at the private entrance to your residence more than once." John thought it best not to reveal the source of his information.

Patriarch Epiphanios sighed. "How is it that our God should choose a man to serve him in the highest capacity, and yet allow such a servant to remain enslaved by the same appetites as bedevil any man?"

"You may want this." John held out the silver necklace he had found in Leukos' pouch. The Patriarch took it in a shaking hand, and brought it closer to his tired eyes until he could see the entwined fish.

"Yes. Thank you, Lord Chamberlain. I gave it to Leukos as a keepsake. It was his mother's. She is dead."

"He kept it with him. I will give you the pouch and the rest of its contents when I am done with them. It appears you took good care of your son, even if you could not acknowledge him publicly."

"Indeed, that is so. I realized that the resulting scandal would be more than just grist for the gossip of old women, for his very existence flew in the face of the teachings of the church fathers. His mother, y see, was married." A shadow seemed to cross the Patriarch's face. "Given your position, Lord Chamberlain, you surely understand how careful we all must be. So finally I had to ask the Emperor to end the investigations into Leukos' death."

John had seldom heard such pain in a man's voice. There was silence for a while. Then the old man turned to John and asked about his interest in Leukos' death.

"Leukos was a good friend," John responded softly.

"Yes, I know that. He sometimes spoke of you."

"And I wanted his death avenged."

"But by all accounts it was the soothsayer, and I have heard that he is dead."

"I don't believe he was murdered by the soothsayer. I think his murderer is still free. I have a suspicion as to who it might be, and it may be that you know something that will help me to be certain."

"But the soothsayer stabbed Leukos. His dagger was in Leukos when you found him, wasn't it?"

"You did not reveal to me who actually identified the weapon."

"The keeper of the inn where the old beast made his lair had seen him using it."

"Can one believe an innkeeper? It's commonly said that those who thrive at such an enterprise do so at the expense of personal honesty."

The Patriarch sighed. "That may be, Lord Chamberlain, but it seems that other people who had seen the dagger—members of the court—subsequently confirmed his identification of the weapon."

John asked what had persuaded the authorities to question the innkeeper about the soothsayer.

The other shook his head. "I was informed it was as the result of an anonymous note. I have no experience in investigating murders, Lord Chamberlain." The Patriarch paused. His lips tightened and his hand crept furtively to his side, fingers whitening as they pressed into his ribs. He made no sound and in a moment the spasm had passed, but when he spoke again his voice was a dry whisper.

"Do you know what I had planted there?" He indicated the plot he had been examining when John arrived.

"I've never been very skilled at identifying plants." John wondered whether this was a calculated digression or whether the old man's attention was wandering.

"It is monkshood. I hope to see it reach its full growth one more time. My physician has been giving me a concoction of it. For the pain. It makes me very cold. I think it numbs the soul as well as the body. The Greeks say the plant springs from the spittle of Cerberus. Were I a pagan I would expect to be seeing the beast soon. As it is...." The weak voice trailed off.

"As it is?" John finally prompted.

"I am afraid when my angel leads me up to heaven, the demon tollkeepers on the way will charge me heavily for my sins. You are quite right, Lord Chamberlain. It was not the soothsayer who murdered my only son. It was I."

It was obvious the Patriarch was near death. Had he lost his mind as well? Or was it the effect of the medicines he was taking? John asked for an explanation.

"I murdered Leukos," the Patriarch repeated. "Oh, it was that vile soothsayer who wielded the dagger, but it was I who placed Leukos in its path. You see, I asked Leukos to consult him for me."

"It did seem an uncharacteristic thing for him to visit a soothsayer twice. Leukos was a good Christian and in no need of magic to order his life."

The Patriarch gestured toward the mass of the building looming above the walled garden. "When th

Great Church is completed it will house the greatest relics in all the world. Neither Jerusalem nor Antioch will rival the sacred collection gathered here for the glory of the Emperor and our city. You may know that Leukos had obtained more than one relic for the church. He dealt with earthly valuables, and merchants are often not discriminating as to the goods they handle. The seller of fine silver sometimes acquires other sorts of treasures. Leukos was in a position to know when such valuables became available."

John looked toward the partly completed church. Whereas inside one was struck by a sense of light and insubstantiality, from outside the impression was one of weight and immensity.

"Leukos' servant mentioned that he occasionally had visitors at night who brought him gifts, summoned him," he said. "They were your messengers, weren't they? "

The Patriarch nodded.

"But why send him to visit the soothsayer?"

"To inquire about this Grail that was rumored to be in the city."

"You would believe such a man?"

"I didn't, but he had ingratiated himself with several powerful people at court, and they spoke of his skills to me. The soothsayer was a remarkably, in fact carelessly, garrulous old man," the Patriarch added, apparently blind to the irony of his words. "Full of rumors."

"What did Leukos report?"

"Leukos found him unconvincing," the Patriarch admitted. "At least on the subject of the Grail."

"But you sent him back to the soothsayer for another interview?"

The Patriarch paused, and again his lips tightened ₁ pain, this time with the agony of a bereaved heart.

"Yes, God forgive me. I might have discounted the tales, but then the foreigner Thomas arrived and began asking about the relic."

"He too may have been deluded," John pointed out.

"And if not? And he managed to obtain it? Even Justinian's reach does not extend to Bretania. How could I take such a chance?"

John said that he understood.

"Perhaps not entirely. Did you know that this relic is said to be a heal-all?"

"So I have heard. But, according to this person Thomas, its power could not properly be directed at an individual."

The Patriarch's eyes looked glassy in the thin light filtering out of the cloudy sky. John could not tell whether it was the sheen of tears or the effect of physicians' concoctions.

"He may well be right. My son died because I was so afraid of death that I grasped at the chance to preserve my own life." A quaver had entered the Patriarch's voice. He smiled wanly. "You realize I am only telling you this because I am a dead man, Lord Chamberlain?"

"You are not dead yet." John was beginning to fear that he was learning things that might considerably shorten his own life if the Patriarch were to reclaim the senses he had apparently lost. "And indeed the holiest of all relics would bring great honor to Constantinople."

"Will bring great honor, Lord Chamberlain. Will bring."

The old man lurched to his feet, his thin hand searching inside his plain white robes. He produced square, jewel-encrusted box.

"Come closer, Lord Chamberlain."

John stepped forward.

The Patriarch's hands trembled as he opened the lid of the box. "The Grail," he breathed. "It cost me dearly, but now the most holy relic in Christendom will reside for all eternity in the empire's greatest church. Perhaps now I will be forgiven for all my sins."

John stared down into the box. Inside lay a round stone, green, flecked with red, perhaps three times the size of the stones Ahasuerus had given his clients, but otherwise identical.

❊   ❊   ❊

If there was one thing Peter truly disliked, it was sharing his kitchen with anyone, so he was doubly distressed to have both Felix and Anatolius in the small room as he was attempting to cook. Thankfully, Felix did not seem inclined to stay long.

"I had hoped to find John home," he was saying. "I wanted to thank him for his assistance the other night."

"You look grim today, Felix," observed Anatolius.

Felix grunted. "I have made some difficult decisions, and now a hard task awaits me."

"And what is this? Have you brought a gift?" Anatolius' stared pointedly at the small bundle Felix was carrying.

"Oh, this? Madam Isis gave me some mementos of Berta. Jewelry. I did keep a bracelet I'd given her, but the rest... who knows where or who they came from? I'd rather not think about it. But I happen to know a merchant who deals in such things, who'll give me a good price. Enough to cover the cost of Berta's funeral, at least."

"Then you know a merchant I don't, it seems," 'd Anatolius. "Could I take a look?"

Peter frowned as Felix undid his bundle and laid

out its contents on the table.

"Your Berta favored green," Anatolius said, leaning forward to examine the jewelry. "I know two ladies these could adorn, and I wager I can give you a much better price than your merchant."

"I would not accept a favor."

"No favor, Felix. We can bargain later."

Felix looked uncertain for a moment. "That would be acceptable," he finally said. "I must go now. I have other business to attend to." He turned abruptly and left. Peter, sighing, abandoned his cooking to see him out. When he returned, he was unhappy to see that Anatolius had seated himself at the kitchen table and was closely examining the jewelry. He picked up a necklace and showed it to the old servant.

"What do you think, Peter? Would Europa like this? Or is it more to Cornelia's taste, do you think?"

Peter sniffed and said nothing.

"Am I the only one in his right senses, Peter?" Anatolius went on. "There's Felix, who's usually so sensible, acting very mysteriously, if you ask me. And John's looking for the murderer in the wrong places. Sometimes he's too intelligent for his own good. He can't see what's right in front of his face."

Peter stirred the boiling mixture in the pot hard enough to slop a few drops over its side. They hissed as they hit the charcoal in the kitchen brazier. He added more liquamen, sniffing at the rising steam. Was it too fishy? Had he already added the liquamen?

"I expect the Lord Chamberlain won't be returning until later," he said. "Perhaps you shouldn't wait for him. And Europa isn't up and about yet," he added pointedly, giving the mixture a vigorous stir.

"Yes, you mentioned that." Thinking of Europa reminded Anatolius of their walk around the city with Thomas. Impulsively, he asked Peter what he though of the redheaded foreigner.

Peter sighed, trying to recall if he had added wine to the sauce. "It isn't for a servant to say."

"It is if you're asked," Anatolius pointed out.

"I don't like Thomas, to be honest." Peter checked the small whole fish boiling in another pot next to the one containing the sauce. He preferred not to talk while he cooked; it distracted him. He preferred to sing hymns.

Anatolius tapped impatient fingers on the table. "Now there I agree with you. Why can't John see through the man?"

"That—"

"—is not for you to say. I know, I know."

"Could you hand me that bowl of raisins?"

"Ah, I'm afraid I've eaten a few, Peter."

Peter snatched the half empty bowl from Anatolius' hand and poured its remaining contents into the sauce. It would have to suffice. He sighed again.

"Thomas has been behaving suspiciously ever since he arrived in Constantinople," continued Anatolius obliviously. "He's been following John and me about like a shadow. Now, consider this, Peter. He's staying at the Inn of the Centaurs, which is also where Leukos, like me, visited the soothsayer. The soothsayer's dagger was used to murder Leukos. But couldn't Thomas have stolen it, followed Leukos to the alley, and then killed him?"

"I don't like the man, or trust him. But I do not see him as a murderer," Peter responded, stirring his sauce thoughtfully.

Anatolius scowled and then banged his fist down on the table. "Well, I do! I must confront him, Peter! If John won't, then I must. In fact, I shall go around to he inn right now and demand to see Thomas immediately."

The young man leapt from his chair and bolted out of the kitchen, leaving the jewelry on the table. Peter shook his head at the impetuosity of youth. As he added boiled fish to the sauce, he wondered if Thomas would even be at the inn. Then, putting the thought aside, he turned his mind to matters of more immediate concern, and tasted the sauced fish. It might be possible to make a passable dinner, after all. If John ever returned and if the women ever emerged from their rooms. A little more oregano, perhaps?

There was a loud rapping at the house door. "The devil take you, whoever you are," muttered Peter ungraciously as he hastened to the impatient summons.

The old servant did not recognize the caller, but the man's rough tunic and breeches did not speak of the palace.

The stranger held out a folded sheet of parchment and spoke without preamble.

"Thomas has asked me to bring this urgent note."

❊   ❊   ❊

Anatolius strode into the courtyard at the Inn of the Centaurs. A heavy, unfamiliar scabbard rubbed painfully against his leg and he kept his hand on the sword hilt, less to be ready for action than to attempt to keep the scabbard from swinging about in such an irritating fashion. He was greeted just inside the courtyard by the imposing, albeit unarmed, Mistress Kaloethes.

"I must speak with the innkeeper at once," Anatolius demanded. "It concerns one of your guests."

"My husband isn't here," she snapped. "What's your business?"

"I am investigating a murder."

Mistress Kaloethes glared at him. "You're the

second inquisitive visitor I've had today. You won't be wanting to rummage through my clothes too, will you?"

Anatolius was given no time to respond to this unexpected question because Mistress Kaloethes, bristling with rage, swept on, her shrill voice rising. "He went through everything! He even examined the marks on my silver plates and tossed my personal belongings about.

"And can you imagine the gall, he stole one of my best table linens! My husband is a good provider. I have elegant things, even some silks. How dare some stranger come here and paw through them?"

The woman had moved very close to Anatolius as she ranted and her indignation was nearly palpable.

Anatolius, alarmed, took a step back. "I assure you, I am not here with any such intent. I am here to speak to Thomas."

"Him?" Mistress Kaloethes gave a sudden laugh. "What would an emissary from the court of the king of Bretania have to do with such a foppish youngster as you?"

"I am secretary to Justinian, madam." Anatolius stood on his dignity.

"So you're from the palace?" The chubby woman looked at Anatolius appraisingly. "Still, scribblers aren't paid much, are they?" Her tone of voice suggested she suspected Anatolius might be less than trustworthy if he should find himself in proximity to her valuable possessions.

"Is Thomas here?" Anatolius persisted.

"I am here, Anatolius."

Thomas had just entered the courtyard. He moved over to the fountain. "Mistress Kaloethes," he addressed the woman, bowing slightly. "If you would leave my friend and me alone for a moment?"

"Certainly, sir. Let me know if you need anything," she simpered, and retired into the inn.

"I see you are bearing arms, Anatolius," Thomas observed coldly. "Is this the custom now you are a Soldier for Mithra?"

"No! I mean, how would you know?"

"I know many things, my boy. Now what do you want of me? Is it about Europa?"

"No, it's...."

"She is a very attractive young lady. But like myself, she must travel from country to country. Soon we will all go our separate ways, she and I included. Did you think you would be able to convince her to stay here with you?"

"That is none of your business," Anatolius responded hotly. He grasped the hilt of his sword more tightly.

"I did not come to your city to have romances with young ladies, my friend. I came on a much greater quest, a quest that requires many sacrifices. Indeed, for it a knight must sacrifice even love."

"And will a knight kill to further his quest?"

A hint of a smile flickered behind Thomas' mustache, but his green eyes had a hard look. It was then that Anatolius saw that they were rimmed with red. "Of course, if it should become necessary," Thomas finally said.

Anatolius gathered his courage, and finally blurted out, "I believe it was you who killed Leukos."

"People entertain many strange beliefs in this city," Thomas replied mildly.

Anatolius reached for his sword. Before it was even free of the scabbard, Thomas' blade was resting against the young man's chest.

Ice closed around Anatolius' heart. In the win' an eye, he would be covered not with the hot blo a sacrificed bull, but his own. At the imperial court, violent death lurked around every corner, but Anatolius had never expected to come face to face with it so soon. He drew what he expected would be numbered among his last breaths.

Then, rather than driving the sword home, Thomas spoke. "You are fortunate that I am beyond feeling the sting of your petty insults, lad. I have just met a traveler from Bretania. He told me the High King is dead." His voice cracked. "It seems it was a soldierly death, a good death, if any can be called good. Not that you would understand. It was in battle, although there are rumors of treachery, they say by one of his own blood. I should have been at the king's side, not here. Now I must return as fast as I can. For me, at least, this quest is ended. I shall take the first ship home that I can find."

Thomas lowered his sword.

As he did so, John burst into the courtyard. "Peter said I'd find you here, Anatolius," he called out. "Both of you, make haste! Cornelia and Europa have been abducted!"

"What... How... ?" Anatolius was at a loss for words.

"When I returned home," John explained rapidly, "Peter told me that a note from Thomas had been delivered for Cornelia and Europa. Despite her mother counseling caution, Europa rushed off and so of course Cornelia had to follow. They're on their way to the Cistern of Hermes."

Thomas blurted out an obscene oath.

Anatolius looked toward John in confusion, then back at Thomas.

The knight snorted impatiently. "Of course the e wasn't from me, you hotheaded young fool. I write!"

Chapter Twenty-eight

John, Anatolius and Thomas hastened into the forum on which stood the Cistern of Hermes. The dying sun cast a confusion of shadows through numerous marble statues, the very collection which Anatolius had so recently mentioned to Thomas and Europa. Living figures stirred dust as they moved between the statues toward shelter for the night in the half-abandoned building housing the entrance to the cistern's underground chamber.

John wondered if the crowd of beggars concealed men waiting to waylay them or, more likely, a sentry posted to warn of their arrival. The scene was so hellish he almost expected a pack of devilish black dogs to erupt from the gloom and leap snarling and snapping onto them.

Anatolius, whose thoughts were running along similar paths to John's, drew a deep breath. He felt he was embarking on an adventure not unlike those recounted by the great poets of antiquity. The deepening shadows beneath the cistern portico suggested an entrance to the underworld, a dark abode where were held captive not only Persephone-Europa but also Demeter-Cornelia. Such arrogance, he though hotly while admiring his own cleverness in linking the women to the goddesses. After all, Hades had only kidnapped the daughter. What villain would have the temerity to also take the mother?

"What are we waiting for, John?" Thomas, the man of action, demanded. "The women are in danger."

"So are we," John responded curtly. "Or rather, so am I. They've set a trap baited with Cornelia and Europa. Let me go after them while you summon the Watch."

"You're not thinking right, John!" Thomas snapped back. "There's no time. And while we don't know the number of our foes there may be only two, perhaps three. They'll be ready to fall on us, no doubt, but we are forewarned."

Anatolius ended his musings to nod enthusiastic agreement.

John shrugged. "Then it is time."

The sun was vanishing, leaving a glorious orange and gold streak low on the horizon. Raven-like black clouds were scudding over the livid gash of the sunset. But as the men reached the building they sought, sunlight flashed off what remained of the flaking gilt on the statue of Hermes set above its entrance.

"Mithra blesses our attempt," John murmured.

The building's atrium smelled of smoke, dampness, and unwashed bodies. Voices echoed in its cavernous space, barely illuminated by small fires around which ill clad beggars gathered for warmth.

John threw his cloak to the floor. "A soldier fights unencumbered," he told Anatolius. Thomas had already discarded his travel-worn cloak. As soon as the men stepped away, shadowy figures fell on the abandoned clothing in the manner of rats swarming over a discarded bone.

From somewhere in the dimness came a wheezing

laugh. "Does our young hero seek to free more captives?"

John, aghast at their early discovery, turned quickly toward the source of the taunting question.

It was only an old woman huddled beside some wicker cages.

"I purchased some birds from her not long ago," Anatolius' voice shook with relief.

The crone's cackling accompanied them on their way.

Access to the cistern was through an opening little more than a dark rectangular gap in the wall. Beyond, worn stone steps disappeared downwards.

John's stomach lurched as he led the way. "Mithra guard me," he muttered the soldier's prayer. The knot in his vitals was as tight as ever, but having invoked the protection of his god he was ready to fight. Yet his mind leapt and plunged, balking at the task ahead. He was not afraid of battle and bore the scars to prove it. But to descend into the depths of his private Hades, into that dark, water-filled space, the stuff of his wildest nightmares…. It tore at him, knowing that somewhere down in the bowels of the earth his family was in danger. Let it begin, he fretted. The long wait before the attack had always been the most difficult part of the mercenary life.

His knuckles whitened as his grasp tightened on his sword, but his face remained impassive as a sly, echoing voice in his head began to whisper mockingly, "You're going to save your family? Just as you brought Cornelia silk?"

❋   ❋   ❋

As the three descended, the air abruptly grew colder. Faint light from the fires upstairs filtered through chinks in the floor and down the stairwell. Reachin the bottom of the steps, one hand on the stone wall for guidance, John could see his breath ghosting in front of his face but little else. Waiting for his vision to adjust he could hear the magnified dripping of water and an almost imperceptible liquid murmur.

Gradually John could better see the interior of the cistern chamber. The water's ebony surface threw wavering reflections onto concrete walls and up the regular rows of pillars soaring up from its depths to vanish into deeper shadows beneath a vaulted brick ceiling.

John turned back and saw in the dim light that Anatolius' bright eyes burned with the fever of approaching battle—mingled excitement, fear, and anticipation. Or perhaps it was only a reflection of the fitful light straggling down.

"Did you hear that?" Thomas' voice was barely audible. "I think they are on the opposite side."

John had heard nothing. Where the men stood, however, was only a narrow ledge of stone skirting the cistern.

"We'll have to make our way around," whispered John, fighting to control the tremor in his voice. "Quietly."

"They'll probably have seen us already, even in this light," Thomas muttered back.

John did not reply. He stepped away and began to move along the ledge. Glancing down in the semi-darkness he saw the menacing glimmer of the water that gurgled a hands-breadth away. His boot slipped on moisture and he tottered, pressing himself back at the last instant against the rough wall behind him. Heart leaping, he wondered uneasily about the depth of the water in the cistern.

Anatolius licked his lips nervously and glanced ↄck the way they had come. Thomas' face seemed frozen, as if his thoughts were rigidly focused on what lay ahead.

Setting his jaw in a grim manner Cornelia would have instantly recognized, John slid sideways along the narrow ledge, back pressed to the wall, leading the way. The hungry water, so close to his feet, was criss-crossed with ripples journeying to and from the pillars holding up the roof. He was acutely aware of every slight lift and swell in the water. It seemed to him that the huge liquid mass was breathing, a monstrous entity waiting to pull him down into its disgusting embrace. Waiting to devour him endlessly, holding him in its obscenely wet clutches, suspended with his lungs bursting forever and ever, never to mercifully lose his mind or his consciousness.

John's back was wet with condensation and sweat. Again he prayed to the Lord of Light, but somehow Cornelia and his daughter were jumbled into it, so that as he inched along his unspoken petition was incoherent. He knew he might panic, and that if that happened, inevitably he would fall into the waiting water. Then the spirit of that freezing beck, thwarted when he was in Thomas' homeland so long before, would at last claim the prey for which it had so patiently waited through the years.

He heard what he thought was a faint cry, or the echo of one. Cornelia? He signaled to Thomas and Anatolius to stop. All three listened intently. No, nothing there. Just the soft, terrible sound of water lapping against pillars, dulled by the cistern walls.

But again there came a whispering echo. Clearer this time, a woman's sobbing. John tapped Thomas' elbow lightly, attracting his attention. The knight touched his ear and nodded. He had heard it, too.

The wraith of sound sighed again across the wa_ John felt an exultant surge of joy. They were here alive! Mithra be praised!

At this realization, the scorching heat of mingled exultation and rage welled up in his breast. In the semi-darkness of his watery Hades, John began to resemble a demon himself, his thin lips drawn back in a feral snarl. He had taken on the expression of near insanity which had momentarily transformed Anatolius' gentle face when he emerged from the mithraeum pit. For the moment at least John's doubts were gone, and he waved his companions onward.

Abandoning his former crab-like shuffle, he now broke into an even-strided lope, one elbow scraping the wall as he maintained his balance on the narrow ledge, sword pointing down, ready to swing up and forward to stab or to sweep side to side to slash. Thomas and Anatolius kept up the pace.

At the far end of the cistern there was a wide platform, its margins fading into shadow, no doubt a place to accommodate the materials of those who kept the vital water source in repair. Straining his eyes, John could just distinguish two dark shapes huddled at the base of a pillar rising from the platform's edge.

The women had been bound to the pillar. As John stepped forward, intent on cutting their bonds, Europa's head jerked upwards. He had only an instant to register the startled expression on her pale face as she gazed past him, then a low voice—Thomas' voice—growled, "Stay where you are!"

John turned. Seeing the knight's raised sword, he had a sensation of falling, though he could feel his feet still firmly planted on the cold concrete. Had he miscalculated the man so badly?

"I thought I saw movement in the shadows," Thomas said, lowering his weapon slightly. "I think it afe for the moment. Go ahead now. I'll be on the out."

Silently thanking Mithra, John turned back to the pillar. Beside Europa, Cornelia slumped forward against her bonds, silent and still.

"Europa!" John muttered. "Did they hurt you? What about your mother?"

The girl shook her head. "He tried to… well, I kicked him in the groin and he suddenly lost interest."

Her face was bruised. Apparently the man had exacted some physical revenge. Perhaps he had worse in mind for later. Still, John smiled thinly, thank Mithra for his child's courage!

He freed Cornelia. Unconscious, she felt heavy as the dead, heavy as old sorrows. His daughter put a hand on his arm.

"Father, it took two of them to subdue her while the third was busy with me," she said softly. "But she is unharmed, I swear."

"Why don't they show themselves?" grumbled Thomas. "I'll settle the score with the bastards!"

"Cowards!" cursed Anatolius. "They'll pay for this, Europa, I promise you!"

John shook his head. "We must get the women to safety." He looked around, re-orienting himself amidst the water-reflected light snaking across floor and walls.

"The stairway they brought us down is over there." Before John could protest Europa ran in the direction she had indicated. She was brought up short by a booming voice.

"Lord Chamberlain! You of all men should know it is impolite to enter without being announced. However, since you are here, you are welcome to our hospitality!"

Two men emerged from the darkness just in front of the girl. One was a tall, muscular man whom John did not recognize. The other, even larger though not so obviously muscled, was the innkeeper, Mast

Kaloethes.

"We have them outnumbered," growled Thomas.

Even as he spoke Anatolius bellowed. "Europa, watch out!" In a few steps he was past the girl, charging toward the unknown man who sneered with contempt, stepping out of the way. The innkeeper shifted his bulk slightly and deftly knocked Anatolius aside. The young man crashed into a corner and fell to the floor, lying as motionless as Cornelia.

And two previously unsuspected men appeared out of the shadows, cutting Europa off from her would-be rescuers. One of the new arrivals stepped toward the girl.

The innkeeper chuckled. "It appears we have recaptured at least one hostage, Lord Chamberlain. And I expect when it comes to such goods, the price for one differs little from the price for the pair. Don't move, or my friend will skewer the girl."

For an instant John and Thomas stood still. It was Europa who suddenly moved. In the uncertain light she seemed to take no more than a single step forward. Then she had catapulted herself into the air. The innkeeper's accomplice stabbed upwards, too late. The girl's hands barely touched his shoulders as she vaulted over his blade, just as she had vaulted over the equally deadly horns of so many bulls. She completed the move, to sprawl safely at Thomas' feet.

Thomas bounded over her. It was a less graceful leap than Europa's, but one which brought him face to face with the newcomer, who drew one gasping breath before the knight's blade had pierced his throat. Shoving his corpse aside, Thomas engaged the second man. The swordplay was brief.

"Now," remarked Thomas with a grin, "now, my friends, we are even."

John and Thomas instinctively became a fighting

unit, moving forward in concert. The redheaded foreigner trod slowly, unwavering gaze fixed on the taller of the remaining kidnappers, straining to get the measure of him.

John's lips curled back in a wolfish grin. Rage iced his veins. The siren song of combat, so long absent from his ears, sang in his blood. He was prepared to kill and to enjoy the killing.

The innkeeper gestured his sword in a petulant manner as he moved slightly to the right. At the same time, the man at his side stepped left, drawing Thomas away from John's side.

An unholy shriek rebounded around the subterranean chamber. Before its rolling echoes had died John, from whose throat the animal sound had burst, was upon the innkeeper, slapping the weapon out of his hand with the flat of his sword. Kaloethes grabbed for the thin-bladed knife at his generous waist.

John had dropped his sword and was ready, dagger drawn. A sword, he well knew, was too clumsy for hand to hand fighting. But more than that, he wanted the hot visceral satisfaction of closing in on his prey, to slice deeply into the other's flesh.

The men moved toward each other as if to embrace, jabbing and slashing. The innkeeper, now close enough to see John's half-insane expression, was driven by fear for his life. It was a fear which gave him a surprising agility, considering his bulk. He skipped backwards as John pressed his attack.

In his rage, John became careless, allowing the innkeeper to draw first blood. He slashed John across his cheek, opening a welling furrow from eye to mouth. But it brought him too close to John, who seized the opportunity to get under the other's guard, his blade biting into a meaty shoulder.

The innkeeper shrieked with surprise and pain

John yanked out the blade. The quick movement threw him off-balance, and the innkeeper, automatically using a maneuver that had won him victory in more than one street brawl, brought his knee up into John's groin.

The maneuver did not have its usual devastating effect.

John merely grunted with pain and staggered backwards, then leapt forward, to drive his dagger deep into the innkeeper's neck. Kaloethes sank screaming to his knees, but, keeping his wits about him, jabbed upwards toward John's stomach.

John kicked the weapon out of his opponent's hand. The unarmed innkeeper tried to crawl away. John was only dimly aware of Thomas trading sword thrusts with the remaining kidnapper. Now nothing could distract John from indulging his lust to inflict as much pain as possible on the man groveling at his feet—at least, until he slipped in the growing pool of the innkeeper's blood.

John went down on one knee at the edge of the cistern, catching a nightmare glimpse of his reflection springing up at him. His concentration was immediately broken. All he could think about was avoiding the horror of that waiting water.

It was enough. With a shout of rage, Kaloethes leapt up and forward, closing his huge hands around John's throat, thumbs sinking into the flesh. John tore at the innkeeper's death-grip as the pressure was steadily increased. A reddish tint was creeping into what little vision he had. He began to feel faint, gasping for air. His lungs were bursting, the pain shooting hot rivulets of fire across his laboring chest. Blood from his face wound ran down in scalding rivulets.

The fog shrouding John's mind suddenly cleared. He realized he was going to die in this echoing underground chamber. At least it would be an honorable death. And yet what would become of Cornelia and Europa? He knew they could expect no mercy. He began to lose consciousness, his fading thoughts of Cornelia and their daughter, the daughter he had cherished so briefly.

"Ten!"

A voice screamed out of the roaring red darkness engulfing John.

"Ten!"

John could make no sense of it.

"And all of them my fingers!"

Above him, swimming into his blurred sight, was the face of Felix. Felix grinning broadly, both hands facing outwards, all ten fingers splayed as if he were playing micatio and had finally guessed the correct number.

The innkeeper's head snapped back and his hands fell away from John's throat to claw at the stranglehold Felix now had on him.

"Kaloethes," Felix addressed him, his voice eerily calm. "I've just come from the inn. Your widow said I would find you here. She thought I'd come to assist you as in the old days, when you paid me well not to notice things I should have reported. 'Hurry up, they're at the Cistern of Hermes,' she told me. Oh, she was beside herself. It had all gone wrong. You'd been found out, she said. It was all your fault. And you never got the object you were seeking either."

Felix paused. A frown passed across his face, and then he continued, speaking louder to drown the noises the innkeeper was making. "She was angry at Berta, you see, because she wouldn't give the accursed talisman to you. So you killed my beautiful Berta, didn't you, you murdering whoreson?"

The innkeeper pawed ineffectually at the iron

grasp on his throat. John, on his hands and knees, gagged, as the world darkened again.

He heard another voice, more shouting. Thomas had been forced down on one knee. John peered into the gloom. Thomas' sword had gone. Surely it was not possible that such a man, such a soldier, had been vanquished? John knew he must stand and go to the aid of his comrade in arms. But his legs refused to cooperate.

Now Thomas' attacker was grinning, raising his sword to dispatch him.

As if he had simply decided against killing the knight, he paused. A strange expression crossed his face. Then he pitched forward, pulling with him Anatolius, who was still gripping the sword he had thrust into the man's back.

And now there was only the one man left, and he was coming to his end. John, Anatolius and Thomas looked around at Felix. He was straddling the innkeeper's back, pinning down his flailing arms, and began to sing loudly as he held Kaloethes' head under the water.

John gagged again.

Felix, still singing merrily, pulled the innkeeper's dripping head up out of the water. Kaloethes gasped for air, begging for his life. Felix spat in his face, screamed "Did Berta beg?" and pushed the innkeeper's head underwater again.

John recognized what Felix was singing. It was a scurrilous marching song.

Thomas staggered over to John and helped him to his feet. "It isn't a soldierly way to take a life," he muttered. "And yet, who can blame him?"

Felix's singing reverberated louder in the vaulting overhead. There was a frenzied thrashing in the churning water. Reflections leapt madly against walls and pillars, and then the sound of struggling ended as the innkeeper lost consciousness.

Anatolius was on his feet. He was trembling. Thomas clasped his shoulders briefly. "Thank you, my friend. You saved my life."

Anatolius was sobbing. "I stabbed him in the back! All I did was creep up behind him and stab him in the back!"

"And he is dead and we are not," Thomas said gently. "That is the difference between life and poetry. But now you are a true Soldier of Mithra, Anatolius." A frown crossed his face.

"I deserve no honors myself," he continued. "You see, I spoke to the innkeeper about my quest, hoping he had heard something useful. After all, innkeepers hear many travelers' tales. Of course, I didn't know that he was in the habit of visiting Isis' girls where he would hear about the pendant the soothsayer had given to Berta at the palace.

"But with the additional information from the description I'd given him, he realized what Berta called a talisman, which is to say the stone set in her pendant, was actually the Grail I was seeking. And to think we tried it on my leg the first time I met her!

"But once he knew that, he immediately went after it, for he knew he could name his own price for such a great treasure. So you see, because of my loose tongue I was also partly responsible for her murder, Anatolius."

Cornelia had revived and John helped her to her feet, glad she had not witnessed his madness. Thankfully, they left the hellish place. As they climbed back toward the cool night air, they were accompanied by echoes from the semi-darkness below. The echoes of the exultant singing of a man slaking his blood lust, slowly and lengthily drowning the man who had murdered his beloved Berta.

Epilogue

The following afternoon, John and Anatolius sat drinking wine in the Forum Bovis opposite the great bronze bull head Europa had so admired.

"I see you've chosen a good Cretan wine for a change," noted Anatolius. "None of your foul Egyptian stuff."

"Cretan wine in honor of our ladies, though they have sailed away," John replied softly.

Earlier in the day, Anatolius had accompanied the party to the docks. John however contented himself with a few private words in his study with Cornelia and Europa. Although he was a master of elaborate court ceremony, the simpler, unwritten rituals of everyday life such as leave takings made the Lord Chamberlain feel uneasy and awkward. From his window he watched them leave. They did not look back. He had walked down to the docks long after their ship sailed and lingered there, staring thoughtfully out over the water. The sea seemed to him more sinister than ever now it had taken Cornelia and his daughter away.

Anatolius took a sip of wine. "I heard from an

impeccable source today that four men were found dead this morning in a certain cistern. The authorities suspect robbery and aren't inquiring too closely."

"Just as well."

"But refresh my memory, John. How did the innkeeper know about Cornelia and Europa?"

"I believe that when I returned to the inn to inquire about the soothsayer, Kaloethes, suspicious man that he was, followed me to the Great Church and from there to the *Anubis*. Overhearing my conversation with Europa, he realized she is my daughter. I imagine he would have kidnapped her and Cornelia that very night had I not scared him away. He may well have come back later, but the crew returned before I left, and then, of course, the women came to stay with me the following day."

Anatolius looked thoughtful. "So within just a few days Kaloethes not only committed two murders, he'd dug up Berta's grave looking for her pendant and also broken into Felix's house to coerce him into assisting with his schemes?"

"Either Kaloethes or one of his accomplices. Felix had accepted bribes from the innkeeper in the past to pay off gambling debts. Thankfully he's set a new course for himself now."

"But why did the innkeeper wish to murder you, John?"

"He must have feared that when I returned to talk to Ahasuerus a second time it was only a pretext, and that I already suspected that he, Kaloethes that is, was the murderer. If so, he over-estimated me. I wasn't certain until yesterday when I went back to search his establishment."

"Of course! You were the official visitor who insisted on examining Mistress Kaloethe's belongings!"

John nodded. "When I noticed she had a set of

table linens exactly matching the one we found in Leukos' pouch, that is to say with the imperial mark, I was convinced she and her husband had had a hand in his death.

"Imagine the odds, Anatolius, on the Keeper of the Plate going to an inn where, among other things, plate stolen from the palace is in use! He would have recognized it at once. I assume he wanted to take some proof away. A piece of linen is easier to conceal than a platter or goblet."

"And Kaloethes saw him take it?"

John shook his head. "If he had, he would never have left it with the body. No, he must have noted the fine robes Leukos was wearing and realized he was from court. I am supposing that he then observed Leukos examining the plate perhaps a little too closely."

Anatolius frowned. "But how did you know the linen didn't belong to Leukos to begin with?"

"He didn't have it earlier at the Hippodrome because I recalled him wiping his face with his hand."

Anatolius remarked with admiration that only John would have noticed, let alone remembered, such a small detail.

"Small details are essential in court ceremony, are they not, and I have had to cultivate a keen eye."

Anatolius fell silent for a moment, his face darkening. "Stolen imperial goods. Imagine the punishment! Mutilation would be the least of it!" He took a long drink of wine, as if to fortify himself against the thought. "No wonder Kaloethes panicked. I'm surprised he let poor Leukos get as far as the alley before stabbing him."

"He didn't. He drowned Leukos in the fountain at the inn. Held his head underwater, as if he were reviving an intoxicated reveler like the charioteer I saw him bringing to his senses."

John closed his eyes for a moment, trying to control his emotions, and then continued. "I should have realized at once when I saw Leukos' dead face, the blue lips. I'd seen it before, when my brother in arms died in that icy beck in Bretania. Perhaps I didn't want to be reminded."

Anatolius asked how the innkeeper transported Leukos' body to the alley in which it was found.

"It isn't far from the Inn of the Centaurs to Isis' house. I was reminded of how small Constantinople is that night I climbed the stylite's column. During the celebrations the streets were full of reeling drunkards, many of them in costume. Kaloethes put on a mask and staggered through the streets dragging Leukos along. They would have looked like just another pair of revelers. However, I found a young woman who saw them from a tenement window although she mistook them for demons."

"But the soothsayer's dagger?" protested Anatolius.

"Stolen from his room easily enough," John replied. "It was Kaloethes who sent the anonymous note pointing the authorities in Ahasuerus' direction. After all, the old man was a foreigner and a soothsayer to boot, and there was no one to speak for him."

Anatolius fell silent but did not contain his natural curiosity for long. "What do you think of this Grail business?" he blurted out. "I hear that the Patriarch has acquired some holy relic more remarkable than any in Constantinople. It's being talked about all over the palace. Do you suppose... ?"

John laughed softly. "When I visited the Patriarch he showed me a stone. He believes it is a thing of great value, at least judging from the amount he said he paid for it."

Anatolius inquired where the Patriarch had found such a treasure.

"I gathered, from the little he revealed, that it was a very sensitive transaction. Now consider, did not Ahasuerus have at least one audience with him?" John sipped his wine, evincing no more pleasure from it than he took from his customary harsh Egyptian drink.

Anatolius was amazed. "You mean that soothsaying old scoundrel did have the Grail? Not a cup or a platter but rather a stone, and he sold it to the Patriarch?"

"Tell me truthfully, did you ever desire something because someone else wanted it?"

A puzzled look crossed Anatolius' face.

"Did it ever occur to you," John continued, "that our friend Thomas talked a lot? I gather he attempted to get audiences with every person of importance at the palace. Would you go about a quest like that?"

"I've never thought about going on a quest. Perhaps Thomas is something of a simpleton?"

"Is he? His attention to Europa certainly increased your pursuit of her," John pointed out.

"You wrong me, my friend." Anatolius blushed. "But are you saying that Thomas was trying to persuade people to take an interest in the Grail?"

"What better place than Constantinople to sell a priceless relic or, for that matter, a counterfeit? Especially now, with Justinian completing his Great Church and the Patriarch so ill. A dying man may grasp at straws. No doubt the Patriarch believes that the stone he purchased is indeed the Grail."

Anatolius looked down into his wine for a long time before speaking.

"Surely you don't think Ahasuerus and Thomas were working together?" he finally said.

John shrugged. "I made inquiries as to the destination of the ship Ahasuerus took this morning. It was bound for Crete."

"And Thomas is accompanying Europa and

Cornelia that far. But that isn't proof."

"I admit, I have no proof. Thomas may well have been on a real quest. And perhaps Ahasuerus is indeed the keeper of the Grail. And perhaps he must live until the end of the world and that was how he escaped drowning if he actually fell into the harbor."

Anatolius shook his head wearily. "I don't know what to believe, John."

"The soothsayer cast the pebbles for me, you know," John said. "He told me I would find my treasure underground."

"An accurate prediction."

"Indeed. And what if Ahasuerus did, after all, possess the Grail? And what if rather than selling the real Grail to the Patriarch, he gave it to Berta for safekeeping, to retrieve later?"

"You mean Berta's pendant? The one with the green stone? But John, I purchased that from Felix. I gave it to the ladies." Anatolius' eyes widened with sudden understanding. "That explains why Ahasuerus went to Crete. He followed the ladies to retrieve the pendant."

John smiled thinly. "I wonder, has the soothsayer yet foreseen the disappointment to which he is doomed?"

Anatolius gave his friend an inquiring look.

"Before she left," John explained, "Cornelia gave that pendant to me and asked that it be returned to Berta."

In thoughtful silence the Lord Chamberlain contemplated the bronze bull head which, as twilight fell, reflected dancing light from the torches in the forum. He could not help wondering about the pendant he had had reburied with Berta. Could a Holy Grail truly exist?

For an instant, as he mused over his lover and his

daughter—lost, found, and now lost again—regret breached the barricade of John's self-control and he allowed himself to think what he would never have spoken. Mithra forgive him, but did there live in Constantinople any man who had more need of such a mighty heal-all than he?

Afterword

One for Sorrow was inspired in part by evidence for the existence of a historical King Arthur who defended Britain against Germanic invaders around the time of Emperor Justinian I. The well known legend of Camelot and the Knights of the Round Table solidified during the Middle Ages. Although the Holy Grail is generally considered to be the cup from which Christ drank at the Last Supper (Robert de Boron in his verse romance *Joseph d'Arimathie*, late 12th/early 13th century) it has also been envisioned as something very different: a platter (Chretien de Troyes, *Perceval or Le Conte du Graal*, ca. 1190), a cauldron (Celtic legend), and even a water-filled glass ball (Lady Flavia Anderson, *The Ancient Secret*, 1987). In *Parzival* (ca. 1210) Wolfram von Eschenbach presented an interpetation of the Grail as a stone from heaven which provided sustenance and protection from death.

GLOSSARY

ATROPOS

One of the three Fates, daughters of Zeus and Themis. Clotho the spinner formed the thread of a person's life; Lachesis, the allotter or dispenser of time, measured the length of the life-thread, and Atropos, the inexorable or inflexible, cut it with her shears at the time for death.

AUGUSTAION

A small square near the CHURCH OF THE HOLY WISDOM, graced by a column topped by a bronze statue of JUSTINIAN. The square was not accessible to members of the general public.

BELISARIUS (505-565)

JUSTINIAN's most trusted general. His exploits included retaking northern Africa and successful campaigns against the Vandals and the Persians. He also assisted in putting down the NIKA RIOTS in Constantinople (532) at a cost of 30,000 dead. He is said to have relied heavily upon advice from his wife Antonina.

BLUES see **FACTIONS**

BYZANTINE EMPIRE

After the western Roman Empire fell in 476, the eastern part of the Empire continued. Although Christianity became the state religion and Greek replaced Latin in everyday speech, the citizens of the Empire still regarded themselves as Romans. The Empire was finally conquered by the Turks in 1453, but for much of its nearly 1,000 years of existence, it remained one of the world's great powers. Hundreds of years after the Empire ended, scholars derived the name "Byzantine" from the city of Byzantium, which the Emperor Constantine had made his capital and renamed Constantinople.

CARIA

Caria was in south-west Anatolia (now Turkey). Carians often entered the mercenary trade. Certain areas were still largely pagan as late as the 5th century. It was chiefly famous as the site of one of the Seven Wonders of the Ancient World, the tomb built for King Mausolus in 353 BC.

CHALKE

One of many structures destroyed during the NIKA RIOTS and rebuilt by JUSTINIAN. The main entrance to the GREAT PALACE, its roof was tiled in bronze. Its interior had a domed ceiling, and was decorated with mosaics of JUSTINIAN and THEODORA, as well as military triumphs, including those of BELISARIUS.

CHELANDION

Smaller form of the DROMON, used for transport or as a warship, and powered by oar and sail.

CHITON

A tunic, sometimes belted, which men wore short and which on women reached the ankles. Wool or linen were common materials, although imperial chitons were made of silk. As with all clothing at court, its decoration revealed the social rank of the wearer.

CHURCH OF THE HOLY WISDOM (Hagia Sophia)

Still one of the world's great architectural achievements, the Hagia Sophia, completed in 537, replaced the church burnt down during the NIKA RIOTS. The structure is most notable for its immense central dome, about 100 ft in diameter. It was also commonly referred to as the Great Church.

CISTERNS

Constantinople had difficulty supplying sufficient water to its populace, especially when under siege. To this end, a number of cisterns were built in various parts of the city, some above ground and some underground, often below buildings. The cisterns stored rainwater as well as water brought in by aqueducts.

CONCRETE

Roman concrete, consisting of wet lime, volcanic ash and pieces of rock, was used in a wide range of structures from humble cisterns to the Pantheon in Rome, which has survived for nearly 2,000 years even without the steel reinforcing rods commonly used in modern concrete buildings. One of the oldest Roman concrete buildings still standing is the Temple of Vesta at Tivoli, Italy, built during the first century BC.

CURSE OF THE 318 FATHERS

It was customary to invoke this curse to prevent the theft of documents, and it was also regularly used in documents of sale, a curious blending of pagan and Christian belief. It is derived from the First Ecumenical Council, held at Nicaea in 325 and attended 318 bishops.

CYRENAICA
A Greek colony in north Africa.

DROMON
Fast warship (its name means "swift") which could carry up to 200 aboard, propelled by fifty oarsmen in one or two banks. It was equipped with two, sometimes three, triangular sails and a ramming device.

DORKON
Similar to a DROMON, having triangular sails and a capacity of some 135 or so tons. It was noted for its maneuverability.

EPARCH
Equivalent to a city governor. He oversaw the city police and was held responsible for public order.

EQUES
A knight of classical Roman times. The equites (plural) were a class of mounted soldiers. A lower order of aristocrats, the equites ranked between plebeians and senators. During the empire the role of the equites evolved into administration of the civil service.

EUNUCH
Eunuchs played an important part in the army, church and civil administration of the Byzantine Empire. Many high offices in the palace administration were typically held by eunuchs.

EUTERPE
One of nine Muses, Zeus' daughters by the goddess of memory, Mnemosyne. Euterpe was the muse of lyric poetry and of music.

EXCUBITORS
The imperial guard, approximately three hundred in number.

FACTIONS
Supporters of either the Blues or the Greens, taking their names from the racing colors of the faction they supported. Great rivalry existed between them, and they had their own seating sections at the HIPPODROME. Brawls between the factions were not uncommon. and occasionally escalated into city-wide riots.

FUNERARY PORTRAITS
Paintings on wooden panels, from what is now El-Fayyum in northern Egypt. They were painted in the second and third centuries and are particularly striking for their realistic style, in

contrast to the more stylized portraits of much Egyptian funerary art. Because of this, they also provide a valuable record of contemporary clothing, jewelry, and hair styles.

GREAT CHURCH see **CHURCH OF THE HOLY WISDOM**

GREAT PALACE

Lay between the HIPPODROME and the sea walls of Constantinople. It was not one building but rather a number, set amid trees and gardens. The palace grounds included barracks for the EXCUBITORS, ceremonial rooms, meeting halls, the imperial family's living quarters, sports grounds, churches, and housing provided for court officials, ambassadors and various dignitaries.

GREENS see **FACTIONS**

HIPPODROME

U-shaped race track near the CHURCH OF THE HOLY WISDOM. The Hippodrome had tiered seating, and could accommodate up to 100,000 spectators. The dividing barrier, or spina, down the middle of the track included statues and obelisks. The Hippodrome was also used for public celebrations and other civic events.

HYDRA

A kind of organ, commonly used for ceremonial rather than religious events. It appears to have been of the type fed by bellows.

ISAURIAN PIRATES

Isauria was a largely mountainous country in Asia Minor. Its natives were notorious rebels.

JUSTINIAN I (483-565)

Justinian ruled from 527 to 565. His ambition was to restore the Roman Empire to its former glory. He regained North Africa, Italy and southeastern Spain. He codified Roman law in the Justinian Code. After the NIKA RIOTS, he rebuilt the still-standing CHURCH OF THE HOLY WISDOM (Hagia Sophia) as well as many other buildings in Constantinople.

KEEPER OF THE PLATE

In addition to ceremonial items, plate included tableware such as spoons, platters, ewers, goblets and various types of dishes. In wealthier households and the GREAT PALACE they were made of richly-decorated silver.

KOLLYBA

Small cakes made chiefly of wheat, nuts, herbs, and raisins, given to the congregation when prayers for a departed person were said. The prayers and kollyba distribution would usually be on the third, seventh or ninth days after the death, and again a year later. The practice is thought to be connected with funerary meals at pagan burials and can be likened to the modern custom of holding a wake for the departed.

LIQUAMEN

A salty fish sauce extensively used in Roman cooking.

LORD CHAMBERLAIN

The Lord (or Grand) Chamberlain, typically a eunuch, was the chief attendant to the emperor. He supervised most branches of those serving in the palace. He also took a large role in court ceremonies, but his real power arose from his close contact with the emperor, which allowed him to wield great influence.

MASTER OF THE OFFICES

Oversaw the civil side of imperial administration within the palace.

MAY FOUNDING OF CONSTANTINOPLE

The city was founded in 324 by Constantine I (288-337, r 310-337) and dedicated six years later on 11 May 330.

MESE

The main street of Constantinople, running from the MILION to the city walls. The Mese connected, among other places, the forums of Constantine, Tauri, Bovis and Arkadios. Its entire length was rich with columns, arches and statuary (including secular, military, imperial and religious subjects), fountains, religious establishments, workshops, monuments, public baths and private dwellings, making it a perfect mirror of the heavily populated and densely built city it traversed.

MILION

A marble obelisk near the CHURCH OF THE HOLY WISDOM. It was the official milestone from which all distances in the empire were measured.

MITHRAISM

Of Persian origin, Mithraism spread throughout the Roman empire via its followers in the various branches of military forces. It became one of the most popular religions before it was superseded by Christianity, perhaps in part because women were excluded from Mithraism. Mithraic temples were underground and have been excavated in sites as far apart as northern England

and what is now the Holy Land. Followers were required to practice chastity, obedience and loyalty. Some parallels have been drawn between Mithraism and Christianity, because of shared practices such as baptism and a belief in resurrection. Mithra, in common with many sun gods, was said to have been born on December 25th. Mithrans advanced through seven degrees. In ascending order, these were Corax (Raven), Nymphus (Male Bride), Miles (Soldier), Leo (Lion), Peres (Persian), Heliodromus (Runner of the Sun), and Pater(Father).

MONOPHYSITES

Adherents to a doctrine holding that Christ had only one nature, (a composite of the divine and the human) rather than two which were separate within him. Monophysitism, condemned by the Fourth Ecumenical Council of Chalcedon (451), nevertheless remained particularly strong in Syria and Egypt during the time of Justinian.

NARSES (c 480-574)

A eunuch, Narses served JUSTINIAN I both as Lord Chamberlain and general. He was among those responsible for subduing the NIKA RIOTS and in 552 was commander of the Roman forces which temporarily reconquered Italy.

NIKA RIOTS

During these riots (532) much of Constantinople was burnt down They took their name from the mobs' cry of "Nika!", meaning "Victory!", and almost led to the downfall of JUSTINIAN.

NOMISMA (plural NOMISMATA)

Meaning "coin", it also referred to the standard gold coin of JUSTINIAN's era.

OWLS TO ATHENS

Equivalent to "carrying coals to Newcastle," or taking something to a location already possessing an abundance of the item in question. The bird was considered extremely wise, and wisdom was said to be particularly plentiful in Athens. In addition, owls were sacred to Athena, goddess of wisdom and patroness of Athens.

PATRIARCH

The head of a diocese, or patriarchate. In Justinian's time these were (ranked by precedence) Rome, Constantinople, Alexandria, Antioch and Jerusalem. The patriarch's palace in Constantinople was connected to the CHURCH OF THE HOLY WISDOM.

PINDAR (522BC-438BC)

Classical poet known for commemorating athletic champions such as the wrestler Aristomenes.

QUAESTOR

An official who administered financial matters.

RANKS OF THE POOR

A person was legally considered poor if he or she had less than fifty nomismata (see NOMISMA). Laws sometimes discriminated against the poor in that punishments differed according to status. This meant, for example, that for some offenses a poor person would undergo corporal punishment, whereas a wealthy person could escape with a fine.

SAINT PROKOPIOS

Martyred in 303 during the persecution of Christians by Diocletian (245-316, r 284-305). St Prokopios was martyred after his refusal to offer sacrifices to the gods or to the emperor. Two incidents involving hands are recorded in his hagiography. In one instance, St Prokopius held up a handful of flaming incense, and in the other his tormentors' hands became paralyzed.

STYLITES

Holy men who often spent years living atop columns, also known as pillar saints, from "stylos," pillar. The most famous is probably St Simeon Stylite. Born in Antioch, he became a hermit, and later lived on one pillar or another until his death in 459 atop one 60 feet high. Constantinople boasted numerous stylites.

SYRINX

The water nymph Syrinx escaped the pursuit of the god Pan by metamorphosing into a reed, which Pan cut and made into a musical instrument, the Pan pipes, also known as the shepherd's flute.

TAUROBOLIUM

Bull sacrifice. A ritual of MITHRAISM.

THEODORA (c 497-548)

The influential wife of Emperor JUSTINIAN, whom she married in 525. The contemporary writer Procopius alleges that she had been an actress and a prostitute. Her father was said to have been a bear-keeper for the GREENS, a FACTION she subsequently supported. During the NIKA RIOTS she and BELISARIUS were reportedly instrumental in persuading JUSTINIAN to stay in Constantinople, thus saving his throne.

TRIREME

From "tri", three, the trireme is one of the oldest known vessels. A galley with three banks of oars, it was commonly used as a warship by a number of nations.

WALLS OF CONSTANTINOPLE

Constantinople was protected by a series of land walls, the first begun by Constantine I (see MAY FOUNDING OF CONSTANTINOPLE). In 413, to accommodate the city's expanding population, Theodosius II (401-450, r 408-450) added another set of fortifications, an inner and outer wall and a moat, west of Constantine's wall. The coastal side of the city was protected by sea walls.

ZEUXIPPOS

A Thracian deity whose name combines "Zeus" and "Hippos". The public baths named after Zeuxippos were erected by order of Septimius Severus (146-211, r 193-211). A casualty of the NIKA RIOTS, they were rebuilt by JUSTINIAN. Situated to the northeast of the HIPPODROME, they were generally considered the most luxurious of the public baths and were famous for their classical statues, numbering between sixty and eighty.

ZURVAN

In Persian mythology, the father of Ahura Mazda and his twin Angra Mainya, who represented good/light and evil/darkness respectively. Zurvanism, a form of, but opposed to, orthodox Zoroastrianism, appeared between the third and seventh centuries. Zurvanism influenced MITHRAISM, among whose deities Zurvan was numbered.